# GENEVRA

*Recent Titles by Elizabeth Ann Hill available from Severn House*

THE KENDRICK GIRLS
REMEMBER RACHEL

# GENEVRA

## Elizabeth Ann Hill

This first world edition published in Great Britain 2002 by
SEVERN HOUSE PUBLISHERS LTD of
9-15 High Street, Sutton, Surrey SM1 1DF.
This first world edition published in the USA 2002 by
SEVERN HOUSE PUBLISHERS INC of
595 Madison Avenue, New York, N.Y. 10022.

British Library Cataloguing in Publication Data

Hill, Elizabeth Ann
  Genevra
  I. Title
  823.9'14 [F]

  ISBN 0-7278-5803-3

Typeset by Hewer Text Ltd.,
Edinburgh, Scotland.
Printed and bound in Great Britain by
MPG Books Ltd., Bodmin, Cornwall.

# One

Was it foreknowledge which fleetingly chilled me the night I arrived at Trenarwyn? I shall never be sure. I only know that I suffered a moment of panic as the red tail lights of the taxi receded up the lane and the purr of the engine faded away. I watched the lights become ever more distant and tiny and then they were gone.

Alone. I had never been so completely alone before, with all connections severed and a whole way of life left behind. But now here I was, at the back of beyond, in the darkness with my luggage and the key to an empty house. All around me was silence, save for a quiet swish and flutter, the stirrings of branches still half-clothed with dying leaves.

Alone. By choice, of course. I had wanted this, planned it for nearly a year, looked forward to it. Yet dismay had seized me as soon as the cab driver wished me goodnight and drove off. As I stood with my hand on the latch of the gate, I asked myself: What have you done? My God, Christine, whatever possessed you to give up so much and come to a place like this! Are you out of your senses?

Doubts, misgivings. They had to be squashed. It was too late to turn back now. Trenarwyn was mine, paid for in cash, and its purchase had tied up most of my money.

Looking up at the shadowy bulk of the house, I had to remind myself how pretty it was in daylight, and that this was the start of my dream, my idyllic new life. Just at this moment, it didn't seem so wonderful after all. I hadn't expected to feel this way: lonely, cut adrift.

I was tired by the journey, I told myself firmly, and I hadn't planned to arrive after dark. A two-hour delay on the London

1

to Penzance line was to blame for this ebbing of courage. A good night's sleep and the morning sun would bring it flooding back.

As if in agreement, there suddenly came a spreading of silvery light as the clouds uncovered the moon. Before me, the lines of the house now stood out clean and sharp. Scrawled up and across the white-painted walls were the dark, woody stems and tendrils of the wisteria I had seen in full bloom five months ago, the day I first came to view Trenarwyn. Turning, I looked towards the bay, and there lay the great white crescent of the beach and the grey shine of the sea.

At once I felt fine again, eager and excited. This was a good place, a beautiful place, and I was going to be happy here.

I was carrying a cat basket, and a heartbroken wail from inside interrupted my thoughts. Poor Lucinda, my tortoiseshell, imprisoned since noon and desperate to be let out.

'All right,' I said, 'all right, Lucy, we're here at last, we're home.'

Opening the gate, I hefted one of my cases and walked up the front path. Unlocking the door, I pushed it back, groped around for the light switch and found it – only to learn that the power was off. The place had been disconnected since the last occupants left eight months before, but I had written to the electricity company, telling them the date of my arrival, and they had promised to have it reconnected by today.

Staring down the blackness of the hall, I softly swore and was just about to say something even stronger but stopped myself. For briefly I fancied that there was a listening atmosphere, not unpleasant, but just as if the house were aware of me and curious. I hesitated on the threshold, biting back a foolish urge to call 'Hello?'

Of course, it was merely my imagination. All I heard was another tragic howl from the basket, and at that I collected myself and stepped into the hall. Dropping the suitcase, I fumbled in my bag for my cigarette lighter, and its flame lit my way to the sitting room.

A beautiful, spacious room, this one, with a high ceiling, fine cornices, and a six-foot fireplace with a slate hearth. The latter

2

looked like a shadowy cavern in the feeble light, and my footsteps echoed loudly on the naked floorboards.

Stooping, I opened Lucinda's basket. Her head popped up, staring this way and that, and then she flowed cautiously out, slinking and sniffing around.

Going down to the gate again, I fetched in the other two cases. One of them contained an oil burner with a couple of dumpy candles. I had thought the house might smell stale after being locked up for so long. In fact the air was fairly fresh, but I was very glad to have the candles, one of which I lit and placed on the mantelpiece. The wavering flame threw dancing shadows on the walls and ceiling. The house around me felt benign, despite its dark, half-empty rooms, and I savoured a silence more profound than I had known in many years. It was still a mite hard to believe I was here, that I'd actually made the break and embarked on this new way of life.

It was only a quarter past eight, but without electricity there was little to do except get straight to sleep. Tonight and for several nights to come I was going to have to rough it, even though I had bought Trenarwyn part-furnished. The items which came with the house did not include a bed or sofa, and the best I could do for myself at present was a roomy basket chair. I would have to sleep in it, wrapped in my coat and a blanket I'd packed in a suitcase. I didn't mind too much; it was mild for October.

Lucinda had disappeared into the dark of the house and was doubtless enjoying a good nose around. I tipped out a snack of dry food for her, settled down in my chair by the fireplace and quickly fell into a doze.

Scenes and faces came before me on the borderland between waking and dreams, images of all the people and places left behind. The expensive avenue where I had lived. The flat with all its comforts. Neville, my partner for nearly nine years, smooth, well-heeled and vain. My office and the leaving party, all my colleagues wishing me good luck – with those flickers of doubt in their eyes and their voices which said they thought I was totally mad and that I was going to be sorry for throwing so much away. Yes indeed, at thirty-eight I had simply abandoned

3

what most would call an enviable life, an affluent, smart life, and come to this house on a remote Cornish bay to make an uncertain living as a weaver.

After the dreams came deeper sleep, which carried me past midnight and into the small hours. I was still soundly off when a sudden shock awoke me, the thump of something weighty landing squarely on my stomach. Jerking in the chair, I gasped and almost gave a scream – but then let out a sigh and a murmur of welcome instead. It was only Lucinda, soft and purring, looking for a lap.

As she curled herself around and settled, I glanced at my watch. It was just after two and the candle was burning low. The room had a large bay window and the panes were squares of blackness. No street lights here, and no moonlight now. Total darkness beyond the glass; I couldn't discern a thing. I wasn't used to that and it bothered me a little – perhaps because, with no curtains and my candle burning, I would be clearly visible to anyone outside. The thought produced a slight unease, although I wondered why it should. After all, I had no neighbours. No one lived within a mile and the lane was not a thoroughfare but a dead-end, just an access to my house. All the same, I suddenly felt on show, like a tropical fish in a tank. And as if in response to my thought, the wick of the candle suddenly slid over sideways into its puddle of wax and the flame went out.

Just as well, perhaps – though I hadn't intended to extinguish it myself. It was not in my nature to pander to nerves.

'*You won't like it, Chris, living on your own, particularly if the house is isolated, as you say. It's asking for trouble, a woman alone, especially an attractive one. I'm warning you . . .*'

Neville's cultured, cajoling voice. I could hear it in my head as I settled down again. He wasn't used to having women leave him. He had tried everything he could think of to change my mind. When all else failed, he had even tried to frighten me. Stroking Lucinda, I smiled in the darkness. Though not without caution, I wasn't the type who scared easily.

I was woken next day by the cries of gulls, briefly bewildered to find myself here, heart thudding a few times with shock at the strangeness of the house. Then, moving stiffly, I threw off the blanket and sat up, shrugging a shoulder at the soreness of its muscles.

Lucinda was sitting in the bay window, daintily washing a paw. A comical kitten grown into a gorgeous green-eyed cat, long haired and silky, exquisitely patterned with patches of white and bright orange and black. Once, in the course of an argument, Neville said I loved her more than I loved him, and he was right.

The room was filled with a rosy light which told me the sun was just rising. I went to the window to look at the day, and saw a sight that will always stay with me. The lawn sloped away to a low stone wall, and beyond that lay the broad sweep of the bay. A little above the horizon, the sun was a perfect ball of crimson hanging in a sky the shade of buttermilk. The tide was at its lowest ebb, the sea no more than a distant glitter behind a low line of surf. Ribbed and patterned by the receding water, the bay was now a vast expanse of amber sand criss-crossed with rivulets and dotted with shallow pools. Tawny in the sunrise, it offered the most unearthly view. In my quest for solitude, it almost seemed that I had come to the very edge of the world. I could well imagine what Neville would say.

'*Why didn't you simply go to Mars, darling, and have done?*'

I must have stood gazing for half an hour, until the sun climbed higher and the early haze dispersed, and the weird sandy waste became merely a beach again in the clearer light. Turning away from the window, I focused my mind upon matters more practical. Most urgent of needs were food and coffee. I would have to walk into the village first thing for supplies.

Taking one of my cases, I went upstairs to wash and change, and was grateful to find that the water company, at least, had heeded my letter. The bathroom mirror said I appeared no worse for my night in the chair. People tell me I'm good-looking. Well, I do have nice hair, dark blonde and somewhat curly. I wear it in a shortish mop and it's never any trouble.

Some time later, refreshed, in a clean pair of jeans and a jersey, I put on a jacket and set out to walk to the village,

5

Polvean. It was as I opened the front door that an upward glance made me pause. There, just inside, was the electricity meter and the mains switch for the power supply. It was up, in the 'off' position. I reached and pulled the lever hard. A metallic clunk and the hallway was flooded with light.

So the power had been on all the time. Shaking my head, I called myself a fool and went on my way. I felt buoyant this morning, exhilarated by the coolness and earthy-decay smell of autumn. The garden was all crinkly husks and dry brown stalks, a mess of exhausted life, bordered at the sides by hedges of escallonia. There wasn't a breath of wind and my rubber-soled shoes made scarcely a sound on the flagstone path, but a crowd of starlings flew up from a nearby elm as I approached, and the flap of their wings was startling in the stillness.

At the gate, where a big amelanchier grew, I paused and turned to admire my house. Trenarwyn was eccentrically pretty with its single bay window downstairs and a balcony running across the upper storey, serving the two front bedrooms and the bathroom which lay between them. One could walk along this balcony on to the semi-circular roof of the bay window jutting out below. The front door had a deep porch, to the right of which was a fan-shaped trellis wreathed about with climbing jasmine. A paved terrace ran the full width of the house, with a couple of steps leading down to the path. Almost from the instant I had seen the photograph in the estate agent's window and read that sing-song name, Trenarwyn, I had fallen for this place. One viewing and I was helplessly caught. It had been for sale for just three months and would doubtless have been snapped up faster if the property market had not been sunk deep in the doldrums at the time. How lucky for me – just as if I were meant to have it.

A few yards down from the gate, the lane ended where the beach began. There was just space enough at the bottom to turn a car and park. For the time being, however, I was without a vehicle. Beyond the gate, I turned up the lane, doubling back past the rear of the house, then striking off obliquely to the right on a footpath through the woods. The walk took twenty minutes, leading me up and over a ridge, then down to the narrow creek around the headland from the bay.

Here was Polvean – expensive Polvean – nestling on the wooded flanks of this deep-water inlet where yachts and sailing dinghies rode at anchor. Halfway down the hill was an Anglican church, St Martin's. A little lower, among the trees and well separated by their private acres, large houses could be glimpsed, while down beside the water's edge were granite cottages, small but still high priced. Picturesque Polvean, exclusive, full of retired professionals from out of the county, who had moved in and made it their own. There were some native Cornish too, bemused to find the values of their little homes pushed to such heights, but Polvean was first and foremost a colony for the well-to-do.

A van was due to arrive with my possessions that afternoon, but I had plenty of time. Famished, I went into a café and had a hot breakfast, then wandered around for a while, exploring all the quaint and carefully tended corners of Polvean. Finally, I made for the cluster of shops which fronted the quay, found a grocery store and went inside to buy a few essentials. There were no other customers and only the hum of refrigerators broke the silence. I filled a wire basket and went to the till, where an elderly man in a blue overall stood waiting.

He nodded and smiled and said, 'Morning, dear,' as I handed the basket over. Ringing the goods up, he eyed me curiously, remarking, 'Late in the year for visitors.'

Thrusting the groceries into a carrier, I said, 'I'm not on holiday. I'm moving in.'

The old man's eyebrows lifted. He hit the total button and £15.83 sprang up in luminous green figures in the window of the till. 'That so? Bought a house, have you?'

I nodded. 'A wonderful house, just right for me.' Delving in my purse, I plucked out a twenty and passed it over.

'On your own, are you?'

'Happily, yes.'

'Whereabouts is this house, then?' he asked, counting out my change.

'Overlooking the bay. It's called Trenarwyn.'

7

'Oh . . .' The sound emerged long and low. 'You've bought that one, have you?'

'Mm – lovely place, I'm delighted with it. The setting is out of this world.'

I went on to mention the sunrise that morning, the wild and spectacular sweep of wet sand. However, he pulled a dubious face and frowned at me.

'Yes, but you want to be careful out there. Know about the quicksands, do you, and the potholes?'

I looked at him.

'It's dangerous, the bay, when the tide is low. There are soft spots and currents and pits. Don't ever swim when it's on the ebb, and don't walk out too far, stay close to shore.'

Blinking, I said, 'The estate agent never mentioned any of that.'

A chuckle. 'Well, he wouldn't, would he?'

I must have looked dismayed, for then he added, 'Oh, I don't mean to frighten you, dear. It's all right to go for a dip at high tide. Just be careful, that's all.'

'Do I take it there have been drownings out there?'

'A few, I'm told. Long time ago, mind. Nothing recent. Don't know who they were or how it happened, but the bay has a grim reputation and needs to be treated with caution.'

'I see.'

'My name's Dennis Trelease, by the way. I own this place.'

I clasped his outstretched hand. 'Chris Elford. I'm planning to start up in business myself – sort of a cottage industry. I'm setting up as a weaver.'

'Oh yes?' Unlike my friends in London, he didn't appear to think me insane. 'Well, good luck to you.' Then, with a grin: 'Mind, I wouldn't have taken you for the arty-crafty type. Most of them look like hippies.'

'Give me time. I've only just quit office life in London.'

'Mm.' Again he was thoughtful and not quite at ease about something. 'It doesn't bother you then, being all on your own out there?'

'Why should it? Very quiet around here, isn't it? Safe enough, I mean?'

'Oh certainly, yes. I wasn't thinking of anything like that.'

'What, then?'

A shrug. 'It's just the idea of another solitary woman living out at Trenarwyn, I suppose.'

I was ready to go now and only half listening.

'Solitary woman? I bought the house from a family called Dean.'

'Yes, yes, of course, I knew the Deans. But I was thinking about poor Genevra, the lady who lived there before.'

I hadn't quite caught the name. 'Jen . . . ? Who?' I repeated vaguely. 'Jennifer, did you say?'

'Genevra,' corrected Mr Trelease, stressing the second syllable. 'A spinster, a Miss Penhale. I used to supply all her groceries. Eccentric, she was, reclusive and funny in the head. She died twelve years ago.'

'Oh? Well, it's people who drive me mad. Too many people, too many demands. I don't think the solitude's going to hurt me. It's largely what I came here for.'

He chuckled again and with that I bid him good day.

Heading homewards, I gave just a passing thought to the woman he had mentioned. It appeared that I wasn't the first to retreat from the world at Trenarwyn. Well, it was the perfect place for that. If the truth were told, there was probably nothing so strange about – what was her name – Miss Penhale? To me, the wish for seclusion was quite understandable, but people always thought you odd if you liked your own company.

# Two

I was finishing off a cold lunch when the van arrived with my belongings, and I passed the afternoon emptying the packing cases. It was reassuring to have my things about me. Although, when I sat down and looked around me at the totality of what I owned, it didn't seem all that much to show for fifteen years in a well-paid job. Very well paid, in fact, a salary of which most working women could only dream. What had happened to it all?

Well – buying Trenarwyn had taken the bulk of my savings, even though I had bought it cheaply, thanks to the slump in property values. I had about nine thousand left in cash; but how had the rest of the money been spent, all those big rises and fat bonuses paid to me over the years? On style and good living, I supposed, on running a smart little car and replacing it every eighteen months, on two or three foreign holidays each year, and eating out and dressing well, on the sheer cost of living in London. Despite my good earnings, Trenarwyn was the only substantial thing I had ever owned. Fortunately, Mr Dean had been in a hurry to sell. His proper field, the estate agent said, was hydraulic engineering – dams and irrigation systems, things like that. An offer of a job in Saudi at some fabulous salary had prompted a quick departure. He must, I thought, have taken a loss on Trenarwyn, but presumably the contract abroad was enough to compensate.

Anyway, the upshot was that Trenarwyn was mine, all mine, along with some items of furniture and kitchen fittings the Deans had seen fit to leave for a modest extra sum. However, the place was still half empty and I was going to have to buy a lot of furnishings. And rugs – the rooms were painted beige and cream throughout and all the floors were nicely woodstained, but apart from the one on the staircase there wasn't a carpet in the house.

So, what had I brought with me? Books and pictures, records and tapes and a music centre, a small television and some personal odds and ends. Essential household stuff. Nothing much else. Like a travelling circus, I'd been able to pack up quickly and just move on. I had never been settled, I realised, not properly anchored anywhere. No marriage, no children, merely portable possessions and some money in the bank, as if something in me had known all along, deep down, that this change would come.

Next day I walked into Polvean again and caught the bus to Truro, where I bought myself a bed. In the fortnight that followed, I went to some auctions and spent about three thousand pounds on furniture, mostly dating from the twenties and the thirties. Delivery vans came and went all the time until I decided I had enough to serve my needs for the present. Some of the rooms were still half bare, but there was no hurry to complete them. In the meantime, my sitting room was finished, my chosen bedroom too, and my kitchen adequate.

The final effect was shabbily cosy. Neville would not think much of it. A curl would come to his lip and a twitch to his nose. He would baldly call it second-hand and tatty. He liked a stark and integrated modern style, a new-pin shine. Neatness – maintained, of course, by me. Now I was free to indulge my own tastes and enjoy the luxury of disorder. I wanted my own special kind of clutter, and clutter I would have. Not to mention dust, if I felt like it. By nature, I was always a bit unkempt, a trait long suppressed in the interests of career and domestic harmony. Neville couldn't stand the sight of an unwashed dish or an unmade bed or a couple of crumbs on the carpet.

Neville was a solicitor, a suave and immaculate man, sleekly good-looking and utterly a creature of the city. And I had played the part of something similar. Christine Elford, keen to get on. One of those smart young women with a briefcase and a list of useful contacts. I'd spent most of the eighties living with

Neville, entertaining clients, his and mine, to dinner. Being one of the winners, a success.

So when had the change begun? Or, to be more accurate, when had the real me started to fight her way out? Before the bubble burst, before the recession came. Even before I signed up for those evening classes in textile crafts. Yes, well before that, a morning had come when everything about my life began to weigh on me. The dressing up, the endless to and fro, being nice to the clients and grubbing for deals. All of a sudden I wanted to walk away from it. I didn't, though, not immediately. It took an extra push – which came when I discovered that Neville had not just one but two other girlfriends on the side.

I had never been lucky with men. I had lived or had affairs with several, all of them misfits in one way or another. One was married and strung me along with the usual yarn about leaving his wife – which, of course, he never did. Another was a musician, a second-rate keyboard player, who allowed me to pay all the bills, and finally decamped with fifteen hundred pounds I'd 'lent' him. There were one or two others who didn't last long. All in all, they were a sorry lot, of whom Neville, I have to confess, was far and away the best.

Even with him there were stresses and strains. I must admit to a hot temper and a tendency to explode at times. He, in response, would be calmly stubborn. I would scold and he would shrug and in the end we would patch it up, so despite the tensions nothing ever changed and we rubbed along together almost like a married couple.

Lucinda was a cause of many arguments between us. The day I brought her home, he made a fuss. He said there would be fleas and cat hairs everywhere, and I must get rid of her straight away. Well, I put up a fight and kept her, but the poor mite was always a bone of contention. I can't describe the rage I felt when I learned he had other women, at the same time be-grudging me a harmless pet.

That was when I finally decided to take the great step. The night I told him, he was teasing at first, and then appalled. I can still, to this day, see his face and that little one-sided smile.

'Christine, my sweet,' he said, 'you can't be serious. Look,

I'm sorry about the girlies, all right? Just a couple of tiny lapses, didn't mean a thing to me.'

At which I snapped back: 'Nor do I. I give good dinner parties and look right with you when we go out together, that's all.'

'Oh come! You're being cynical.'

'I'm being realistic.'

Thereupon, he tried to scare me. 'You'll never make a go of it. You'll be sorry, very sorry. Within a month you'll be kicking yourself for what you've sacrificed, and it won't be easy – perhaps not possible at all – to come back here and pick up the threads. You could end up in poverty, mark my words. Be reasonable, Chris, grow up. Dropping out was a fad for youngsters twenty years ago. Look, I'm sure you're overtired. A holiday's all you need. We'll go somewhere nice for a fortnight – no, three weeks. How about that?'

'I'm going somewhere nice for the rest of my life, without you,' I said.

Whereupon, he became quite testy, which was very satisfying, because it only happened on rare occasions when he was really rattled.

'Down among the hayseeds? Going to wear tie-dyed skirts and live on chickpeas with the rest of the homespun, back-to-nature brigade? Christine, you can't, you're not one of those types!'

Ah, but he was wrong. I was always that type. It had simply taken me a long, long time to realise it. Significantly, the day I handed in my notice was also the day I stopped smoking. Release was in sight and no more pacifiers were required. Instead I had the promise of a future more fulfilling. For sure, the evening classes had been a revelation. I discovered in myself a special aptitude and love for handweaving, quickly progressing from simple work to pieces more and more complicated, then going on to design my own patterns. At first even Neville admired what I made – never suspecting that my little hobby was destined to rob him of his handy housekeeper.

The day I left, he glumly drove me to the station. 'Fancy choosing Cornwall,' he sniffed. 'How very unoriginal, Christine. What's this house like, anyway? Cob walls and a midden?'

'An absolute hovel,' I said cheerfully. 'Not the sort of place where you'd want to come and stay.'

He gave me one of his injured looks and told me I was being very selfish. Then he tried another tack.

'Joking aside, sweetie, haven't you asked yourself why it was going cheap?'

'I've told you, the owner was taking up a job in the Middle East.'

'Verify that, did you?'

'Certainly not. Why should I?'

'Price was too good to be true.'

'A bargain, pure and simple.'

'There must be something wrong with it.'

'The survey said not. It's in fine condition.'

'Perhaps it's too close to the sea. You'd better watch out for the next spring tide.'

'I checked on that. No danger.'

'Then the ground underneath it is probably riddled with mine shafts. You'll wake up one morning and find half the house gone.'

'Oh Neville, don't talk such rot!'

'Has to be something amiss,' he said darkly. 'Has to be. There is no such thing in life as a free lunch or a genuine bargain, Christine. Believe me, there's always a catch, as I fear you will soon find out.'

That was just like Neville, dry old cynic that he was. I, however, knew I'd made a very canny purchase – a fine four-bedroomed house in a magnificent setting, some of which was my own private ground.

Trenarwyn came with an acre of land, mostly composed of mixed woodland at the rear of the house. On a day at the start of November, I decided to explore it thoroughly. According to the estate agent, there was a boundary fence, albeit in poor condition, and I took it in my head to search for it that morning.

I set out after breakfast, clad in boots and jeans, following

14

what remained of a footpath. The land went uphill, running parallel with the lane and separated from it by an ancient Cornish stone hedge. Sad to say, however, it was not the pretty walk for which I had hoped. The further I went, the thicker and darker the woods became. Some of the trees near the house bore the scars of bygone loppings, but those more distant had never been tended in any way and some had attained massive size. No doubt in sunshine some light filtered through to render the woods a little more pleasant, but on that day of overcast skies they were dank and chill.

The boundary turned out to be a slack wire fence, all but lost in the undergrowth. Just a token border, beyond which the woodland continued unbroken. Stepping over, I carried on, if only to see where the path would lead.

It must have been a good mile from the house that I reached the end of the track. Suddenly in front of me was a shaft of brighter light, a glimpse of asphalt between the trees and a leaning concrete post which barred my way. Squeezing round it, I emerged on to a road – the one which ran from Polvean into Truro. On the other side of it, the woods began again. To my right there was nothing except more trees. To my left, in the distance, a cluster of cottages and a large barn fronting the road, buildings I had seen before as the bus passed by.

So that was it, then. On the whole, I was disappointed with my ground. Perhaps I had hoped to find some airy dell, or else a lovely stream upon my property. The reality could not have been more different. The woods were – well – disagreeable. Certainly not a place for a pleasing stroll. Going back, I told myself that I ought to have come on a brighter day, but given even the best of weather, the atmosphere among these trees would probably still be creepy.

Approaching Trenarwyn again, I stopped and looked up at the back bedroom windows. I hadn't yet bothered to furnish those two rooms at all. One of them was quite attractive, but the other, above the kitchen, was somehow rather glum. For myself I had picked out one at the front, above the dining room.

Crossing the yard, I went in by the back door, entering the kitchen which was large and still old-fashioned. The only incongruous modern touches were a gas cooker and neon strip light. There were walk-in pantry and larder cupboards, and yet another door which led down to a cellar.

Despite an unpleasantly steep flight of stairs, this cellar was a perfect place to keep all my mordants and dyestuffs. They resided on shelving in rows of big glass jars, labelled in my own untidy scrawl. Just three weeks after moving in, I already felt fairly well organised and ready to start at my trade.

Although there was ample space for a separate workroom, the big sitting room was to serve me both for weaving and relaxation. I had a four-shaft Ashford loom, thirty inches wide, and this was set up on a sturdy table in the corner. Handy nearby, stood a shelving unit crammed with skeins of wool, and a big rack of spools bearing coloured thread. Although wool was the principal yarn, I sometimes mixed it with other fibres or wove exclusively in cotton or linen or silk. Even when I wasn't working, I loved to have my rainbow of materials around me, and no other room in the house was so congenial.

That very same day, after lunch, I set about dyeing skeins of wool for my first commercial piece. I wanted shades of navy, magenta and pink, so I weighed out quantities of alum and cochineal, logwood and copper sulphate, and passed a happy afternoon grinding away with a pestle and mortar, mixing up potions in jugs and simmering little muslin bags of dye. It was hot work and I thought I must look like a witch at her cauldron, hovering over my bubbling pans, lank-haired in the steam. The notion pleased me. I didn't have to care too much any more about how I looked. I was finished with make-up and business suits and high heels. From now on I would have two modes of dress – jeans or long skirts, sloppy and comfortable.

The process went well and one after another I lifted out the newly tinted skeins with an old cricket stump, plunging them into the sink to be washed with olive oil soap. The day was breezy, perfect drying weather. I took the hanks of wool outside and pegged them on the line which stretched between the kitchen window and the outhouse.

As I finished and turned to go inside, I paused for a moment and once more looked up through the woods. It might have been the memory of my morning walk which gave me a sudden shiver. Then again, perhaps it was only a cold gust of wind. Somehow, though, the trees now seemed possessed of a dour and watchful presence. Those which grew close to the house were mainly laurels. They tossed and hissed in the breeze, their branches whipping up and down. There was something oppressive about the way they clustered thickly round the yard and overhung the roof of Trenarwyn. I wondered that Mr Dean hadn't had them felled, and vowed to arrange it myself at some future time, when I felt I was on a firm footing and had the money to spare.

# Three

It can't have been many days afterwards that I saw the old woman, a trespasser – or so I thought – within my gate.

I had spent the day at the loom, working on a cushion cover. The aim was to make up a set of samples to take to town in the hope of securing orders from suitable shops. There were quite a few outlets in Truro and one or two in Falmouth I thought might buy my wares. I could turn out shawls and lacy stoles, bedspreads, tablecloths and throws, as well as clothing. For hours I sat throwing the shuttle and beating and working the shafts, producing a square of waffle-weave in linen. I worked to the sound of a tape of Strauss waltzes, which I later changed for *Carmen* and then *Swan Lake*.

It was close to half past four when my arms began to ache too much, forcing me to stop. I stood up and went to change the tape again, then stoked the fire. In the window, my basket chair was positioned to face the garden gate, beyond which the bay curved away, sickle-shaped, its far point tapering into the sea a mile distant. I liked to sit there in the evening and watch the sun go down. The day was a bright one for late in the year, almost cloudless, but cold.

Flopping into the chair, I put my feet up on a hearthstool, then settled back to enjoy the last hour of light and my favourite selection of Ralph Vaughan Williams.

The sinking sun grew a darker gold, shining through the naked branches of the trees which overhung the lane. The tide was coming in, steel blue and scarcely ruffled by the glancing wind. Half an hour went by, the music played and the sun dipped lower, shadows like dark fingers stretching out across the garden. It was time now to close the curtains, but I felt too lazy to move. And then for several minutes I was lost in the strains of a piece of music I specially loved. Slow and sweet, an emotional rising and falling of strings – to me inexpressibly lovely and somehow sad. It was *Fantasia on a Theme by Thomas Tallis*, and I closed my eyes to concentrate and take in every note.

After it ended, I sat for a moment, unmoving. Then came the click of the tape switching off. Stirring, I rose to draw the curtains . . .

And I saw her.

An elderly woman, thin and bent, stood within the garden gate, staring out to sea. Dusk was falling, but nevertheless I could see her fairly well. Her back was turned, but I knew she was old, knew by her stance and by the scragginess of the hand she rested on top of the gate. Her hair was very dark, streaked grey, pinned up untidily. She wore a dowdy, calf-length dress. It might have been dark blue or green, I couldn't say for sure.

Somebody come to see me, I wondered.

I waited, but the woman made no move. She was, indeed, unnaturally still – like someone posing for a photograph.

What could she be looking at? There was nothing to see except calm water, an empty beach and the far headland blurring away in the fading light.

I tapped at the window.

No response.

Perhaps she's deaf, I thought, but tapped again anyway.

Still no sign that she had heard, still no movement, not a muscle. The obvious course was to go out and speak to her. Yet I hesitated, reluctant, although for no good reason I could pinpoint.

A minute went by, perhaps two, and suddenly I became aware that I was clutching a handful of the curtain, almost dragging on it. Whereupon, I grew annoyed.

I would go out and ask what she wanted, I decided, collecting myself. Briskly, I drew the curtain, reached for the other – then halted again.

The woman had turned round. She was looking up at the house and – oh, her face!

Beauty, sapped by age and sorrow, that was what I saw. Beauty worn away by time and self-neglect. A face which must have been exquisite once, in youth, in happiness. It wore an expression, grotesque and piteous, of childlike hope.

She was looking straight at the window now, but apparently unaware of me – or merely, perhaps, indifferent to me. Whoever she might be, I had the strongest feeling that she hadn't come to pay a social call.

A certain indignation seized me, because the woman kept standing there, on my private property, for no discernible reason. And because she upset me, unnerved me. That face, that lost and yearning face.

Whisking the second curtain across, I marched out into the hall, flung open the front door and called: 'Hello? Can I help . . . ?'

She had gone. In a matter of seconds. Just vanished, as quickly as that.

I ran down to the gate and peered up the lane, then looked across the beach. There was no one in sight. A quick search of the garden and back yard yielded no trace of her.

Puzzled, I went in and locked the door. It was nearing dark and I supposed the old girl had gone up the lane, where she would swiftly disappear in the shadows under the trees. I mused for a while over who she might be and why she had come here, but finally shrugged it off as simply odd. Probably someone from Polvean, perhaps a little peculiar thanks to her years, poor soul. Just a harmless frail old woman, no reason why she should worry me.

Strange, though, how that air of sorrow about her depressed my mood. It took me quite some hours to shake the feeling off.

I'd forgotten about her by next day, and worked hard on my samples the rest of the week. When Saturday came I felt ready to sally forth and make some sales. Once more I caught the bus into Truro, carrying my wares in a suitcase. Before too long I would have to buy myself a little car. Something old would do, something cheap to run.

The ride into Truro was long but pleasant, following narrow

country roads. The bus was usually half empty, which was no doubt why there were only three a day on this route. Official stops were few, but the drivers would frequently halt on request. On that particular day, an old man was waiting outside the cluster of cottages I had seen from the end of the woodland path behind my property. The bus pulled in to pick him up, and while the driver took his fare I noticed that what I had previously taken for a large barn was nothing of the sort. Instead, a sign above the door announced it as 'Jennings' Foundry'. Glancing into the yard, I saw a couple of broken-down solid fuel stoves and a Cornish range. Hankering after a wood-burning stove, I wondered if they had any decent ones, second-hand, and made a mental note to pay a call some time.

Arriving in Truro at half past ten, I spent the next four hours traipsing round its streets and alleys and mews arcades, trying to interest the shopkeepers in my samples. They were all, I explained, my own designs – home-dyed, hand-woven, no two pieces ever quite the same.

The response was poor, to say the least, utterly dispiriting. By two o'clock I had one timid order for table mats. That, after walking the town from end to end. Some of the shopkeepers were pleasant but apologetic, others brisk, and one woman downright rude, but it all added up to No, No, No, whichever way it came.

Routed, miserable and footsore, I retreated to a café for a lunch of soup and rolls. As I ate, I could mentally hear Neville saying: 'Well, sweetie, I told you so.' For the first time my confidence faltered and pessimism briefly overcame me.

Fell at the first fence, I thought morosely, and kicked myself for not investigating the whole business more thoroughly before diving into it. The doubters, it seemed, had all been wise and right, while I, pig-headed, had made the greatest mistake of my life. If I couldn't sell in prosperous Truro, I couldn't sell anywhere. So much for my new life, scarcely begun and already a failure.

But then, at the last, the day was saved. Heading for the bus station, I took a short cut down Cathedral Lane and there found a very smart shop which sold fine household linens. Still with half an hour to spare, I went inside. When I came out I was walking on air, or rather, running: I had to dash for the bus. I climbed aboard, panting but happy, and full of smiles for the driver. With orders for bedspreads and tablecloths, sideboard runners, even curtains, I was in business after all.

Things go right – and wrong – in batches. That's my experience, anyway. For further proof that they were looking up, a little more income came my way the next time I was in Polvean. I'd been to the dairy and the greengrocer's and was making my final call at a shop called Good Harvest. It was one of those places which sold wholegrains from sacks and bins, home-made preserves, and honey and cheeses, nuts and dried fruit. A health-food store and a delicatessen combined, fashionably spartan, with no-nonsense brown paper bags, and glass bottles which one was expected to return and have refilled. The side window was plastered with advertisements for homeopathy, acupuncture, crystal healing and the like, not to mention sundry protest meetings – everything from saving the whale to stopping some by-pass or other. I was going in anyway, and a fresh notice down in the corner gave me an added incentive. It said:

Assistant Required
One Day a Week
Apply Within

It would certainly help, some extra money, immediate money. It wouldn't be much, I supposed, but if it only kept me fed that would make it worthwhile. Anyway, no matter how I loved my solitude, a break from the house and some regular human contact were no doubt advisable. One day a week would suit me perfectly.

I went inside. The shop was crammed with stock, all in big jars and barrels and baskets. From the ceiling hung a wooden frame, festooned with strings of garlic bulbs and dried herbs. Behind the delicatessen counter, a pleasant-faced, brown-haired woman was carving up boiled ham. She was young and wore spectacles and a rather odd patchwork dress.

I bought some flour and yeast, and a bag of dried apricots just as a treat. As I paid her, I nodded towards the notice.

'You want someone part-time? Which day of the week would it be?'

She looked at me. 'Fridays. Are you interested? Thirty pounds for the day.'

Thirty pounds. After what I'd been earning in London, it was a shock to realise just how little some jobs paid. It told me, too, how spoilt I'd been.

I don't know what showed on my face, but she plainly took it for disapproval.

'And discount,' she added quickly. 'Thirty per cent on everything.'

'Well, that sounds fair enough. What would I have to do? Just serve?'

'And restock the shelves.' She was sizing me up as she spoke. 'Have you any experience?'

'Not in this kind of job, but I'm sure I could do it.'

The eyes behind the spectacles regarded me uncertainly. 'I know almost everyone hereabouts, but your face is new to me.'

I told her my name and then delivered a potted history. She gave a cough of laughter on hearing about my past career.

'No wonder you blinked at thirty pounds a day. Still, I'm afraid it's the best we can do.'

'It's all right, really, it's fine, and I think I'd like it here.'

She looked me up and down, this girl young enough to be my junior secretary, and briefly I felt very keenly the loss of prestige, the come-down which had resulted from walking out on my job.

But then she said: 'Look, I'll call my husband. We've never hired anyone before. You certainly seem all right to me.' Opening a door at the back of the shop, she shouted, 'Trevor? Here a minute.'

A man aged about twenty-two, wearing denim jeans and shirt, appeared.

The girl introduced me. 'This is . . . Sorry, is it *Mrs* Elford?'

'I'm single, and call me Chris.'

Smiling, she said: 'Trevor, the job – I think we may have found our lady.'

He went through the same questions with me again, and finally agreed to try me out.

'I'm Trevor Moffat,' he said, 'and this is Jane. Can you start this Friday? Good. Won't take us long to show you the ropes and you'll soon be able to cope by yourself. We don't get much time off, you see – only Sundays at the moment. We set this place up two years ago and we're only now feeling rich enough to employ someone.'

'It'll be a good way for you to make some friends,' Jane said. 'Just about everyone comes in here. You'll soon get to know them all. Must be lonely for you, living out there by the bay.'

It would feel strange to be working for people virtually half my age, but they were a nice little couple, even if Jane did seem to think that my solitary life was a cause for concern. She mentioned several times the opportunity for making friends, as if it were the best perk of the job.

I started the following week, and in truth I did enjoy my Fridays serving in the shop. A social interlude, just enough to make me feel a part of Polvean and 'in touch'. Before long I was picking up bits of gossip and some grasp of the network of intrigues and feuds which pervaded this little community just like any other. Weighing up lentils or slicing cold cuts, I would learn that so and so was carrying on with guess who, that a certain old man was sueing a neighbour over the height of his hedge, or a certain young girl would hop into bed with any man she met. Over the baskets of chilli peppers and root ginger, I would hear that so and so's son had been kicked out of university, or that sundry other folk were pregnant, bankrupt, alcoholic – all human life was here.

It was good for me, a counterbalance to the quiet of Trenarwyn, and I was surprised what thirty pounds could buy if I was careful, especially with my discount at Good Harvest. With my orders to fill for the shop in Truro, I really felt optimistic now, and considered it time to lay out for the car I had promised myself. One Saturday morning I bought a banger by way of the classifieds in the *West Briton*. It was ten years old but the engine was good and the back seat folded down to give plenty of carrying space. When I brought it home and parked it in the lane outside the house, I felt my life was coming together fast.

# Four

This spirit of optimism made me decide I could also afford to buy the stove I wanted. Recalling Jennings' Foundry on the Truro road, I drove up there one morning to see what they had in stock.

Parking on the verge outside, I went in through the gate. On close inspection the place seemed even more like a junkyard, a weed-infested court with rusting oven doors and hobs and stove-pipes dumped in heaps against the sides of the building. For a moment I wondered if it had been a mistake to come here, and stood half poised to go away again.

But then there came a clank from within the workshop, followed by a terrific crash of falling metal and a string of curses.

No harm in asking, I supposed, seeing I was here. Stepping inside, I encountered a man in dungarees and a cap. He was gathering up bits of scrap iron from the floor and slinging them on to yet another heap in the corner. Middle aged, sandy haired and broad featured, he took in my appearance, top-to-toe, with one candid and slightly familiar glance.

'Mr Jennings?' I asked.

He nodded his head.

'I've just moved into the area. I'm looking for a wood-burning stove.'

'Oh.' Another jerk of the head, this time indicating a sort of cubicle back in the shadowy depths of the foundry. 'Come into the office, madam.'

The formality fell as lightly from him as 'dear' had come from Mr Trelease and carried no subservience whatever.

I followed him through the workshop, and over his shoulder he shouted, 'Mind how you go.'

The warning was apt, for the foundry, like the yard outside, was a mess. From the rafters hung pulleys and chains and crucibles, while tools and moulds lay strewn about everywhere. There was no fire in the furnace that day, but the floor was crusted with coils and rolls of what had been molten metal. Almost everything was rusty or dusty or burnt.

The 'office' was a corner of the foundry sectioned off by a flimsy wood partition. It contained a desk almost buried under chaotic piles of paper, and was miserably lit by the glare of a naked bulb.

Mr Jennings pushed a chair at me. 'Sit down, then. What are you looking for? Something custom-made?'

'Depends on price. I'm just shopping around at the moment, you understand. You're my first port of call.'

'Well now . . .' He rummaged through the mound of papers and finally drew from the bottom a dog-eared booklet. 'This is our brochure and current price list. We can cast any of these models for you here on the premises, no trouble at all. The cost includes the installation.'

I flipped through the booklet and shook my head. For such a scruffy place, the prices were surprisingly steep.

'A bit beyond my pocket.'

'You could pay by instalments.'

'Thank you, no. What about reconditioned ones?'

Clearly disappointed, he said reluctantly: 'Second-hand? Well, we've a few . . .'

He had the salesman's knack of making one feel vaguely guilty for asking about cheaper options. Knowing the tactic, I said stoutly, 'May I see?'

A sigh. 'Of course. They're in the yard. No, this way.'

I had risen and moved to go back in the workshop, but Jennings now opened a back door leading from the office into yet another court. This one had a perspex canopy and all around it stood an array of stoves. I pointed out one with glass fire doors and a brown ceramic finish. It looked almost new.

'We've overhauled that one,' Jennings said. 'It's all in good order now, last you for years. Burns wood, coal, anything.'

Squatting down, I opened the oven doors to peer inside, then straightened up and lifted the hob covers, inspecting everything. It all seemed very clean and sound.

'How much?'

'Eight hundred, plus labour. Only take us a day to put it in, providing we meet with no problems. What kind of house is it?'

'Old. Granite-built and rendered. You probably know it, everyone else seems to. It's called Trenarwyn.'

Something crossed his face. 'Oh yes, the Penhales' place, that was. Used to be a Cornish range in the kitchen there. My great-grandfather made and installed it, then Grandfather took it out again when they changed to gas back in the twenties. Your stove could go in the same place and use the same flue. Is the recess still there?'

'No, but I know where you mean and where the chimney is.'

'Just bricked over, I expect. We can easily open it up again. You're looking at about three hundred for the labour, I would think.'

I walked on around the yard to see the rest of Jennings' stock. Some of the stoves were falling to bits, while others were almost pristine. I hovered over a huge Aga, fire-engine red, but decided it would take up half the kitchen. A cream-coloured Rayburn held some appeal, but in the end I returned to the brown one again.

I was giving it a second examination when the office door opened and a workman came out of the foundry. A young man, dark and about twenty-five, dressed in jeans and sweatshirt. He was carrying some tools and a small oven door. At the sight of me, he paused very briefly, looking, then passed by and knelt down beside one of the stoves to fix the door.

Jennings, by now, was becoming very genial, intent on making a sale. He was clearly well practised at soft-soaping women and told me to call him Phil.

'And you are . . . ?' he asked hopefully.

'Miss Elford.'

'Ah.' He took the hint but was unabashed, his eyes and his grin still over-friendly and seeming to admire. It was hard to tell if this was just a sales technique or if he had really taken a fancy

28

to me. At any rate, he was a man of great persistence. Some women, no doubt, would be flattered and a weaker creature might have placed an order there and then.

'I don't know,' I said, wanting time to consider. 'As I told you, I'm shopping around.'

'You won't get a better deal.'

'Perhaps. If not, I'll be back next week.'

'That stove you like could be gone by then. Can't hold it for you, see, without a deposit.'

'I'll have to chance that.'

I didn't like being pushed, even though the stove was attractive and within my means. Anyway, I hadn't had a chance to look anywhere else.

Jennings pressed a little more as I made to leave. The young man was listening, grinning, and I flushed as I caught his eye. He was not bad-looking, but he appeared coarse and too unyielding in his stare. The word 'insolent' came to mind.

Getting away was difficult, as Jennings talked on and on, and my gaze kept flickering down to the other man, pulled by his unrelenting stare. He was screwing a hinge on to the front of the stove to take the door. His fingers worked the screwdriver with a delicate slowness, peculiarly lewd. I couldn't keep from looking back, and his grin grew wider. As the screw went in, he applied more pressure until the movements were twisting jerks of the wrist. He grunted softly with the effort, glancing between his boss and me as if to convey some meaning.

Suddenly aware that his customer was being distracted, Jennings abruptly turned and the younger man swiftly looked away, eyes intent now on his work. Seizing the chance to make my escape, I hurried off, thanking Jennings for his time.

'I may come back to you,' I called as I beat a retreat.

Eight days later, that was what I did, after a tour around other suppliers who wanted two or three times the money for something similar. I rang the foundry, learned that the brown stove was still available and said that I would take it.

Jennings and the other man arrived at Trenarwyn one morning in early December to do the job. I found their presence a bit discomforting, especially since the younger one soon proved to be as forward as his boss. He had a lot to say about himself and to ask about me.

He told me his name was Noel Kinsman, tried to find out how old I was and if I had a manfriend. He played rugby, he informed me, and kept himself extremely fit. Well – couldn't I see? Laughing, he flexed his muscles for me. It was pretty obvious that he was keen to make an impression, but his boasting got on my nerves, along with that intrusive stare and grin. I summed him up as an over-sexed clod, the sort who would find mere vulgarity hilarious.

As for Phil Jennings, he admitted he was married but stressed that it didn't hinder him socially – did I understand? I surely did and disliked him for it. Neville probably said something very similar to his 'girlies'. Jennings, however, did not have Neville's charm. There was often something slyly lecherous in his eyes and tone – a manner he probably thought seductive. To me, it was merely annoying.

For the day and a half that it took them to finish the job, I stayed out of the kitchen as much as I could, venturing in there only to make snacks for myself and cups of tea for them. They had to smash open the bricked-up recess, and the thud of sledgehammers seemed to shake the very house.

At lunchtime Noel roared off somewhere in the lorry, while Jennings stayed put in the kitchen, drinking his tea and eating his sandwiches amid all the debris. Not once in all the time he was there did he ask to use the lavatory, and I wondered how he could hold himself so long, especially since the younger man was always up and down the stairs to the bathroom.

And in and out of the sitting room where I was working. He kept coming in to ask trivial questions, glancing all around him with curious eyes. It roused a sudden fear in me that he might be looking to see if there was anything worth stealing. Once, while I was at the loom, I thought I heard the creak of a floorboard overhead and suspected that Kinsman might be prying in my bedroom. I was on my way up to look, ready with a reprimand, when I heard the lavatory flush, then met him coming down the stairs, so couldn't say a thing.

Finally, though, when the work was complete, there came a harmless explanation for his interest in the house. He called me into the kitchen to see, and there, all neat and gleaming, stood my stove. The men had even swept up most of the mess, leaving just a pile of grit and brick dust in a corner.

'There then, how's that?' Jennings said. 'All ready for you to light.'

I was pleased. For a while I had feared I might have hired incompetents, but they had done a good job after all. Relieved, I beamed at both of them.

'It's splendid. Thank you so much. Shall I pay you now?'

'We'll send you a bill,' Kinsman said. Then, with a jerk of his head which somehow encompassed the whole house, he confided: 'I've always wanted to see what this place was like inside. Because of the old girl. Know about her, do you?'

I had to think for a moment. 'Miss Penhale? Mr Trelease at the grocer's mentioned her.'

He nodded. 'Weird, she was. I used to come out here and play in the woods sometimes when I was a boy, on my own or else with other kids. Used to see her outside now and then. We thought she was an old witch, what with that long black hair and her old-fashioned clothes. Used to make up kids' stories about her and what we imagined went on in this house.' He let out a loud guffaw. 'We reckoned she had skulls and cauldrons, books of spells and jars full of dead things in here.'

Jennings, however, looked sombre for once and nudged him reprovingly.

'Shouldn't laugh, Noel. Poor old creature. Shouldn't laugh at anything so sad.'

Kinsman scratched his nose and shrugged. 'Aw, well I suppose not. Anyway, the house was a terrible den, all right, and full of horrors – dry rot, cockroaches, that sort of thing – as we all found out years later when she died. Worse than a slum upstairs, it was. Hope you don't mind, I had a quick look round. Sorry for being nosy, but I can hardly believe it's the same place.'

So that was it. I knew, of course, that the house had been done up. There was a lot of new woodwork, a new roof and wiring. Still, Kinsman made it sound as if Mr Dean had bought Trenarwyn practically derelict. I asked about that, and Jennings confirmed it.

'Awful, it was, and went worse again after she died. It was empty a long time, see, till that young family took it on.'

'Did a good job, I must say that,' Kinsman declared. 'Dry and solid now as when the Penhales built it.'

'The same people lived here a long time?'

'Hundred and fifty years or so,' estimated Jennings with a thoughtful suck at his teeth. 'The Penhales were what you would call a leading family hereabouts until the First World War. Plenty of money, certainly.'

'Did they lose their wealth? Is that why the property fell into disrepair?'

'I don't think so. They just died off and the house went downhill when only Genevra was left. She was addled, see, couldn't take care of things.'

For some reason, the name intrigued me more this time. A pretty name, romantic. Hardly evocative of a crazy old woman – more suggestive of a young girl, beautiful, a social butterfly. Yet also it seemed to leave wistful echoes, aftersounds like 'never' and 'forever'.

'She should have been looked after, surely?'

'There's always a few the do-gooders miss,' Kinsman shrugged. 'Anyway, about this stove – you got any fuel for it?'

'Not yet.'

'My brother can help you with that, then, supply you with logs. It's one of the things he does, see, tree-work, lopping and felling and so on.'

'Oh? Well, perhaps . . .'

'He's easy to find. We live in the cottages there by the foundry, he and I. Jimmy's place is second from the end.'

He was smiling now, hopeful. Not such a bad sort, I thought, in his doltish way.

'Really? All right, I may call in and see him about it sometime soon.'

Off they both went, rattling away up the lane with all the rubble from my kitchen wall in the back of their lorry. I looked again at my new stove, delighted now the job was done. The wall would need repainting round the hole, but otherwise the operation had been very neat. The recess itself was lined with red brick – rather ugly, as it always is when it starts to discolour. I would paint that as well, give it a nice fresh coat of cream.

A few strands of cobwebs still clung here and there at the base of the chimney flue, so I set about them with a duster. It was while I was wiping the bricks at one side of the alcove that I came across a little carving of a heart. Roughly incised and a bit misshapen, but there was no mistaking what it was. A heart, with a name inside, scratched on the face of a brick. Squinting, I fingered it, tracing the letters. The name was David.

I had an overwhelming feeling that it was the work of a child, or else a barely literate kitchen maid. Many servants, anyway, were scarcely more than children themselves in the old days.

David. A sweetheart. A follower, or someone worshipped from afar? Object of somebody's dreams and affections, some very young girl. It was oddly poignant to see it there, revealed to the light after so many years, and just for a moment it moved me. They were probably dead now, both of them, or very old indeed. Love fulfilled or unfulfilled, I wondered. Or merely a fickle fancy, quickly forgotten – like the 'Michael' I once carved inside the lid of my desk at school?

Yes, probably nothing more than that. Shaking myself, I rubbed over the brick with my duster. Almost at once a chip of the surface flaked off and the name was half gone.

I had said I might call and see Kinsman's brother about some logs. Next morning, however, there came a loud knock at the door and when I answered it I found on the step a middle-aged man in grubby old clothes.

'Morning, miss.' He pulled off his cap and waved it towards the lane, where a pick-up was parked. 'Casanova tells me you want some logs?'

I stared at him. 'What? Who did you say?'

He pulled at his nose and grinned. 'Noel, my brother.'

'Oh! You're . . .'

'Jimmy Kinsman.'

'Yes, I see.' Eyeing him again, I repeated, 'Casanova?'

A chuckle. 'That's what we all call him. Four or five girl-friends on the go. Thinks he's it. You must have noticed?'

'Mm,' I said, laughing.

'Anyway, he says you'd like some logs, so I've brought a load.'

'How much?'

The price was fair. I might as well have them, I decided. He carried ten sackfuls into the outhouse and filled up one of the stalls.

'Applewood, that is,' he said when he had finished. 'Gives off a lovely scent as it burns.'

'Yes, I'm sure.'

Pausing in the yard, he looked up at the overhanging trees. 'Ought to have these down, miss, and sawn up. I could do it for you.'

'I was thinking I would, but I can't afford it yet.'

'Aw. Well, you know where to find me when you're ready.' He nodded his head at the house, as if there were someone in there. 'I offered to do it for her, you know, long time ago. The old girl, I mean. Wouldn't have it, though. She wasn't short of a bob or two, but she wouldn't have anything done.'

'So I gather.'

'All went to the taxman, it did. Everything she had. I read about it in the paper. Makes you want to weep.'

So saying, he went on his way. It was, I reflected, strange indeed that someone who came from a family of means should care nothing about what happened to it all when she was gone. If I were the last of an affluent line, I would at least wish to benefit some charities. She must, without doubt, have been queer in the head, poor old thing.

# Five

The stove soon proved itself to be an excellent investment. It would run all day on a few good chunks of wood. I felt I had all I wanted now – and so quickly too. My home, some transport, orders for work, and a pleasant acquaintanceship with quite a lot of local people. I felt I was liked and accepted, which was very gratifying.

And then I became a bit of a joke. I made a fool of myself – or so everyone thought.

But I know what I saw.

It was on a morning in mid December. I'd risen with a headache at first light. Experience had taught me it was best to get up and have some tea. Had I stayed in bed any longer, it would have progressed to a migraine and knocked me out for the rest of the day.

The stove had been burning all night and the kitchen was too warm for my sick head. I took my tea and toast into the sitting room instead, and sat in my chair at the window to eat and to take some tablets. The dawn was still grey and the morning quiet, the tide was coming in. I had put on a tape of Gregorian chant, and the gentle, ethereal voices of nuns filled the air with soothing music. The tablets quickly took effect and very soon my head began to clear. At least, I thought, I would make a good early start on my weaving.

But I was to do no work that day, because of a strange and very upsetting occurrence.

The morning was cold and revealing a mottled sky of heavy cloud. It was what I called dirty-white weather, making everything colourless and indistinct. I wasn't really noticing the view. I'd been staring out across the bay, unseeing, just listening to

35

the music. I was looking towards the far headland when suddenly a vague awareness intruded of something closer, in the foreground, something upright in the water a few yards out from shore.

Abruptly, I shifted my gaze and focused, and saw the girl.

She was standing thigh-deep in the rising tide, facing out to sea. An elegant figure, unmistakably young.

And stark naked.

I couldn't believe it. In December! Everyone knows, of course, that there are hardy people who swim the whole year round, but all the same I was astonished to see her standing there – not least because I hadn't noticed her walking down the beach. Any such movement should surely have caught my eye, but no. She seemed to have come from nowhere, simply appearing in the place where she now stood.

So very still. Already the water was lapping her hips, but she made no move. I couldn't see her face, not even the curve of her cheek. Her hair was dark and straight, cropped short at jaw length. At the back of her neck I could make out a pale gleam – a necklace, most probably pearls.

A glance at the clock told me it was just past eight. Breakfast time on a cold December morning. Naked swims, to my mind, were for summer and for moonlight, and in the company of a nice attractive man. But there she stood, alone, the freezing water now around her waist.

Why didn't she plunge right in, if that was what she had come here for? I began to feel very uneasy. Nothing about this seemed right.

The tide was coming in so fast, reaching her midriff – and now she moved, wading forward, going to meet it, up to her shoulders, her neck . . .

But instead of launching into a stroke, she simply allowed the water to swallow her. I waited to see her come up, but the seconds ticked past, drawing into a minute, then longer still . . .

And suddenly I knew she wasn't going to surface. I remember the crash as I dropped my cup and plate and dashed for the door.

Flying down the path, I wrenched open the gate and took off across the sand.

The girl had completely disappeared and now I wasn't exactly sure of the spot where she had been. Still in my pyjamas, I floundered to and fro in the shallows, searching for some sign to show me where she had gone under.

But there was nothing. The tide was almost at its height and nothing disturbed the lazy swell. The girl had gone without a trace. I remembered what Mr Trelease had said about the currents here. And yet, he had claimed it was safe at high tide. Well, perhaps after all it was not, which deterred me from plunging in and swimming about in search of her. Unless there was an undertow, how could she vanish just like that?

I had no answer, but knew I had to call some help. Rushing back to the house, I picked up the phone and dialled 999.

'Emergency, which service?' said the voice at the other end.

Panting, shaking all over with cold and shock, I blurted: 'Coastguard, please!'

The rest of the day was spent waiting and watching and chewing my fingernails. From my window I saw the coastguard launch cruising back and forth across the bay. Then, for a while, a helicopter swept to and fro overhead. As the afternoon went on, however, it was clear that they weren't going to find anything. Around half past three, a couple of uniformed policemen called at the house and I showed them into the sitting room.

'I was here at the window,' I said, and described yet again what it was I had seen.

The older man was open-minded, the younger one more sceptical.

'You're certain she couldn't have gone up the beach?' the latter said dubiously.

'Positive. Truly. There wasn't time and I would have seen her.'

'Well, you say she had nothing on, but we haven't found any clothes on the beach or in the woods behind.'

'Then I don't know where she left them, but I'm telling you

most definitely that she wasn't wearing a stitch. Just a necklace of pearls.'

They eyed me silently, both of them, the young one from under his brows and the peak of his cap. Then the older man spoke.

'This is a dangerous bay, Miss Elford, no question of that. I won't be adamant that you didn't see someone drown. Yet, the tide was high and calm, she just walked out into the sea and sank. It's odd, to say the least, hardly typical. A person takes some minutes to drown and you say she didn't even churn up the water. Doesn't usually happen that way. People fall out of boats or they're swept off rocks or they get cramp while swimming. They fight and they stay afloat for a while, but this . . .'

'Well, it has occurred to me that it may have been a suicide.'

'Possibly, but I wonder if you realise how difficult it is to stay down unless you're weighted or caught on something? She wasn't even clothed. There's nothing but sand out there, and no current close in to shore.'

In agitation, I looked from one to the other. 'What do you think, that I made it up?'

The younger one was poker-faced. The other said quickly: 'No, nothing like that. It's not impossible that a body will turn up. Enquiries will be made to see if anyone's gone missing hereabouts. You did your plain duty in calling for help, you couldn't ignore what you saw.'

The other man chipped in. 'I take it your eyesight is good, Miss Elford? May I ask how old you are?'

'Thirty-eight.'

'You don't wear spectacles?'

'No.'

'Haven't been tested recently? Always done a lot of close work, I expect?'

'I am not short-sighted!'

'Just a thought.'

'Wouldn't be somebody having a joke on you?' suggested the older man.

'Absolutely not.'

38

The young man sucked his teeth. 'You mentioned you had a headache this morning. Wasn't a hangover, by any chance?'

'No, it bloody well wasn't! I'm not a drunk!'

'Merely wondered. It must be lonely out here.'

'I like it that way, and I don't invent stories to get attention, if that's what's on your mind. I am not cuckoo, and if you were thinking of bringing up the menopause, you can forget that too.'

He went a bit pink and his partner coughed.

'All right. We shall see in due course what comes in with the tide, if anything.'

I was sorry at once for the outburst. They weren't to be blamed, I supposed; probably all too used to cranks and hoaxers and people who got themselves into trouble by doing stupid things.

'I saw a girl walk out into the sea and vanish,' I said helplessly. 'God's truth. May He strike me dead if it's a lie.'

When they left I felt utterly drained. I watched them walking off down the path and heard the young one muttering about what it cost the taxpayer to put a helicopter in the air for a couple of hours. Wretched, I slunk inside and closed the door.

After dark, the moon came up in a sky which had cleared of cloud, and by its radiance I went down to the beach for one more look. The tide had gone out during the day and now it was high again. Cold, cold sand crept into my shoes as I walked to the water's edge. The surface of the sea, unbroken, rolled and shone like mercury in the ashen light. It had closed about her and swept her away without so much as a splash of struggle, and somewhere in its depths her body lay, the dark hair and her string of pearls stirring in the currents.

I was not mistaken. I was not!

Local people, sad to say, were not much inclined to believe me. I knew the word had spread as soon as I went in to work at Good Harvest that Friday. True to their promise, the men had asked around to see if anyone was missing, so everybody in Polvean knew I had called out the coastguard and why. A dozen times in the course of the day, customers asked me about the incident. Brows were raised and heads were shaken, eyes were doubtful, puzzled, amused. Worst of all, jokes were made.

'You'll have all the local lads out there now, hoping to spot a naked woman. Ho, ho, ho!'

Or, 'Never mind women, Chris, didn't you see any naked men?'

Or, 'Haven't eaten any funny-looking mushrooms lately, have you, dear?'

And so on and so on. I could tell they all thought me a daft city type with a wild imagination.

'They don't mean any harm,' said Trevor, paying me at the end of the day. 'Shouldn't let it get you down. You know how people are.'

'I saw someone in trouble and tried to help. Now I'm being treated like a fool for it, or else regarded as a fraud. The police weren't convinced at all. I've been horribly worried, you know, afraid they might prosecute me.'

'Hardly, Chris. You're scarcely the sort to play practical jokes. They must know you made the call in good faith.'

'I hope so. Still, I'm sure they went away with the notion there was something wrong with me. One of them asked me if I needed glasses.'

'Perhaps you do.'

Indignant, I stared at him.

'No, don't take umbrage. Jane and I both wear them, don't we? Thing is, Chris, you don't always realise your sight's deteriorating. It can happen so gradually you just don't notice. Wouldn't hurt to find out, would it? Why don't you make an appointment?'

'I wasn't looking at a fuzz, it was all quite sharp and clear. If she truly wasn't there, then . . . I had an hallucination.'

Scarcely a comforting thought. More alarming than bad eyesight. I squeezed my aching temples and muttered, 'Oh, perhaps you're right. I'll have them tested as soon as I can, and get a medical check-up too.'

In the days that followed, I kept a close eye on the newspapers and television, but nothing was heard of a corpse or a missing girl. In the meantime, I checked on myself. A general overhaul at a clinic produced a clean bill of health, and soon after that I went into Truro to see an optician, who told me there was nothing wrong.

These results came as no great surprise, but left me with uneasy questions. If I was physically fit and my sight was good, then what of my mind? Had I been 'seeing things'? Was it possible to imagine something and have it appear before me, so detailed, so real?

As I put on my coat to leave the optician's, a question occurred to me: 'I once read somewhere that what we see is, how shall I say, not necessarily what's there. Is that true?'

He considered, frowned. Then: 'Yes and no. The picture is constructed in the brain. Not entirely objective, therefore, more an interpretation of the signals. Furthermore, the signals received vary widely from species to species. Depends on the optical equipment. We can't see ultraviolet, for instance, but a bee can. Your eyes don't tell the whole story, if that's what you mean.'

He hadn't realised what I was getting at, and I didn't pursue it any further for fear that he, too, would think me cracked. Thanking him, I left.

Christmas was just a few days away and the city streets were strung with tinsel garlands and coloured lights. All the shop windows were gaudily dressed and the town was a pretty sight.

Sight. A picture constructed in the brain, an interpretation, not necessarily the whole story. Or the true one?

In part, he had answered my question. Walking back to the car, I wished I hadn't asked him.

# Six

Christmas came and still nothing was heard. Resolved not to let it spoil the season, I pushed the matter from my mind, decorated my tree and prepared for a few days of solitary self-indulgence. I bought a duck and roasted it for Christmas lunch. Neville had always wanted goose and this was the first time in years I'd been able to suit myself. Lucinda and I made short work of the bird and the afternoon was spent on the couch with a bottle of apricot brandy, watching *A Christmas Carol* on television. How I laughed at Scrooge's terror when Marley's ghost appeared. I had never believed in such things, of course. A thorough sceptic, that was me.

On Boxing Day I made a lunch of gammon and pineapple, played carols for hours and had a lovely, chuckling time curled up with *Cold Comfort Farm*. Christmas alone in front of the fire. No parties, no guests, no visits to kin – thank God.

On New Year's Eve, however, I was tempted out. The telephone rang and it was Jane.

'Chris? How about coming down to The Outrigger this evening? Have a few drinks and sing "Auld Lang Syne"? Oh come on, you must! Everyone's going to be there.'

Yes, and I might come in for a bit more ribbing. Still, perhaps it was best to laugh it off, laugh along with the rest of them. No good taking umbrage, that was certain. No good standing on my dignity.

I took the car and drove down to The Outrigger around ten o'clock. It was one of those carefully preserved waterside inns where all the beams and panelling were original, and comforts like carpets were chosen to be unobtrusive.

As might be expected, the place was crowded. Trevor and

Jane were saving a seat for me at a table near the fire. There was someone else with them, a man I had never seen before.

They all shifted their chairs to let me in. 'What are you having, Chris?'

I asked for a glass of white. Trevor went to buy the round and Jane introduced the stranger. 'Chris, this is Jack Roskear.'

I said hello.

Nodding, he smiled. 'I've heard all about you.'

Inwardly, I groaned, afraid he was going to start on about the girl and all the fuss. But, instead, he continued: 'Must have taken plenty of nerve to give up a good job and come down here. Handicrafts are always a chancy way to make a living.'

'True, although I already have some customers.'

'That so? Good for you. It matters, doing what you're made for, what you enjoy. Hate your work and no amount of money compensates.'

'Yes, so I've found.'

Another nod. He sipped his beer. I very much liked his face, thinking it slightly comical, very brown and smiley. He was fortyish, wearing a navy blue jersey and jeans, and his hair was just beginning to show some grey.

'Jack has a boat,' said Jane. 'He takes people out for fishing trips in the summer months.'

'Really?' I said. 'Is there good trade in that?'

Putting the glass down, he smacked his lips. 'Patchy, but I get along.'

'What about the winter?'

'I do a bit of gardening work, lay down paths and put up walls or fences. Never did have any ambition,' he added, grinning. 'It's a pleasant life and it'll do.'

Neville would have dismissed him at once as a failure, but the man was happy enough with himself, satisfied, and there was something very attractive about that.

Trevor returned with the drinks and sat down. The pub was already quite rowdy and more people kept pressing in all the time. Trelease, the grocer, was there with his wife, quietly downing stout in a corner. There was much noisy talk about boats and the weather in the confident up-country accents of

Polvean's incomers, and as the time moved on past eleven there were outbreaks of singing.

At one point Phil Jennings came over to ask if the stove was all right. At the bar, a little dark woman – no doubt his wife – was perched on a stool, keeping a suspicious eye on him. He leaned over me, beery and rather too close, shouting to make himself heard above the din. I noticed a look pass between him and Jack which was less than friendly. The latter took a swig of ale and twisted his mouth as he swallowed it, as if it suddenly tasted bad. I said I was very pleased with the stove, and as Jennings went rolling off back to his wife, saw Jack mouthing something about him to Jane, something with which she clearly agreed.

From the first I had wondered, and soon I was sure that Trevor and Jane had brought Jack Roskear especially to meet me. I found him a lovely man, but didn't know whether to laugh or be annoyed at this very transparent attempt to 'fix me up'. If he had also tumbled to it, he didn't seem to mind, chatting on, growing more and more mellow with every pint.

As midnight approached, Noel Kinsman arrived with a bosomy redhead in tow. He was wearing a purple shirt, open halfway down to the waist, and a gold medallion nestled in his chest hair. I caught Jane's eye, she jerked her head at him and we both laughed.

'I hear they call him Casanova.'

She chuckled. 'That's right, they do. Great conceited fool. Of course, his girlfriends are all just as dim as he is.'

At five to twelve, I pushed my way through to the bar to buy a last round. Noel was there in loud voice, showing off, he and the redhead all over each other. When he saw me, he insisted on helping me carry the drinks to the table. We had barely put them down when the clock began to strike and everyone stood up, jostling and linking arms for 'Auld Lang Syne'. I found myself with Jack on one side, Noel on the other. As the singing ended, Kinsman pulled me round and delivered a very unwelcome, sloppy kiss. He bellowed, 'Happy New Year, maid,' and looked hugely pleased with himself.

Covertly, I wiped my mouth . . . then turned on Noel in fury as he suddenly bawled out: 'By the way, if you see any more naked women out there, you let me know. I'll resuscitate them, don't you fret.'

Rolling his eyes, he made a kneading motion with his hands. There were ripples of laughter all around. Everyone seemed to be grinning at me and my cheeks burned red. So much for my resolve to take the teasing in good part. It was all I could do not to slap Noel Kinsman across his silly face. Then the redhead, petulant, was pulling at his arm and off he went, still roaring at his own wit.

Later, when we left the pub, Jack was sympathetic as he walked across the quay to the car with me. 'Shouldn't pay any heed when they pull your leg, Christine.'

'Easier said than done.'

'I know, but they're the stupid ones.'

In the light from The Outrigger's windows, I paused and looked at him.

'*They're* stupid? Does that mean you believe me? You'd be about the only person in Polvean.'

'Not entirely. The bay's claimed several lives, and some of the old villagers still remember. Point is, you see, there was one before whose body was never found. My grandfather says he recalls it. Long time ago it was – seventy years or so. Young man, name of David Lanyon. He drowned out there within sight of your house and the body never did turn up. I don't disbelieve you, Chris. What's happened once can happen twice.'

'Is that a fact? He was never found?'

'Not hide nor hair of him.'

'And it's certain he drowned?'

'Witnesses, three of them, saw it, the crew of a lugger heading into Polvean from a night's fishing. They said he was way, way out on the sand and got caught by the incoming tide. They came about and searched for him, but he was gone without a trace.'

I pondered a moment, then murmured, 'Well, that's a comfort of sorts. If their eyes didn't deceive them, nor did mine.' We walked on to where I had parked the car. 'Can I give you a lift home?' I asked, taking out my keys.

'Thanks, but it's just a short way.'

45

Opening the door, I got in. Jack leaned down, peering in at me.

'Nice pub, The Outrigger, eh?'

'Very.'

'Like to go again some time, with me? Perhaps one evening next week?'

I'd been afraid of this. Awkwardly, I said: 'I don't think so, Jack. You're very nice and I enjoyed meeting you, but . . .'

'But?'

I sighed. 'Look, it was pretty obvious that Trevor and Jane were trying to do a bit of matchmaking tonight, but I have other priorities.'

A slight, disappointed delay. Then: 'Oh, I see.'

'I'm sorry.'

'That's all right, it was just a thought. No matter, maid.'

He dismissed it in that cheerful way which fails to hide a man's embarrassment when he's been turned down. I'd heard it countless times before and it always made me feel guilty of dire cruelty.

'See you around, then.'

'Yes, of course. Goodnight, Jack.'

I watched him walk off up a sidestreet until he was lost in the dark. A very agreeable man, but the last thing I wanted was any involvement with anyone just yet.

The drive home was a couple of miles, for the road took a twisting route. It must have been about twenty to one when I parked in the lane by the gate.

Cool and peaceful after the evening's noise, the air felt almost pensive when I got out of the car. The gate gave a little squeak swinging back and the iron latch closed with a clang. Starting up the path, I fumbled in a pocket for my doorkey.

Just as my fingers closed upon it, I saw the light. A haloed glow from my sitting room – as if there were a candle burning on the window ledge.

I can't describe the shock and fright of it. Somebody was in my house and not afraid to advertise the fact.

Horrified, I stood there on the path, staring up at the window. Around me, the garden seemed watchfully silent, as if all the shrubs and trees were waiting to see what I would do.

I was at a loss. Was it best to get back in the car? Drive off and get the police? There was no police station in Polvean. Truro was the nearest, and since I'd had quite a lot to drink, the idea didn't appeal.

What was I to do, then? Stay outside until whoever it was had left? It would seem mad to go and confront the intruder, who might be large and dangerous.

And then, quite suddenly, the light was gone. I didn't actually see it go out, but one moment it was there and the next it was not. I'd been looking up at the bedroom windows, wondering if more than one person was in the house, and briefly the light was out of my field of vision. When I looked back, it had disappeared.

Perhaps whoever it was had heard my car and the sound of the gate and was clearing off.

Either that or he was waiting in the dark for me.

Just for a moment, I found myself wishing that I was back in London, safe with Neville. And that was when anger took over, when I imagined his gloating 'I told you so', and pictured some thief, some trespasser in my house, rifling through my things.

I had spent that morning trying to fork over the flowerbeds – without much success, for the ground was hard. The fork was still where I had left it, stuck upright in a patch of earth. I marched towards it, pulled it out, went up to the front door and let myself in.

A flick of the switch and the hallway was flooded with light. Catching sight of myself in the hall mirror, I thought I looked pretty threatening, woman or not, with my garden fork upraised.

I shouted: 'Who's there? Get out of my house!'

It didn't sound like me, that strident, angry voice. It didn't shake the way I was shaking inside.

There was no response. No sound, not a bump or a scrape or the softest of footfalls from anywhere.

Going forward, I turned the light on in the sitting room. It was undisturbed. I had quite expected to find it ransacked, but nothing had been touched. I went around all the rooms, turning on every light, examining windows and doors. I had left them locked when I went out and locked they all remained. No entry had been forced in any way and nothing appeared to be missing.

I should have been relieved and in one sense I was, for plainly no one had broken in. But then what of the light?

I returned to the sitting room, looking around me, trying to account for it – and finally seized upon an explanation. On the sideboard, facing the fire, a copper kettle stood. Flames licking up round a log in the grate threw dancing reflections upon it from time to time, constantly shooting up, dying away, then springing to life again.

That was it, that was the cause. It had to be. No other possibilities presented themselves, except for the one I least wanted to entertain. It had to be the kettle. Or I was 'seeing things' after all.


When I went to work the following Friday, Trevor asked hopefully, 'What did you think of old Jack, then? Good sort, isn't he? Makes you laugh.'

I was weighing out black-eyed beans, sealing them into cellophane bags. Pausing, scoop in hand, I eyed him severely.

'Very pleasant, yes, I liked him. But Trevor, I really don't care to be paired off. I don't need or want anyone making arrangements for me. If and when I'm ready, I'll find someone for myself. All right?'

He was so abashed, poor thing. I wished at once I hadn't been so sharp. Taking refuge behind the opposite counter, he busied himself pricing trays of tomatoes and courgettes and yams.

'Oh, well Jane and I just thought . . . I mean, Jack is single and so are you and you're both about the same . . .' He floundered, reddening.

'Same advanced age, yes.' I was grinning now.

'We thought it might be nice if you took to each other, that was all.'

'I do appreciate your concern, but I'm quite self-sufficient.'

'You may be. I think he's lonely.'

'I'm very sorry. Has he no one at all?'

'Just his grandfather. Jack's wife left him, see. Proper little no-good, she was. Had flings with two other men while she was still married to Jack. That chap from the foundry was one of them – Jennings, the boss.'

'Ah.' I looked at him. 'Yes, there was an atmosphere between them, I noticed that.'

'Phil's an alley cat,' nodded Trevor. 'He's even tried it on with Jane. He and Jack's wife were two of a kind. When Jack found out what was going on between them, he went up to the foundry one morning and flattened Phil. Of course, it wasn't worth his trouble. The woman cleared off three weeks later with someone else she'd met. Never did like the quiet life, and she wanted plenty of money.'

'Poor Jack,' I murmured. 'How is it that nice men often get involved with such bad lots?'

'Precisely because they are nice, I suppose. They don't see someone's rottenness until it's far too late. She was pretty, of course, slightly porky, but pretty, and he just fell for her. Everybody else knew they were terribly mismatched.'

'And you consider me more suitable.'

Trevor shot me a shifty glance. 'It was Jane's idea, really.'

That was very probable. I carried on measuring out the beans.

'He liked you, Jack did,' ventured Trevor. 'I could tell he was impressed.'

I smiled but had nothing to say.

'Jane said she'd be afraid to live alone out there as you do. She has a point. Doesn't it worry you, Chris?'

About to respond with a definite 'no', I faltered. What had my first reaction been to the sight of that light in the window? Wouldn't I have given a lot to have a man there with me then? Still, in the end I'd been brave and was proud of that.

'It's damned hard lines,' I said, 'if a woman can't live alone simply because she's afraid. To my mind, it's intolerable.'

'Point is, your house is more isolated than most. And a person needs company. You've only been there – what? Three months? Give it a year and the solitude might start to pall.'

49

Once again, I grew irritable. 'Precisely, Trevor, let's give it a year, let's not prejudge.'

He fell mournfully silent.

I carried on with my work, but a mixture of vexing suggestions now went swirling around in my mind. That I wasn't safe at Trenarwyn, and that guarding my privacy was somehow selfish – as if I had some duty to team up with lonely Jack. As if we were both loose ends who should be neatly tied together, because the animals went in two by two and the orderly world of couples feared or pitied loners. That I might become increasingly unhappy as time went on. The cure for all these ills was a partner, a mate. But I had only just escaped from Neville.

Jack was certainly attractive in a well-worn way, and I had to admit I'd never done well at picking out men for myself. Jane, perhaps, had better instincts than mine in that respect. Yet, wasn't Jack a needy case? So it seemed from all that Trevor said about him, and I'd already succoured more than my share of misfits, waifs and strays.

# Seven

The end of the month brought storms. Bad weather was truly impressive here. Wild winds came shrieking in from the sea, beating and bending my trees till I thought they must surely snap. In the front garden the shrubs and rose bushes strained away from the gale as if they would tear themselves from the ground and flee. The sky was a boiling of white, black and grey, flinging down hard, slanting rain. Heaving and booming, the sea was a cauldron. Breakers came charging like runaway horses headlong in to shore, hurling themselves on the beach and exploding in founts of spray.

A tremendous show; I watched and enjoyed it for hour after hour, playing Mussorgsky's *Night on the Bare Mountain*, Saint-Saëns' *Danse Macabre*, *The Flying Dutchman* by Wagner, and many another orchestral tempest. Disgusted with it all, Lucinda stayed in the kitchen and slept by the stove, only venturing out when she had to, and rushing straight in again afterwards, looking peeved.

The storms went on for the better part of a week, with only short lulls in between. After them came a chilly fortnight, overcast and still. One morning I walked across the beach, where the waves had thrown up heaps of seaweed, and driftwood which must have come from the creek. At the end of the headland some sloe bushes grew, and below them the point tapered down to a jumble of rocks. I looked up the inlet as far as the bend which hid Polvean from view. Close to the opposite bank, a small yacht wallowed on its port side, half-submerged. Several broken branches floated in the water, and near the tideline was an oak tree, cleft in two by lightning.

51

So much damage, so much wreckage pitched up by the surging tides.

But no body, no dark-haired girl.

It had been at the back of my mind that the churning seas might finally have cast her up, if not here, then somewhere further along the coast. But the news still carried no reports of a corpse being found. Although reassured to some extent by what Jack had told me, I was still much troubled by the matter. Unlike the light I had seen in my window, it couldn't be explained away. Sad though it would be to hear of a body turning up, it would certainly set my mind at rest – and prove to everyone that I wasn't a crank.

I scanned the bay, so placid now, and felt an urge to cry: 'Where is she?', as if the sky and sea could hear and answer me.

Clouds and water gently rolled, bleak, inscrutable. Standing there in that lonely place, I feared the mystery might plague me till my dying day.

Yet . . . It was not long afterwards that I began to guess and to understand.

In mid February there was snow. I woke one Monday morning and found my bedroom window frames crusted with white. Out in the garden, a pristine eiderdown of snow lay six inches deep on the grass. The hedges were stiff with a crunchy frosting and the hips and haws of the shrub roses looked like crystallised fruits, all heavily sugared.

The fire in the sitting room was nearly out when I went downstairs, and it took me half an hour to coax it into a decent blaze again. Because of the weather, I turned on the television in hopes of hearing a forecast, and shortly saw a news report with aerial film. It seemed the whole south of the country was blanketed in snow and more was expected before the end of the day. Villages up around Bodmin and down on the Lizard had lost their electricity, so I felt very lucky indeed to have mine, as well as the wood stove and open fire. The house was well stocked with food and the shed was full of logs, so being snowbound was not a disaster.

I spent the morning at the loom, listening to *The Barber of*

*Seville* and placidly happy among my coloured yarns. The house felt protective around me, and the scent of burning apple logs came sweetly from the grate. Away from here, in the world I had left, people were struggling to get from A to B on icy roads, crawling along with chains on their tyres, or getting stuck and trudging off in search of telephones, ringing around and cancelling appointments they couldn't keep, fretting over schedules and backlogs. Panic over disruption, dismay at falling behind. Thank God I had given up that life. Thank God I was here in this warm room, at peace with my quiet, satisfying work and my music.

Just before two, feeling hungry, I went to put some tinned soup on the stove. While it was heating, I thought I would fetch in some logs from the shed, so I put on a quilted jacket, boots and gloves, and ventured into the bitter wind outside.

Coming out of the woodshed, arms full, I kicked the door shut behind me, and was just about to go indoors when I noticed the tracks leading down at the side of the house. Animal tracks, possibly those of a fox. Mildly curious, I followed them around to the front garden, where they disappeared through a hole in the escallonia hedge. Whatever it was had probably been poking around the dustbin at the back door, seeking food, and I made a mental note to leave something out this coming night.

I was just going to turn and go back in the house when I realised I had another visitor, a human one.

She was young, I knew that straight away, even though her back was turned. Young and tall and graceful, with black hair – glossy, glossy hair – rippling down her back. She was standing by the bottom wall, looking out to sea. Yet again, someone in my garden, someone trespassing. The shock of her presence, however, had little to do with the fact that she had no right to be there. There was something else and just for a second I couldn't pinpoint what – something incongruous, not quite real . . .

Of course – her clothes. All she wore was a dress of a very thin cotton, like muslin. A summer dress on a freezing day. She was standing in snow to the ankles, yet she didn't shiver, not a tremor, and not so much as a hair of her head was stirring in the wind. No, nor the flimsy fabric she wore. It fell straight and hung still. Unnaturally still.

To speak, I think, is human instinct, even when we are confronted with something we know to be very strange. We speak, it's just a reflex. I know I called something out to her, something idiotic, like: 'Excuse me? Can I help you?'

There was no response. She didn't turn, seemed unaware of me.

'Excuse me? Who are you? What do you want?'

Again she paid me no heed, so I took a few steps forward. I was careless, I suppose, so intent on the woman that I forgot the path was slippery with ice. A second later I was on my back, shocked and winded, with logs strewn all around me. I cracked an elbow against the ground as I went down, and a slamming pain went through me from hip to shoulder.

After a moment I sat up, wincing, and looked around for her.

But she had gone.

Cautiously, I got to my feet. Treading more carefully this time, I walked across to the spot where she had been.

No sign of her in any direction. She seemed to have melted into thin air, just vanished. Like the girl in the tide, and like the old woman a few months before . . .

What entered my head turned me shaky inside, and when I looked down at the ground my mouth went dry.

For she had left no footprints anywhere. There were mine and mine only. The fox made tracks and so did I, like all mortal things. But not she. Not a mark.

When I went indoors again my first desire was a drink, and a large one at that. I was still rather shaken by my fall and horribly rattled too, so when I entered the back door and met with a smell of burning I almost shrieked.

I'd forgotten the soup, of course, and the saucepan had boiled completely dry. A black sticky mess coated all the inside, from which rose a pungent smoke. Still, it hardly mattered now; I'd lost my appetite.

All afternoon, over a bottle of Scotch, I argued with myself. I didn't believe in ghosts or hocus-pocus. Never had, never would. Never, never, never. Yet, perhaps . . .

It would explain so much, especially the girl with the necklace of pearls.

The notion both attracted and repelled me. I liked to have answers. I liked to have whys and hows, to know and not be puzzled. Such an explanation, though, was scarcely comforting. I was never a superstitious person, rather a hardheaded sceptic, in fact; a scoffer at horoscopes and tarot cards, magic and omens and visions. I, who prided myself on being down-to-earth, was surely the last person likely to see a phantom?

Only one? Weren't there three of them? Three generations of ghosts, I thought, laughing aloud as I grew tight. Probably all related.

Indeed, perhaps they were. Each, after all, was dark haired and tall. The old woman was stooped, but she would have been tall in her youth. I recalled she had worn her hair roughly pinned up and there had seemed to be a lot of it. Released from its clips, it could well have reached right down her back, like that of the young woman out in the snow . . .

A memory half surfaced, teasing me, something about long black hair. Musing, I twirled the whisky bottle round and round by its neck on the table before me.

'. . . *that long black hair and her old-fashioned clothes.*'

Noel Kinsman's voice.

'*We thought she was an old witch . . .*'

He was speaking, of course, of Miss Penhale.

Genevra. She of the lovely name.

I ceased to spin the bottle, stared unseeing at the label and sipped a drop more Scotch.

Which one would be Genevra?

The old woman, naturally.

Then who were the other two? Not the same person?

Not possible, no, for the girl had drowned.

Hadn't she?

The whisky began to fuddle me. I couldn't sort it all out in my mind and grew frustrated, angry. Here was I, hitherto sensible Christine, drinking myself silly and entertaining fantastic ideas about spirits and spectres. I was actually, seriously, debating the possibility that I had bought a haunted house. It was ludicrous, absolute rot!

So reason said. Instinct told me something else, and I slept with the light on that night.

# Eight

I didn't speak to anyone of what I had seen or what I suspected. If Trenarwyn were known as a haunted house, then someone would surely have mentioned it to me, and no one had. Apart from me, only the Deans had lived there since Genevra died, and there had never been any suggestion that they had experienced anything odd. If I were to go around saying that Miss Penhale was haunting the place, I'd be judged even more batty than the old girl herself. Living down the business with the coastguard was hard enough. I didn't care to compound it with talk of ghosts.

So I kept my own counsel, remaining alone with my unease. Not even Lucinda shared it. She seemed untroubled by anything inside the house or out. A few days after the snow had gone, I watched her sniffing around the front garden in her normal, casual way. Did she spit, did her fur stand on end, did she turn tail and run from some lingering presence? No. On the contrary, she sat down almost on the spot where the long-haired woman had stood, and placidly started to wash. I did find a certain reassurance in that. Animals, after all, were supposed to sense things humans could not. If my cat was unconcerned, at least it seemed fair to conclude that nothing malign was involved.

Late in the month I went into Truro again, this time to try my luck with a stall at the Saturday fleamarket and craft fair. I took along a folding chair, plus a pasting table and a hatstand on which to display my wares, and was lucky enough to get a pitch out of the draughts which blew through the doors at each end of the hall. Mine was one of a dozen handicraft tables, where pottery and leatherwork, dried flowers, patchwork and silver jewellery were represented. The other stalls were a glittering show of bric-à-brac and collectables. The tables were crammed in end to end and the aisles were filled with slowly milling crowds. The twinkle of silver and china, coloured glass and paste jewellery was interrupted here and there by stands of books, their cloth and leather covers faded to washed-out reds and greens and browns. Out-of-print novels, the pages foxed; out-of-date reference books, quaint in their notions and attitudes. In front of them, in cardboard boxes, lay gaudy modern paperbacks and bundles of *National Geographics* tied around with string. I loved the world of the second-hand. It was one of treasure hunting, of rescuing things unwanted and forgotten. It suited my penchant for scruffiness and I liked to imagine the objects around me had stories to relate. Better a chipped old Toby jug with faded paint and a history than a brand new one out of a smart china shop.

In view of this, I supposed I ought to be positively pleased to think Trenarwyn might be haunted. For it meant that it wasn't just any old house, but an interesting one, something special. Most old houses had some tale to tell, but that of Trenarwyn must be exceptional, something for me to investigate – quite exciting, really.

I mused on these things as I sat behind my table, interrupted now and then by someone wanting to buy. Of course, in surroundings like these, it was easy to take a cheerful view. I doubted it would be any fun to confront a spectre when I was alone in the house at night.

Around midday I went for a walk around the hall, leaving my pitch in the care of a neighbouring stallholder. I found a man selling wind-up gramophones, old seventy-eight speed records and sheet music. He sold me a long-player of *The Merry Widow*. For a while I browsed among collections of postcards and cigarette cards, then moved on to a bookstall. It was there, while foraging in the depths of a packing case, that I chanced upon a volume called *The Night Side of Nature*, sub-titled *Or Ghosts and Ghost-Seers*. The author was called Catherine Crowe, and although the book dated from 1848, the style and content appealed to me. The man let me buy it for just thirty pence.

Another stall yielded a wonderful teapot, moulded and painted to caricature a beaming Winston Churchill. He cost twenty pounds and was very heavy, but I had to have him. At home in the kitchen I had a Welsh dresser, where he would take pride of place.

That was a good day altogether: several splendid little finds and – better still – a very worthwhile order from a large interiors store in Exeter. It was my good luck that a buyer had chanced to travel to Truro that day on personal business, and took the opportunity to pop in and look at the craft stalls. Driving home in bouncy mood, I whistled all the way, and felt ready to deal with the White Lady, the Headless Horseman, or even the Baskerville Hound, if they cared to call on me.

Around six, I sat down at the kitchen table with a cup of coffee and an apple doughnut. Wreathed in smiles, the Church-ill teapot gazed across at me from its place on the dresser, and I smiled back as I ate my doughnut, delighted with this latest addition to my home. I tried to buy a little something for the house each time I went into town. The best touch in the kitchen was probably the wooden rack suspended from the ceiling above the kitchen table. I hung my herbs and saucepans on it, and often skeins of wool as well.

Licking the sugar off my fingers, I started flipping through Catherine Crowe's book, scanning a passage here and there, then skipping on again. It struck me as worthy of careful study, and I decided to spend the evening reading it. On most subjects, old books could be dismissed because they were rendered obsolete by new outlooks, new knowledge. On the matter of hauntings, however, no one was very much wiser today than at any time in the past. We were simply more inclined to deny the possibility out of hand. The idea was not disproven, merely brushed off without much thought.

Well, I had reason now to think about it, so I took the book into the sitting room, made myself comfortable by the fire and started at page one.

I had put *The Merry Widow* on to see what it was like, but in truth I paid the music scant attention and didn't bother to turn it over when the first side ended. I was far too absorbed in what

I was reading. According to the introduction, the author had been both praised and scorned for this volume in her time. It was easy to see why. There was much I couldn't swallow – but also much I recognised from recent experience. On the whole, I felt the book was the work of an open, agile mind, albeit slightly too religious for my taste. I had quite a few reservations, but Mrs Crowe's enthusiasm was infectious and some of her reasoning made very good sense.

By the time I put it down, there were only forty pages left and it was nearly midnight. In bed, still eager to finish it, I managed to read another twenty pages before the book fell from my hands and I was fast asleep.

If I had harboured any lingering doubts that my house was haunted, *The Night Side of Nature* had put an end to them. Thereafter, I was on the lookout, constantly alert for anything odd. Of course, it's often the case that when one awaits or seeks a thing, it declines to appear. So it was with me. Yet, as winter turned into early spring without any further visitations, I became more and more exercised in watching for Her or Them, as the case might be. For hours I would sit at the window, keeping vigil, but to no avail. Going about my daily tasks, I was watchful, and would think sometimes that I glimpsed a movement, a shadow, a shape, from the corner of my eye, but when I turned to see there was never anything there.

That first reaction of dismay, that early case of the creeps, had long since turned into something else. I was fiercely curious, fascinated. I wanted to know all about the old woman, Genevra Penhale.

Mulling the whole thing over, I'd made a connection in my mind, one which should have hit me sooner. That name I had found in the chimney recess – 'David', enclosed by a heart. The same name as that of the young man who had drowned in the bay years ago and whose body had never been found, according to Jack Roskear. Of course, there might not be any link, but I couldn't help remembering how intently those women, all of them, had stood just staring out to sea.

I wished I could talk to Jack again and wondered how I

might arrange it. Then I recalled he did gardening work and thought he might care to do some for me. Now and again he bought stuff at Good Harvest, though rarely on Fridays when I was there, so I left a message at the shop for him to call round if he felt so inclined.

He turned up one morning in the third week of March, a bright day with a lively breeze whisking through the catkins and the primroses. I was out in the lane with a sponge and a bucket of soapy water, cleaning the car, when I spotted him coming, an unhurried figure in faded jeans and an army surplus jumper. Dropping the sponge in the bucket, I wiped my hands on my old jersey, leaving it smeared with foam.

'Hello, Jack.'

'Morning, maid. Jane says you want your garden dug?'

Hands still wet, I brushed back a floppy strand of hair, leaving froth on that too.

'Yes, I've had a go, but it's a bit too much for me. Very heavy and stony, really packed down hard. The poor plants must be choking.'

He nodded, looking over the gate, eyes narrowed against the sun. 'I'll prune back your shrubs and roses too, shall I? Especially that buddleia – should have been done last month.'

'If you would. I'd be glad, as well, if you'd spike the lawn. It's holding water and full of moss.'

'All right.' He looked at me and smiled. 'Keeping well?'

'Fine, thanks. And you? Must be nearly time for you to get the boat out?'

'April,' he confirmed. 'First trippers come around Easter. Well then, where's your toolshed?'

I showed him round to the old stable, then left him to it. While he clipped and pruned, I threw a couple of buckets of clean water over the car, then went inside to get on with the crackle-weave curtains I was making.

He laboured hard without a pause, and it took him a couple of hours to deal with the shrub and flowerbeds, for the ground was like concrete. Every time I stopped working the loom, I could hear the scrape and clink of shovel on stone. At twelve, I made tea and sandwiches for us both and took them outside.

61

Sipping my tea, I sat down with him on the top step of the terrace.

'Hard going, wasn't it? I could tell.'

'Hasn't been done for a couple of years,' he said. 'Earth soon gets impacted when there's heavy rain. You've got some beautiful species here, especially the shrubs. They're young as yet, but you'll have a fine show in a few years' time.'

'Mr Dean must have planted them. I'm surprised he got around to the garden, with so much to do to the house. I heard it was pretty dreadful when he bought it.'

'So I believe.' Finishing a chicken sandwich, Jack reached for another. 'Never used to come out here myself. Hadn't been out here for years till today.' Thoughtfully, he added: 'I can't pretend I like this beach. Never did, even as a boy.'

'Because of what your grandfather told you?'

'Partly, yes. That and the atmosphere of the place when the tide is out. It's a wide open space and yet it's a trap. The sand seems to go on for ever, but you know the water is there, just out of sight and waiting to catch the unwary.'

After a brief hesitation, I ventured: 'The man you spoke of on New Year's Eve, the one who drowned here . . .'

'David Lanyon?'

'Yes, that's right. Did your grandfather know him?'

'Knew of him. Wouldn't have been acquainted with him, though. They were better class, see, the Lanyons. Wealthy people – had a big house about three miles the other side of Polvean.'

'Bigger than Trenarwyn?'

'Oh yes, by far. The National Trust owns it now, along with all its gardens. Very fine gardens.'

I was silent a moment, thinking. 'Someone told me that the Penhales, who built this place, were quite an important family. The Lanyons must have been even more so. Do you think they knew each other, socialised?'

'Seems likely. Moneyed people always mix with their own kind, don't they? Why do you ask?'

Lightly, I said: 'It's just that I've become quite interested in the old lady who lived here.'

'Oh yes, she was touched in the head, according to local rumour.'

'It's hard to imagine someone of that background ending up the way she did, living in squalor, isolated. I don't suppose she was always strange. There must have been a time when she was normal, had friends and a good life. Something must have happened, something dreadful.'

'Not necessarily. She could have been born with a screw loose, simple as that.'

I was doubtful, somehow, but didn't bother to argue the point. 'This David Lanyon,' I said, 'how did he come to get drowned?'

'No idea – except, as I've told you before, he did what no one should do and walked far out on the sand when the tide was low. Ought to have known better, being a local man. Mind you, I believe Grandfather did say there was something a bit wrong with him, can't recall what. It was something to do with the war.'

I looked at him. 'The Great War?'

'Must have been.'

'Do you happen to know who else was drowned out there?'

He thought for a moment. 'One, I believe, was a naturalist chap, the other a man who'd been digging for bait. Those incidents both happened right back in Victorian times. Their bodies turned up a few miles down the coast.'

Two other victims, both of them men, I thought.

'You never heard of anything involving a woman?'

Turning, he frowned at me slightly in puzzlement. 'Not till the one you reported. Why?'

'Oh, just wondered.'

'It's more often men who take silly chances,' he shrugged. 'Anyway, that's all I know of it, and I'd best get on. I'll go and prick over your lawn with the fork to give the grass a chance.'

I murmured absently, 'Thank you, yes,' and he went back to his work.

Still sitting there drinking my tea, I chewed over what he had told me. '. . . *something a bit wrong with him* . . .'

Did that mean David Lanyon hadn't known what he was

doing? Or could it have been that he wanted to die? Impossible to say.

However, one question was probably answered. It was on the cards that David and Genevra had known each other. Whether they were close was another matter. Anyone could have carved that little heart on the chimney brick – and it could have meant another David altogether. After all, it was a very common name. Yet, why had Lanyon died, and why had Genevra ended her days as a poor old recluse? A shared tragedy, or separate misfortunes? I still knew too little to make a confident guess.

Going inside, I ploughed on with my work. At just after three, I looked round in response to a tap on the window and there was Jack, mouthing 'All done.' I waved him towards the front door, making signs to come in.

When he appeared at the sitting room door, he looked around him with approving eyes.

'Made it nice here, haven't you? Very homey.'

'I'm pleased with it,' I said, hunting around for my purse.

'I like this sort of place, plenty of comfort but no spit and polish.' He sounded wistful.

'What's it like at home?'

'Rough,' he said, grinning. 'Grandad and me, we're any old how.' Ruefully, he confided: 'I did rent a decent little house when I first married. Wife wanted all new stuff, couldn't wait, so I went in debt for it. Devil for catalogues and credit cards, she was. Then I had a really bad season, couldn't keep the payments up, so half of it had to go back. Not long after that, she just pushed off. Left me up to my eyes in debt. Took me nigh three years to clear all the bills she'd run up. I had to move in with Grandad. It was that or live on the boat.'

'Poor you,' I said, and left it at that. It would probably embarrass him if I brought up what I'd heard about his wife from Trevor.

'I'm all right now,' he went on. 'I'm back on my feet again, but the old man's glad of company, so I've stayed put. He'd be lonely and he couldn't cope very well if I were to leave.'

'Of course,' I said. 'Well now, what do I owe you for today?'

What he asked was patently too little.

'Please, you've done five hours hard work.'

'Can't overcharge a friend.'

I pulled out a sum which I thought about right. 'You must take this, or I shall feel dreadful. Come on.'

With a sigh, he accepted the money. Then, as he was about to go, he suddenly paused and turned round.

'Just had a thought. You ought to call up our place and see the old man some time. Little white cottage, top of Viskey Hill. He loves to talk about the old days and he can tell you more than I can about the Lanyon chap and the people who used to live here. They were his generation, see. Funny thing about old people, they get so they can't remember last week or even yesterday, but their youth comes back to them clear as clear. You call, if you want, any time. He's always in.'

# Nine

About a week later I took up his offer. I'd been doing some shopping in Polvean, and on my way back to the car I passed the bottom of Viskey Hill. Pausing, I looked up the road and debated. At the top on the left the white cottage could be seen peering out from between two massive clumps of spotted laurel. It couldn't hurt to go, I thought, and might turn out to be enlightening.

The cottage had a small piece of ground at the front, enclosed by a waist-high stone wall and a wooden gate with one slat missing. Whatever he did for others, Jack didn't bother with his own garden, which was nothing but a bramble patch with just a path cut through to reach the door. I walked up and knocked, and after a minute the door was opened by a very old man. I guessed he was well over ninety, but he still had all his hair, which was white and overdue for cutting. He reminded me of Marley's ghost – except that the latter had not appeared in carpet slippers, dungarees and a tweed cap.

Grey eyes just like Jack's inspected me from behind a pair of steel-rimmed glasses.

'Yes?'

'Mr Roskear? My name's Christine Elford. I'm acquainted with Jack and he said I might visit you for a chat.'

'Oh, yes.' Nodding, smiling, he stood back and motioned me inside. 'Come on, then, this way.'

I followed him down an ill-lit hallway, past a jumbled sitting room from where came a warbling twitter and the ping of a budgie's toy bell.

'Hope you don't mind me just dropping in?'

'Lord, no. Always glad of company. Jack's out a lot, see. Has

66

to make his living, after all. Most of the day I'm stuck here alone, save for the budgie. I believe there was something particular you wanted to ask about?'

'That's right, there is.'

Mr Roskear led me into a chaotic kitchen, its sink piled high with dirty dishes. The floor was spread with newspapers, on which lay parts of an outboard motor.

'He's stripping that down, Jack is,' the old man said. 'Do you want some tea?'

'That would be nice. No sugar, thanks.'

He handed me the brew in a coronation mug – Edward the Seventh and Alexandra.

'Nearly as old as me, that mug,' observed Mr Roskear. He sat down opposite, sipping his own tea from a soup cup with a cartoon chicken on the side. 'It's all I do, day in, day out – drink tea,' he said morosely. 'And watch the box and read the papers. I'm not much good for anything else any more. Used to be a skipper, had a little fishing boat.' A light appeared in his eyes at the memory, then was quickly gone again. 'Nobody fishes out of Polvean these days, not proper fishing for a livelihood. No real working boats left. It's all sport fishing now, and yachts.'

The last word dropped heavily, weighted with scorn.

'And foreigners?' I asked, brows lifting.

He wasn't slow. 'No offence to you,' he shrugged. 'It's just that the proper Polvean folk have mostly gone. Place has been taken over. It's nice, of course, very smart and well-kept, but it's not the village I used to know.'

Yes, I thought, indeed – almost a whole population had gone and been replaced by another which had no connection with Polvean's past and precious little knowledge of it. Names like Lanyon and Penhale, which had once been important, were now remembered only by a few. It occurred to me that my recent experiences had opened a window through which I might never have otherwise bothered to look. A window on years gone by and a different Polvean, a sepia-tinted phantom itself, poorer and even more detached from the world outside. If not for my ghosts, would I ever have taken an interest in local history? I doubted it.

Mr Roskear began to reminisce – about the Great War, his wife, Jack's father and sundry other things. Once in full flow, he was entertaining, many of his stories coloured by a dryness and perceptive wit.

At one point, I remarked, 'You must miss the old way of life and how things used to be.'

He reached out and tapped the back of my hand, and a sharp humour gleamed in his eyes. 'Being young, maid, that's what I miss. That's what nostalgia is really about. There never were any "good old days" – but there was youth. That's what puts the lustre on the past when you're looking back. For most of us, life was poverty and slog. More pain for the body, less freedom for the mind than there is today. Narrow, that's how it was. How you behaved, what you expected, what was open to you – restricted, all of it. And that's how it stayed until after the Second World War.' The old man sniffed and pulled a scornful face. 'I'm not one of those who'll say how wonderful it used to be and how terrible things are now. It isn't so. But being strong and having time before you, yes, that's lost, that and the freshness of everything. The time before you lost your illusions and made all your worst mistakes, the time before you had anything much to regret. That's what you really pine for, maid, no matter how much you talk about old favourite cinema stars, old tunes and fashions and dances, no matter how much you moan about what's replaced them.'

It made me smile, for I sometimes felt a similar longing for the early seventies. He was right, and the yearning was apt to set in long before one grew old. Even a short and fairly uneventful past could take a strong grip on the mind . . .

So what of tragic memories hoarded for a lifetime? Remembering my purpose, I moved on to the subject which had brought me here.

'I suppose you've heard about all that fuss before Christmas?' I asked. 'When I called out the coastguard?'

A faint smile. 'Yes.'

'Jack says you remember a man called Lanyon who disappeared out in the bay without a trace.'

'That's right. Mind you, it happened differently. He walked

right out on the sand at low tide, and just when it was ready to turn, by all accounts.'

'So I gather. Why would he do a thing like that?'

Thoughtfully, Mr Roskear worked his mouth. I could tell he was shifting his false teeth around.

'Well, see, he'd just come home from the war. So had I, as a matter of fact. Course, I was only a private soldier. He was an officer, I forget what rank. Dark chap, good-looking, with curly hair. I was lucky, I came out of it all right, but I recall hearing that he was suffering from shell-shock. Now, how bad it was, I couldn't say. People like the Lanyons didn't broadcast their personal troubles to the likes of us, the lower orders, but it was known that David had – bouts – if you follow me.'

Shell-shock – yes, that would provide a solid, simple explanation.

'I see. How old was he when he died?'

'Not sure. Early twenties, I reckon. Nearly destroyed the Lanyons, it did. He was the only son. His mother, in particular, just couldn't get over it – to have him survive the war and then die like that. People who knew the family said she turned into a real heller. You know – bitter, harsh.'

'It wouldn't have been so bad, I suppose, if they'd been able to bury him. Why did the body never turn up, do you think? Mr Trelease, the grocer, told me there were quicksands, but . . .'

Dismissively, the old man waved a hand. 'Quicksands are apt to cough up what they swallow, sooner or later. It was one of two things, by my guess. He was either carried right out to sea, or he went down one of the holes.'

'The . . . potholes?'

'Yes.'

'Are there a lot of them?'

'Nobody knows.'

'I've never heard of such things before, not on the seabed,' I said.

'Ah, well, this is Cornwall, dear, and there's a reason for it. If you go up the coast by boat from here, you'll see a pair of engine houses built into the cliffs. They're only a couple of miles the other side of Polvean creek. Now, most of the levels of those two mines go right out under the sea. That was the way the seams of tin ran, under the bay. The miners followed them out to their limit, of course, and some of them stretch for a very long way. Well, they're pretty old, those mines. They were worked out by the end of the 1700s and abandoned. Before very long they flooded, as pits always do once the pumps are stopped. Now, the top levels were quite near the surface, and once they were no longer being maintained, shored up all the time, there was subsidence. In places where the roofs fell in, great holes opened up in the seabed. There are two which are very well known, not far out from the cliffs where the engine houses stand. When the sun is bright and the water's clear, you can see them as big dark shadows down underneath. If you didn't know better, you'd think they were rocks or patches of weed, but believe me, they're holes. Out in deeper water, it's likely there are more.'

I was silent, picturing this. There was something horrific about it.

He offered me more tea and I accepted half a cup, digesting this new information while Mr Roskear brought the kettle back to the boil.

'Do you know the house where I'm living?' I asked. 'Tren-arwyn?'

'Not really. Seen it from the water, of course, back in my fishing days.'

That was disappointing. Still, I said, 'Don't know anything of the people who lived there, by any chance?'

His back turned, he was dunking teabags in the cups. He shook his head. 'Penhale, they were called, that's all I can tell you.'

Bringing the tea to the table, he sat down again. 'I did have a bit of a fancy, mind, for one of the maids working there. Used to see her in the village and try to get her chatting. She was never interested in me, though. Posh name, she had, for a servant girl. Earnestina. Earnestina Toy. She was with the Penhales for a long time, but then she left them and moved away. I don't know what happened in between, but somebody told me years ago that she was in a retirement home over St Austell way.'

An avenue of enquiry, possibly, I thought. A servant, Earnestina Toy.

'You don't remember what the home was called?'

'No,' he said, adding, 'She could be dead by now.'

Indeed she could, I thought, deflated. Best not to get too excited about her.

'I'd be in a home myself if it weren't for Jack,' added Mr Roskear. 'I couldn't manage here on my own. He's good to me.'

'I'm sure.'

Eyeing me craftily, he confided: 'Needs a woman, though. Doesn't have much of a life, all told. I shan't be around for ever and then he'll be all on his own. Deserves better, Jack does. Deserved a damned sight better than that thing he married twelve years ago.' Growing irate at the memory, Mr Roskear angrily sucked his teeth, and his eyes became fierce. 'Snubnosed little article, she was. Greedy, selfish little pudding, always eating and always spending.'

'He did mention her.'

'Needs a nice woman, Jack does,' said Mr Roskear, collecting himself. 'Somebody who likes the simple life.'

I could see where this was leading and thought it time to go. Glancing at my watch, I feigned surprise. 'Dear Lord, it's nearly four. I must be getting back. I'm sorry I've kept you so long.'

'My pleasure, dear. Has it helped you at all, what I've said?'

In small measure it had, though I'd hoped to learn very much more. At least I now knew what was wrong with David and where his body could have gone. I also had the name of a servant who must have known the Penhales very well, but I was still a long way from sorting out my mystery.

'I'm a little bit wiser, Mr Roskear, and I really enjoyed our talk.'

'Ah, it was all too much about me. You come again, won't you, whenever you like, and next time I'll want to hear about you.'

Picking up my shopping bags, I noticed once more the heap

71

of dishes and suffered a sudden impulse to offer to wash them up. But I quickly squashed it, horrified at the foolishness of female instincts when confronted by men's housekeeping. Once I started, I'd probably clean the whole kitchen and sitting room too – which was more than I'd do for myself at home.

'I'll tell Jack you called,' said Mr Roskear as he showed me out. 'He'll be sorry he missed you. He likes you, Jack does.'

I had dreams that night, bad ones, about the old mines and the bay. I dreamt the sky was gold again and the sun was a glowering red, exactly the way they had been when I awoke on that first morning at Trenarwyn. But this time I was out of the house and looking back at it from the sands of the bay. The tide was low, drawn out as far as I had ever seen it, and I was standing at the water's edge. In the distance, Trenarwyn looked no more than a doll's house.

In my dream I wanted to get back home and started walking towards the beach. Yet, somehow, the house never got any nearer, and after a while I began to notice a sinister sound. Behind me there was a mounting murmur, becoming a rumble and roar. Turning, I saw that sky and sea had changed to a fuming of black and grey. Rearing and plunging and hissing, the tide was coming after me!

I took to my heels and ran and ran, but the beach seemed ever as far away, no matter how I raced. Over my shoulder, I saw that the water behind me had piled up into a dark, shining wall, its crest curving forward as if it were reaching out for me. It made a sound that was both a boom and a hideous bronchial sigh. Panting with terror, I *ran* and *ran*. My feet were bare and the flat sand flew away beneath them, yet the shore and safety seemed to recede at an equal pace.

Then, abruptly, there was nothing underfoot. The sand gave way beneath me and a gaping shaft appeared. I screamed and went spiralling down and down, seeming weightless now, and finally came to rest in a rocky tunnel. All around me there was rubble, together with toppled beams of pine and discarded digging tools.

The moment I picked myself up there was thunder overhead

and water came cascading down the shaft. Shrieking, I fled before it down endless gloomy passageways, splashing through puddles of rusty-coloured ooze. I knew there were ladders by which the old miners climbed up and down, and frantically I searched for one to help me escape the flood.

But no ladder appeared. The deluge pursued me and all I could do was keep running. The crash and hiss of it was deafening and soon I could feel the leading edge of it licking round my heels.

All at once, ahead, another hole – a vertical shaft with a rickety bridge made out of a couple of planks. Darting across it, I turned to see the water go plunging down like a cataract, leaving me safe on the other side.

I went off in search of a ladder again. More tunnels, going on and on. Then at last a dead end, where . . .

In the crazy, jumbled way of dreams, there was once again sand on the floor. And there, amid serpentine pebbles and seaweed, two bodies lay clinging together and utterly still. A young man with curly hair, and a girl, very dark, wearing only pearls. I stared at them for a long, long time, engulfed by pity and the certainty that theirs had indeed been a shared tragedy. I wanted to step forward, turn them over and look at their faces, but for some reason felt too afraid.

A second later they no longer mattered. The water was coming again and I was trapped. It came bursting down the passage, covering the bodies and rising around me, carrying me up towards the rocky roof, leaving only a foot of air, then just a few inches, then one . . .

I woke up gasping and thrashing about in the bed. No matter how I sucked in air, I still felt I was dying. By the time I was fully conscious, my fingers were prickling with pins and needles brought on by hysterical over-breathing.

Throwing out an arm, I groped for the light, knocking half the stuff off my bedside table before I found the switch. A blaze of brightness and there was my room, my primrose curtains and counterpane, my stuffed toy tiger on the window seat. At the foot of the bed, Lucinda was staring at me in amazement.

Only a nightmare, only a play produced by the subconscious mind. Sitting up, I clutched at a handful of hair as I bowed my head, getting my breath. Lucinda came padding up the bed. Mewing, she pawed at my face, and I hugged her gratefully.

# Ten

It was quite a relief to go into work at Good Harvest that Friday. What a pleasure to see Trevor and Jane and hear of their humdrum concerns. Bills unpaid, supplies delayed, a sack of cereal mouldy when opened. Myriad tiny irritations belonging to the real world. How reassuring it was to return for a while to the petty grumbles and silly mistakes, the jokes and small kindnesses which made up ordinary life. Even more than usual, I enjoyed the tittle-tattle, because it was all about the living – people who were mostly happy or at least well balanced. Their ups and downs were trivial, their sins were peccadilloes, and this was reality. This, and not the bygone tragedy which had started to take a grip on my imagination.

Just before lunch that day, Jack Roskear came into the shop for a piece of pork pie. He was all boots and crumpled clothing, big and easygoing like a St Bernard, and I was glad to see his smiling face. I had an impression, no matter irrational, that calamities never happened to people like Jack. Misfortunes, yes, but rending catastrophes, no. Those were for the highly strung, driven by passion and doomed – not for sensible, practical people who knew when enough was enough, pulled themselves together and got on with life as cheerfully as they could. Jack was of the latter sort, and a perfect antidote to the morbid mood my nightmare had left behind.

The pork pie, he said, was for Grandad. The old man liked a chunk of pie with a spoonful of pickle.

'You went to see him, then?' he observed, as I wrapped it up.

'I was passing, so I thought I might as well.'

'Find out anything useful?'

'We had a worthwhile chat. He's a dear old man, very sharp, and he must be . . . how old?'

'Ninety-five,' supplied Jack. 'Hope I'm as good if I live that long.'

'He's lucky he has you.'

'Well, I couldn't see him put in a home, no matter how nice it was. Some can take to it and be happy, others can't. He'd just decline and die.'

Yes indeed, I thought, recalling that that was precisely what had happened to Neville's mother a few years before.

Jack took a glance at his watch. 'Twenty to one. Be closing up soon for an hour?'

'I might,' I said.

Although the Moffats allowed me a lunch break, I seldom bothered to take it, but kept the shop open and ate my sandwiches there. Today, however, I had been thinking of going out for a while.

'Like to come down to The Outrigger, have some lunch with me?'

He had taken my visit to Grandad as a cue for a second try. The instinct to refuse rose up in me at once.

'Thank you, but I never drink at lunchtime.'

'Guinness and oysters?' he coaxed. 'Don't tell me you can't hold a pint of stout?'

The truth was that I would be glad of some company and the pub atmosphere, just for a change. I was tempted but I stalled, not wanting to start anything.

'Come on, I'm only asking for an hour of your time.'

I guessed I might have to remind him of that later on. However, the invitation was very attractive.

'All right, I'll be shutting the shop at one.'

'Good, I'll come back for you. Just nipping up the hill with the old boy's pie. It'll be nice to eat at the pub today. We can sit at the tables on the quay.'

Off he went with Grandad's lunch. Well, it could do no harm, I thought. I wasn't going to get involved, I'd be careful not to lead him on.

It was the start of April and the weather was warming up.

76

Tables and chairs had been set up outside the pub and would stay there now until the summer season ended. The whole village seemed touched with the expectation of long, warm days to come. Everywhere, walls were being white- or colour-washed, and gardens planted with summer perennials. Sailing boats laid up all winter had received fresh coats of paint and varnish, and now they bobbed at their moorings in the creek, the toys of Polvean's well-to-do, bearing names like *Poco Loco*, *Nippy Today* or *Make a Splash*.

We sat at a table alongside the railings right at the edge of the quay. The air carried scents of brine, seaweed and engine oil, a smell characteristic of harbours everywhere and apt to provoke a hungry appetite.

Oysters, Jack had said. It occurred to me now that they were too expensive, and I wasn't sure I would care for them anyway.

'I've never tried oysters,' I said awkwardly.

He looked surprised.

'Perhaps I ought to have something plain, more filling.'

'Go on with you. Don't turn down a new experience. You can always have something else after.'

If I don't feel bilious, I thought.

'Aren't they awfully . . . ? I mean . . .'

'Pricey?'

'Yes.'

'Never mind that, I'm flush this week. Come on, we'll have a dozen between us. Don't worry. If you don't like them, I can eat the lot.'

They came on the half shells, all neatly arranged on a bed of crushed ice. They looked so plump and wet and raw, I didn't fancy them at all.

'Just swallow one down,' encouraged Jack, 'but take the time to swill the liquid round your teeth. There's nothing else so good, I promise you.'

I can still taste it now, that first one. I can still feel the crusty sharpness of the shell against my teeth and the slippery lump of the oyster sliding off it, bathed in its delicately fishy juice. I gulped it down in haste, almost afraid to savour it in case my gorge should rise, but when it was gone I felt pleased with myself and ready for the next. After a couple more I was seizing them with relish and Jack ordered a second lot. We washed them down with the full-bodied stout, rich and bitter-tanged.

There were just three left when suddenly a shadow crossed our table. I looked up to see Phil Jennings standing over us, beer glass in hand.

'Hello, Roskear. Lucky man.'

This with a nod at me.

Jack was stony-faced and silent. Jennings grinned at him. 'Wouldn't come out with me,' he went on. 'Made it clear I was willing – didn't I, maid?' He leaned down, peering into my face. 'What's he got, then, that I haven't? Eh?'

Jack's voice came across the table, low and hostile. 'You're intruding, Phil.'

Jennings ignored him. Just drunk enough to be playful and flirt with trouble, he waved his glass towards the platter. 'Oysters, is it? Sparing no expense, I see. Jack's wife used to like good things. Now perhaps if he'd bought her a few more oysters . . .'

Straight away, Jack was on his feet.

'Mr Jennings,' I said sharply, 'go away.'

Backing off a yard or two, he blew me a kiss, then smirked at Jack. 'Don't get heated, Roskear. The lady's not your property. Not that it would make a difference – as you know.'

Certain Jack was going to hit him, I stretched out a pacifying hand. 'Please . . .'

Smouldering, he sat down again, while Jennings, chortling, wagged a finger at me. 'Faint heart never won fair lady. I shan't give up on you.'

So saying, he swaggered off back towards the pub.

'Trevor told me all about him,' I said quietly. 'He's just a conceited goat. Dropped some heavy hints to me and I didn't want to know, so he's sour because I'm having lunch with you.'

Gulping down the rest of his stout, Jack muttered something about his ex-wife.

'Trevor told me about that too. I gather you gave Phil Jennings a going-over. I doubt he'd be capable of doing the same to you, so he needles you instead. You shouldn't rise to it.'

'I know, I know, but I hate the man – and I'm not alone in that. He's one of those who can't take no for an answer, prides himself on being able to get any woman he wants, eventually. Once he's had them a time or two, that's the end of it as far as he's concerned, but he leaves a trail of damage behind him. There are plenty of husbands in Polvean who'd like to break his neck.'

'I've met the type before. The surprising thing is that they're so successful – that so many women fall for them. Must be the proverbial attraction of the rotter.'

'And you're immune to that?'

'No, but I've never succumbed to one as obvious as he is. At least my rotters were subtle about it at the start. At least they had some style and plenty of charisma.'

A faint smile lifted his face at that. Quickly his bad mood melted away and we finished off our lunch with a couple of double gins.

'Which is your boat?' I asked him, as he walked me back to the shop.

He pointed out a fishing vessel, tied up by the jetty steps right opposite Good Harvest. She wasn't very large, but she was spick and span, and painted sky blue. The name on the prow was *Thomasina*.

'Had her nearly twenty years,' he said. 'Good little craft. She's made me a living and brought me home safe on some nasty days. You ought to come out for a trip in her.'

He was so nice, and I was feeling expansive. Without even stopping to think, I said, 'That would be lovely.'

By the time I got back to the shop I had made a date for Sunday, a picnic up the river. Against all my intentions, I was going to see him again.

Sunday was a perfect day. The village snoozed in the morning sun and a lazy ringing of bells could be distantly heard from St Martin's when I met Jack on the quay at ten o'clock. He had the engine running and was eager to be off, for the tide was just right. We could follow the river right up to its limit and have plenty of time to eat lunch before *Thomasina* got stranded by the ebb.

Beyond Polvean, the creek continued meandering inland for several miles. All of nature was still as a church, the trees unstirred by any wind, the water unruffled and glossy. The air was balmy, the woods a palette of brilliant greens. All around was a great, soft quiet and even the chug of the engine sounded subdued, as if it were wrapped in cottonwool. I remember how lost our voices seemed, and the gentle rippling of the wash spreading out and away from the bow of the boat.

The journey up-river took an hour and a half, and only once was the peace disturbed. I was watching a pair of herons wading in the shallows by the bank, when a distant buzz from up ahead grew to a whining drone. Around a bend appeared a speedboat, tearing up the satin surface of the water, churning it into a great white wake that sploshed to either bank. The herons flapped away in a panic and *Thomasina* bounced a little in the sudden surge.

As the boat sped by I glimpsed the driver, somehow familiar in spite of dark glasses. He waved at us and yelled a greeting or something of the sort. Beside him sat a blonde-haired girl and she waved too.

'I'm not sure who that was,' I said, as the speedboat snarled on down the creek and disappeared around another turn.

'That idiot Noel Kinsman,' grunted Jack. 'Loves to make a racket. Noise and speed and brainless women, that's what Noel likes. You ought to see him drive a car, it's enough to stop your heart.'

'I've heard about his many romances. Where does he find them all?'

'Oh, pubs and clubs. I know he gets about.'

'Seems he and Phil Jennings are two of a kind.'

'Yes and no,' sniffed Jack. 'Noel's a rowdy article and fancies himself no end, but at least he doesn't go for married women. And he hasn't a wife and a couple of kids left at home wondering where he is.'

I smiled to hear him use that word 'article', loaded as it was with scorn and disapproval. More forceful than 'object' or 'thing', but stopping short of profanity.

*Thomasina* ambled slowly on up to the tiny beach at the very head of the creek. I had brought us a picnic of baguettes, ham and Camembert, peaches and walnuts, a bottle of wine, and a plum pudding with half a pound of clotted cream to spread all over it. We sat on the shingle and ate the lot, even cleaning out the cream carton with our fingers.

I had put on some weight since coming to Cornwall; not a great deal, but an inch or so. In the past I was always a little too thin for my five feet six inches. Even so, Neville used to notice and comment whenever I gained a bit. At work, as well, there had always been the tacit suggestion that people who failed to keep smart and svelte were bad for the firm's image, even a liability it could do without. Nowadays, I gave my appetite free rein. It wasn't gross, but I ate as nature demanded, which seemed a positive luxury.

Neville would have been shocked to see me. His formerly smart Christine, clothed in crumpled cotton trousers and a baggy shirt, drinking wine from a thick glass tumbler and stuffing herself with what he called 'heart-attack food'. He would say I'd gone native.

After a time the water began to drop and a slim crescent of river-mud could be seen at the foot of the pebble beach.

'We'll have to be off or the boat'll get stuck,' Jack said. 'Shall we go up the coast to Polperro this afternoon? There's good scenery on the way.'

'All right,' I said.

It must have been about two o'clock when we reached the river mouth and the open sea, turning to follow the line of cliffs which marched away up the Channel coast. The scenery was dramatic, all right, a very lonely, rugged stretch of shore. Even on a calm day like today the rocks looked threatening, but Jack wasn't troubling to give them a very wide berth, obviously quite familiar with this stretch of water.

'Is this where you bring people fishing?' I asked.

'No, deeper water, a few miles out. Most of them are hoping to reel in a shark.'

'And do they?'

'Often, yes. Chiefly blue shark, nothing spectacular.'

'Can you charge a lot?'

'I ask ninety pounds for the day. For that, I provide all the gear, and teaching if they need it. Given a fine summer, it's not a bad living, but nasty weather means no money coming in. Of course, uncertainty's taken for granted. My family's never known real security. Grandfather had a mackerel boat when he was young. Used to go through some awful hard times, weeks on end when he couldn't put to sea.'

The mention of the old man recalled my dream, and I suddenly realised that we were bound to pass by the engine houses of which Mr Roskear had spoken. I watched the towering cliffs and, sure enough, as we rounded a point, the stacks and buildings came in sight.

Ancient brickwork and dark empty windows looming high among the rocks. Theirs had been serious business, hard industry, and they seemed to frown upon the frivolous, brightly painted little vessel far below. Theirs was the other face of Cornwall, the deeper layer beneath the veneer of leisure and colour and fun. Relics of a long, harsh era – of which Genevra was born at the very tail-end.

I had always felt that people of that generation had one foot in each of two worlds, because they had lived through changes so immense. But Genevra, perhaps, cut off from it all, had remained with both feet in the past, left behind as the county moved on, a remnant like the mines.

Lost in these thoughts, I failed to notice at first that the engine had stopped. Then it filtered through to me that we were not passing on by but just drifting. I looked around for Jack and found that he, too, was standing and staring up at the engine houses on the cliffs.

'Dour, aren't they?' he said softly. 'By God, there were terrible accidents here a couple of centuries back. There's a plaque, you know, in St Martin's church, with a list of all the dead. Damned good thing it was when they closed these mines. I gather Grandad told you about the way the top levels fell in?'

'Yes.'

'That's why I've stopped here. Come over this side and look.'

I had a sudden bad feeling and followed him rather reluctantly. He took me up to the bow at the starboard side, then pointed down through the water.

'There.'

I almost recoiled. It was right underneath us, a gaping black pothole some twelve feet across. The water was no more than fifteen feet deep, and sparkling clear, revealing a seabed of sand and pebbles, rent wide open by that ragged-edged, night-dark pit.

I felt a mite ill and must have turned pale. I don't like heights and the sight of that hole produced a similar sickening effect, as if I were tumbling into it. Vaguely, I heard Jack asking, 'What's the matter, maid?'

Backing away from the side, I didn't answer, just shook my head.

'Here, I'm sorry. I didn't think it would upset you . . .'

'It's all right.' I turned away. 'I just feel a bit queasy. But please can we go?'

'Of course.'

He went and started the engine, and soon *Thomasina* was moving on. I sat down at the stern, looking back as the engine houses slowly receded from view.

'Are there a lot of potholes?' I had asked the old man.

'Nobody knows,' had been his reply.

But the levels ran right out under the bay. There could well be more holes like that within sight of Trenarwyn, and I mused unhappily on the memory of my dream.

We stayed for an hour in Polperro and went for a drink before heading back. Jack was full of apologies once again.

'I thought you'd be interested,' he said. 'Never struck me it would bother you. Stupid of me, I suppose, knowing you saw that poor girl disappear. It was just that you asked the old man, so I thought you'd like to see.'

It was unfair, really, not to confide, but I didn't want to talk about the girl, about what I now guessed her to be. As far as the potholes were concerned, it was the possible fate of David Lanyon's body which saddened me. No one should end up somewhere like that. I only hoped it wasn't so and that he had been carried right out to sea.

Jack continued to be contrite and didn't look too hopeful when he asked to see me again. With hindsight, I think I agreed to the next outing simply to make him feel better.

# Eleven

Make an exception, then make another – before very long you've formed a habit, and so it was with Jack and me. Every Friday, lunch at the pub; every Sunday, a day out somewhere. During the week he would drop by, do an odd job about the house or garden, have something to eat and sit for a while with Lucinda on his lap. She had taken a real fancy to him and knew before I did whenever he was coming up the path. Her eyes would widen, her ears prick up, she would stare at the door and then run to it with her tail held high. Straight away, sure enough, would come the light bump of his footsteps and then the familiar knock.

It was pleasant, cosy. For quite a while I welcomed it. There was a comforting sense of normality, even safety, and everyone approved. His grandad was pleased, Trevor and Jane were pleased. Certain of the customers began to address me in conversation as 'you 'n' Jack', as if he and I had already been fused into a single entity.

'What do you 'n' Jack think?'

'Will you 'n' Jack be coming?'

'That would be nice for you 'n' Jack.'

It didn't alarm me at first. I felt I was still in control and people were just making the usual hasty assumptions. It was all very casual, I explained, just a friendship, nothing more. The fact that Jack might not see it that way was something I avoided looking at for quite some time. It was easy to do so, since he didn't force the pace, and I kidded myself that we could go on like this, that I wasn't being unkind. After all, I had explained that I wasn't in the market for a love affair.

The trouble was, he didn't believe me. He thought it was only a matter of time, and in that he was not entirely wrong. Before long, I began to anticipate Fridays and Sundays with eagerness. Days when he didn't call at the house seemed somehow flat and lonely. The same old pattern was forming again. I'd been through it so many times before and it always ended up in just one way. The man of the moment would move into my place, or I into his, and I'd start playing wife, putting him and his wishes first.

But through April and May, having good times with Jack, I pretended it wasn't so. I wasn't going to fall again. We had a lovely friendship and that was quite enough. It added an extra, bright dimension to both our lives and I was able to take a more detached, less melancholy interest in David Lanyon and Genevra. Brooding about them in solitude, I had seemed to bridge the gulf of years, making bygone events feel so keenly touching that they might have happened only yesterday. Somehow, Jack's company opened that gulf again, distancing it all and taking off that poignant edge.

There were no more apparitions, either, in all those weeks. Perhaps my lighter mood discouraged them, or perhaps they had gone away with the winter weather, finding cold and gloom more hospitable than sunny spring. For me, the warm seasons were always a tonic. Even the music I played was different – especially if I had a new man. Putting my usual favourites aside, I listened instead to Gilbert and Sullivan, Edith Piaf, or Neapolitan folk songs like 'Santa Lucia'.

In my garden many of the shrubs were in full flower, scents of lilac and Mexican orange wafting through the house. For years I had wanted a really nice garden and was pleased with the way it was coming along.

One Sunday in May, Jack took me to see a garden on a grand scale – Roskenwith, once the Lanyons' family home. The grounds extended to seventy acres, thirty of which were paddocks and woodland. The rest was devoted to one of the biggest shrub and plant collections in the county. There was a very large glasshouse full of exotics, and an arboretum said to be spectacular in autumn.

'You told me the Lanyons were better class, but I hadn't

imagined them quite this wealthy,' I said, looking up at the house, a very fine Georgian building.

'Oh yes, they were gentry. The place has ten bedrooms, I believe.'

'What happened to the Lanyons? Are they all dead?'

'Couldn't say. The National Trust has owned this property for a long time now. Chances are, the family simply couldn't afford the upkeep. Where they went to, I don't know.'

'Is it worth having a look inside?'

'We can if you like, but to tell the truth, the house is not especially interesting and it'll take all day to see the gardens thoroughly. We could come again another time, of course.'

I took his word for it and didn't bother with the house. A complex of pathways led from one lovely garden into the next, with seemingly endless nooks and bowers tucked away on all sides. A kitchen garden and rose garden, bamboo jungle and swamp with sub-tropical plants. Italian and Japanese styles, and a palm oasis. It was lucky that Jack did some work here sometimes and knew his way around, or I would have missed many lovely corners.

To my mind, the best was a vale full of rhododendrons, azaleas and tree-ferns. Very still in the hot afternoon, they towered around us, so laden with blossom I wondered how they could bear the weight. Glowing reds and pinks and purples, all the more vibrant against their dark green leaves. A narrow pathway wove among them, going on and on, and soon it began to seem that there was nothing in the world but endless lofty rhododendrons and starry azaleas.

'Grand, aren't they?' Jack said. 'Planted at the turn of the century. That red one there is eighty feet high. You can see it from almost everywhere on the estate.' Then, with a grimace, he added: 'Sorry, must leave you a minute – nature calls.'

He disappeared off into the bushes. Alone, I gazed up at the monster rhododendron. How big had it been, I wondered, when David Lanyon was a child?

As if in answer, there suddenly came a mental image: the whole of this vale more open, all the shrubs miniature versions of the giants they were today. All in their youth – even the red

87

one no more than a dozen feet high. And on the path, in my mind's eye, appeared a little boy. He was clad in Edwardian clothes, a sturdy lad and curly-haired like the young man I'd seen in my dream. He swung down the track with his hands in his pockets, then bent to pick up a stick from the ground and flourished it like a sword.

David would have known this path, he would have played here as a youngster. A boy enacting the role of hero, mercifully unaware that he was destined for an early death.

I blinked and the picture went away. Again the shrubbery towered around me and there was no small boy. Butterflies silently sipped at the flowers and a drowsy humming of insects was all around. The red of the big rhododendron was deep and rich, like blood. All the colours were so intense, the blooms so huge and the fragrance of azaleas so overwhelming. Just for a moment, I felt slightly giddy. Too much beauty, too much sunlight, too much imagination.

A moment later Jack returned, and we walked on down to the end of the path and from there to the arboretum before going home.

I was glad to have seen the Roskenwith estate, but on reflection it did make me question my assumptions about David Lanyon and Genevra.

'Moneyed people always mix with their own kind,' Jack had said.

Yes, but even among the well-off there were strata. Trenarwyn was positively humble compared to Roskenwith, and I wondered if David would really have been involved with a girl whose background was so much more modest than his own.

But then, perhaps he would. Why not, when even aristocrats had been known to marry servant girls? I couldn't help wondering, though, how the Lanyon family might have felt about it.

Later, in the village, I picked up some groceries and went back to Jack's place, where I cooked a meal of macaroni cheese and baked apples for us and the old man. I spent the rest of the evening with them, watching tennis and a thriller on the television. It was all very companionable and it wasn't the first time I had done this. The fourth, perhaps? Or the fifth?

'Take your shoes off, maid, and put your feet up,' the old man would say. 'Make yourself at home. Like a drop of oh-be-joyful?'

Sure enough, I would kick off my shoes and have a few glasses of something. Slipping into yet another habit, hardly noticing.

In the usual way, I was getting in deeper and deeper. Inevitably, the day arrived when I had to face the issue – and I took fright. The whole thing ended miserably, and it was entirely my fault for being so ambivalent all along.

The side of me that shrugged off caution led me into bed with Jack one night. Well, it had been predictable, and after a specially boozy supper at Trenarwyn we staggered upstairs together and that was that.

Next morning I panicked – not least because he had been so sweet. I woke and there he was and that was wonderful . . .

Which was how it always started.

I remember quietly getting up and standing at the foot of the bed, looking at him. It was frightening, the change which came over me as soon as I'd slept with a man. It was rather as if I'd undergone a surgical procedure which cleanly removed my commonsense and all self-interest. I knew what would happen now, if I let it. What always happened. I'd lose myself, my wits, my plans. My preferences, the owning of my life, would cease. Once again, unselfishness would claim and hobble me. Before I knew it, I'd be washing his socks and helping to look after Grandad. Jack would come to expect it, and talk about making it legal. And I would be tempted because, after all, I was thirty-eight and he was very lovable . . .

They were all lovable at first, before they started taking you for granted.

I looked at him lying there on his stomach, broad back and tidy round buttocks uncovered. He smiled in his sleep the way Billy, my cadging musician, used to do. Already, another man in my bed, after less than eight months at Trenarwyn. So much for all my resolutions; I hadn't held out long. Independent, self-sufficient Christine? What a joke. I wanted even now to climb back into bed with him.

89

'He needs a nice woman, Jack does,' his grandad had said.

I'd walked right into the snare and I should have known better.

Putting on a dressing gown, I went downstairs, made coffee and sat at the kitchen table with it, wondering what I could say to him, how to get out of this gracefully and without inflicting injury. The choice was stark now: not see him at all, or else become fully involved. It was no good pretending mere friendship any more, it wouldn't work. We had added the demon ingredient, sex.

Half an hour later he came down while I was frying eggs and bacon. I heard him behind me, and then he was hugging me, whispering, 'Good morning.'

Resisting the reflex to pull away, I said, 'Pass me a plate there, will you?'

He gave me the plate and I heaped it with food – far too much, really, even for him. I think it was half-consciously an apology for what I meant to do.

'Where's yours?' he asked, as we both sat down.

'I only have toast in the morning. Sometimes I like a fry-up at midday, but never this early.'

'Oh. Good of you, then, to cook this for me.' He tackled it eagerly, good-tempered, smiling.

'No trouble, Jack.'

I sipped my coffee. I could feel him watching me.

'That was wonderful – last night, I mean.'

Glancing up, then away, I laughed awkwardly. 'Mm, yes. I don't know quite how, but . . . Well, we drank a lot, didn't we?'

'I should say.' His knife and fork went clink and tap as he tucked the breakfast away. 'Sort of oiled the wheels, eh? I'd been waiting, Chris. Hoping . . . you know.'

'Yes,' I said, 'I know.'

It was hard to look him in the eye. Any moment now, I feared, he was going to ask the age-old question: You're not sorry, are you?

But he hadn't picked it up yet, my disquiet. Poor Jack was happy, thinking this the start of something, not the end.

'You're a lovely woman, Christine. I know I'm a lucky man.'

Puppy eyes across the table. I felt quite sick with guilt. There was a sort of shine about him. I'd never seen that in a man before. In women it's called looking radiant.

Oh God, I thought wretchedly.

'I knew you were my sort as soon as I met you,' he went on blithely. 'We're good together, aren't we? Suited?'

I looked at him, heart-stricken, and his smile began to fade.

'Something the matter, maid?'

'I . . . No. That is . . .'

He laid his knife down. 'Did I do something wrong?' Flickering over my face, his eyes bespoke sudden anxiety. 'Was I rough? See, it's been a long time.'

'God, no! No, of course you weren't rough, Jack. It was fine, truly. Better than fine, it was sweet.'

He took a swig of tea. The glow had gone from him and he studied me soberly now.

'But?'

I mumbled: 'I hadn't intended for things to go this far. You remember what I said to you when we first met, last New Year's Eve?'

I could see him casting his mind back. 'You said you had other priorities,' he murmured slowly.

I nodded.

'Such as what?'

'Well, there's my work.'

'I shan't interfere with that.'

'And I just don't want . . . Look, Jack, I haven't done too well in past relationships.'

'Nor have I.'

'But you want another try. I've had enough, at least for now. As I said, I didn't intend for things to go this far.'

'I'm aware of that. But since they have . . . ?'

'They shouldn't have. I'm sorry, but there it is.'

A silence fell. He pushed a bit of bacon round his plate, considering.

'You feel differently about me now?'

'Of course, and I don't want to grow too fond of you.'

'Why not?'

'I've told you. This simply wasn't in my plans.'

'What plans? What's the grand and precious scheme, Christine? To live alone out here with your cat? Grow old alone?'

'Let's stick to the immediate future. Yes, for the time being, I want my life to myself.'

He grunted. 'Sounds wonderful.'

'You don't understand.'

'Been reading women's movement stuff?'

'No, I've just had a bellyful of being a domestic convenience.'

Both our voices had risen, we were heading for a row. He saw that and drew back from it.

'I wouldn't treat you that way, Chris. You've been choosing the wrong type of man.'

'They all seemed the right type until I lived with them,' I said wearily.

'And I could be the same? That's what you're saying?'

Helplessly, I shrugged. Then, 'Please, Jack, think of this; I gave up everything in London and came down here to try a different kind of life, but everyone, including you, wants to push me straight back into coupledom. It really annoys me and I won't have it.'

Sucking in his cheeks, he eyed me shrewdly. 'But I think you half want it, Chris. That's why you're in such a stew about last night.'

At that I grew angry again. 'Yes, I am susceptible and I have to be on guard. Experience has taught me a lesson or two.'

'That's sad. You know what my wife was like. It hasn't made me cynical.'

Somehow, that touched me on the raw. 'I've been through it half a dozen times, not merely once, so don't you preach to me! How can I tell how you'd behave once I was hooked? You wouldn't be the first one to see me as an amenity and my place as a good billet.'

He stared at me, injured, insulted, incensed. 'Is that what you think I'm looking for? Somewhere to hang my hat?'

I faltered. 'No, I shouldn't have said that. Forgive me, Jack, I didn't mean it. And if I've led you on – as I'm afraid I have –

I'm sorry for that, too. You're a lovely man and I like you so much, but . . .'

He waited. His face was set, but grief was in his eyes.

I couldn't finish – didn't have to. At length he nodded and stood up.

'All right, Christine.'

Swallowing hard, I muttered, 'I don't think we'd better go out any more.'

'That goes without saying, doesn't it?' he sighed.

After he'd gone, I howled for an hour, because I had handled it all so badly, and also because I was going to miss him a very great deal. From its place on the dresser, the Churchill teapot smiled across at me, but the quizzical tilt of its mouth and eyebrows seemed to say: 'You fool, Christine.' I wondered just then if I would ever be able to enjoy my solitude again.

# Twelve

See what happens, I thought afterwards. See what comes of friendships which turn intimate? Upset, arguments, guilt and regrets. Much more restful to be self-sufficient. The sooner I grew used to his absence and settled down again, the better.

In the meantime I decided to take up Jimmy Kinsman's offer and have the trees behind the house cut down. If nothing else, the felling would help remove the lowering gloom of the back yard. It was actually worse now that summer was here and all the trees were in leaf. Even on the brightest days my washing wouldn't dry out there and I'd end up hanging it all from the ceiling rack in the kitchen. It also occurred to me that I might have the ground rotovated and try to grow some of the plants which provided natural dyes. Woad, perhaps. Certainly nettles and elderberry. Possibly weld and madder, dyer's bugloss, dyer's broom. A few, at least, would be bound to succeed.

I telephoned Kinsman on a Thursday afternoon and he turned up the very next morning with a chainsaw. I had marked six trees I wanted down: three laurels, two sycamores and a holly.

Having a great deal of dyeing to do, I spent most of the day in the kitchen amid my chemical mixtures and bubbling pans. I was using indigo stock, together with weld and fustic, to make a range of blues and greens – a process somewhat longer and more complicated than those demanded by other colours.

Absorbed in my tasks, I soon became used to the buzz of the saw outside and the regular rattle of falling branches. At one point, a groan and creak and crash were followed by a sudden explosion of light as the laurel nearest the kitchen window fell. Sunshine streamed into the room and I looked out to see the great tree lying on the earth, still quivering. Mr Kinsman was strolling round it with his saw, casually slicing branches off. Further up the slope lay a sycamore trunk, and the stump of the holly, whose wood and foliage now formed a tidy heap on the ground beside it. Amazing how different the rear plot looked already, how spacious and bright. Excitedly, I thought about growing some vegetables, even soft fruit, perhaps. My own kitchen garden, my own home-grown dyes.

The screech of the saw went on all day as the trees were cut into logs for the stove and the open hearth. At five o'clock, Mr Kinsman came in the back door and said he was done for the day. He brought in a trail of earth on his boots, and a smell of woodland, mushroom-like. His cap and his jacket were sprinkled with sawdust and shreds of bark.

'I've stowed a lot of the wood in the shed, dear. Won't be room for all of it, though, not by a long way. Got a cellar, have you?'

'Yes.'

'Can I put the rest down there? Good place for it, save you going out on a rainy night.'

'All right, Mr Kinsman, fine.'

'I'll be back in the morning to saw up the last trunk and bring it all in. You won't need any logs from me next winter, that's for sure.'

Recalling what he had quoted for the work, I wryly thought he had taken account of that. Still, I was so pleased with the results that I wasn't disposed to complain.

'Been busy yourself, I see.' He pointed up at the ceiling rack, which was garlanded now with skeins of wool in myriad shades from powder blue to royal, emerald to olive green.

'Yes, it's very satisfying, and no two lots are ever quite the same.'

'Nice soft colours, too. Never garish, natural dyes. Be making a jersey for Jack, will you?'

This with a twinkle and a grin. Clearing my throat, I said awkwardly, 'No. I . . . don't see Jack now.'

His head went back and a frown appeared. 'Aw.' The sound contained surprise, concern. His stare was condoling, begging more details.

95

'We're both very busy, you know.'

Another stare, then another 'Aw', unconvinced. Tactful enough not to ask any more, he turned to go. But then, in the doorway, he paused and said: 'By the way, did you know you've got an old stone seat up there on the slope?'

'Seat?'

'Nice little marble bench. Cost you hundreds to buy one today. It's up there under that furthest sycamore. Buried in a two-foot pile of leaf-mould, it was. I wouldn't have known it was there if I hadn't tripped over it.'

'Oh – I hope you didn't hurt yourself?'

'No, no, I caught my balance. But I very nearly went head first, so I dug round to see what was there. Lovely old garden seat. Worth cleaning up.'

'Really? I must go and have a look. I've wondered if the ground at the back was ever cultivated. If there's a seat, then there must have been a nice garden, don't you think?'

'Probably there was, and the old girl just let it run wild. Wouldn't have taken long to turn into woodland. Sycamores, see, and hazels – spread like blazes, they do. Anyway, as I say, I'll be here again in the morning. Eight o'clock suit you?'

'Fine, Mr Kinsman. Thanks very much.'

After his lorry had roared away up the lane, I stood in the yard surveying the empty space on the slope. Sixty feet of open ground before the woods began again. A belt of those hazels formed a curtain of green where the clearing ended. Down one side stretched the rough stone wall which partitioned my land from the lane. On the other ran a border of more trees and scrub. I could hardly believe the difference. Late afternoon sunshine flowed down on the yard, which suddenly seemed to be twice its former size.

I started to wander up over the slope in search of the seat. Twigs and small branches and piles of sawdust littered the ground. The scent of freshly cut wood hung about as I walked between the pale, raw stumps of the trees Mr Kinsman had felled. Underfoot, the earth was springy, made up of long-decayed leaves, years and years of autumn falls, turned to rich brown compost.

Two feet deep, as he had said. I found the little bench amid its hump of humus, and clawed the dirt away with my hands until it stood all but free. A marble seat just big enough for two, quite plain except for an acorn motif on the side of the pedestal each end.

He was right, it was surely worth quite a bit and I was delighted to think I had made an unexpected profit.

It wasn't till late that evening that I started to wonder where Lucinda was. With a cat's customary loathing of noise and upheaval, she had gone out when Mr Kinsman arrived, not to be seen for the rest of the day. As twilight deepened, I went outside and called to her. The air still carried the scent of sawn wood and some of the warmth of the day. Standing at the back door, I whistled, then chanted: 'Lucy-Lucy-Lucy!'

No response. Tired and wanting to get to bed, I tried the ultimate enticement.

'Lucy-Lucy! Fish-fish-fish!'

I waited, but still no answering squall, no chirrups of greeting.

She didn't normally stay out quite so long, and worries began to nag at me. Perhaps the sound of the saw had upset her, perhaps she had wandered much further than usual, even up to the road. She might have been hit by a car, or crossed over and then become lost.

'Lucy-Lucy-Lucy! Come on! Fish-fish-fish!'

Straining to see in the thickening dusk, I scanned the ground Mr Kinsman had cleared, hoping to spot the flash of her white bib and paws up there among the shadows.

What I saw instead nearly stopped my heart.

Ranging over the slope, my eyes picked out the pale shape of the marble bench and . . .

Someone was sitting there.

Against the grey gloom of the oncoming night was a darker outline, upright, human. Head, shoulders, body – the silhouette of a well-built man.

I was sure of it, so sure, and my stomach lurched with fright. He sat there, absolutely still, staring down at . . .

97

The house?

Or me?

Transfixed, I stared back. I could make out no features, just the dim shape of his head. But I pictured the eyes as intent and unblinking, filled with . . . was it challenge or a kind of unwholesome desire?

My nerves were strung as tightly as a warp, and suddenly there came a shock that wrenched a shrill scream out of me. Something bumped against my leg, slithered past and shot into the kitchen.

I spun around and . . . there was Lucinda. She had a mouse. Dangling from her jaws, it looked for all the world like a droopy moustache. She darted under the table with it and crouched there possessively, eyeing me as if she feared I would steal it.

Just then, I was too concerned about the figure out on the seat to feel much relief that my cat had returned. Whirling around, I squinted again up the slope.

There was nothing. No outline now, just formless heavy shadow.

How long had I been distracted? A matter of seconds, no more than ten. As swiftly as that, he had gone.

If he had, indeed, been there at all.

Half-light, I supposed, could play tricks on the eyes. Gratefully, I seized on that, but didn't care to test the theory by looking any longer. Backing inside, I shut the door and locked it.

Almost at once a little uproar broke out, for the mouse was very much alive and escaped the moment Lucinda dropped it. Scurrying across the floor, it took refuge behind the fridge. Lucy bounded after it, pawing madly through the gap where it had gone.

Half an hour of farce ensued, as I tried to flush out the mouse and capture it. I had shut Lucinda out of the kitchen and she scratched at the door all the while, howling protests. After shifting the fridge and two pine cupboards, I finally managed to trap the mouse in a flowerpot and drop it out of the window. When I let Lucy back in, she sniffed around for it, then sat and frowned accusingly at me.

'I suppose that's what you were doing all day?' I said. 'Watching for that poor thing?'

Scornfully turning her back, she began to wash.

'I wouldn't have had such a scare just now if I hadn't been outside looking for you.'

Her ears flattened slightly, she went on licking. Reproaches were always wasted on her.

'What's the expression?' I murmured wryly. 'Nervous as a cat? That's a fine joke, isn't it? I'm the jumpy one.'

It had just been a trick of the light, I told myself again. That and fancy born of fatigue, all muddled up with old associations. That fervid look which I'd imagined – didn't it spring from a memory, the recollection of a man who used to hang about the playground when I was a child in school, a man who would stand at the fence, just staring, staring? The brain was apt to make that kind of connection from time to time, and shadows could so easily be moulded by an edgy mind, reflecting its preoccupations. Weren't there people who swore they had seen the face of God in clouds, or that of a loved one, lately lost, in the embers of a fire?

But what had been bothering me, to make me imagine a man sitting there? Was it something to do with Jack, some wish to see him just once more?

Yes, I decided, it might well have been; probably because I would have welcomed the opportunity to smooth his ruffled feathers and ensure there were no hard feelings.

One evening not long afterwards, I thought I was going to get my wish. It was after dark and I was sitting on the settee, weaving a sample pattern with needles and thread upon a piece of card. I'd been listening to *Peer Gynt*, but the tape had finished and switched itself off and I hadn't yet bothered to go and change it. Profound silence always seemed to follow once the music stopped, despite the faint swish of the wind or the distant tide. I had grown so used to those sibilant sounds that I scarcely noticed them any more. Utter quiet seemed to fill and surround the house. Beside me on a cushion, Lucinda was curled up, asleep. I wasn't thinking of Jack as I worked the needles. It was one of those times when my mind was too absorbed in the task to wander.

I'd heard nothing, not even the squeak of the gate, but all of a sudden Lucinda lifted her head with ears pricked. Then she sat up and stared at the curtains across the bay window, wide-eyed and tense with concentration. I looked at her, then followed her gaze, slowly putting the sample down. Listening hard, I tried to make out what could have disturbed her.

For a minute I detected nothing. But then . . .

A gentle bump of footsteps, slow and very light. So much so that they sounded almost . . . careful. A measured, cautious tread, and very close. I fancied it came from the terrace outside the window.

And there it stopped.

Lucinda sat completely still. Her eyes were fixed intently on the curtain. She seemed not nervous but entranced, the way she did whenever something on the television caught her notice. Then, as now, her eyes would pop. She would know there was something moving there, but out of reach.

Jack, I thought. Is it Jack out there, wondering whether to call or go away?

It was late, though, ten past ten. Hardly the sort of time to call uninvited, even if he felt a compelling need to patch things up.

Then, a few more padding steps, moving towards the front door. Lucinda's head turned, tracking them.

I waited for a knock.

And waited. Waited.

Nothing came.

He could be standing out there in the porch, debating.

I stood up. As I did so, Lucy jumped down, sensuously stretched herself and scratched behind an ear, as if no longer interested in anything outside.

Had he gone, I wondered, frowning. Or had I been mistaken in thinking it was human feet I'd heard?

But what else?

There was only one way to find out. I went straight to the front door, pulled back the bolts and opened it.

Nobody there. For a moment I scanned the dim line of the path and the gloom which wrapped the garden. Hesitantly, I called out: 'Jack? Is that you? Are you there?'

Silence. I felt slightly foolish – and uneasy.

'Jack, if you'd like to talk, so would I. I don't want bad feeling between us.'

Still no response. And as I stood there, mere uneasiness mounted into a truly nasty sensation. Coldness washed all over me and I felt as if something with many legs was sauntering up my back. The night air seemed pervaded with a watchfulness. I had a creeping sense of being observed by something or someone out there in the dark, someone who could clearly see me, framed in the light from the hall.

For dragging seconds I stood rooted, then finally jerked a step backwards and slammed the door, locking it, shooting the bolts.

After that, I was restive the whole of the evening, listening constantly. Those footsteps, I was sure I'd heard them; but whose had they been? Not Jack's, no, surely not. He wouldn't want to frighten me.

Nervously, though, my thoughts went back to the man-shape on the marble seat. Had there, after all, been someone sitting there? Someone who, this evening, had been prowling round the house?

# Thirteen

A s if I were not uneasy enough, soon afterwards a chance remark in the grocer's shop gave me something even more unsettling to think about.

I had gone into Mr Trelease's place to buy food for Lucinda. When I went to pay, I found myself at the rear end of a queue. Only a short one, but since the old man liked to chat with every single customer, it seemed a very long time before my turn came.

Finally, I reached the counter and unloaded my wire basket. As he rang up the nine tins of cat food, he chuckled: 'Costs you a fortune, eh?'

'I'll say she does.'

'Company, though, aren't they?'

'Yes – when it suits them.'

'Hm. I prefer a dog myself. Missis won't have any pets, but if I were on my own I'd have a labrador. I used to tell old Miss Penhale she ought to keep a dog, if only for protection.'

Interested, I looked at him. 'Did you often speak with her?'

'Only on the telephone. She used to ring her orders in roughly once a month.'

'Was she chatty at all?'

'Lord, no. Very polite but always to the point. I used to try and get her talking, but she'd come straight back to the matter in hand, just read off her grocery list and ask me to tot up the account. My son usually delivered the stuff in the van. Now and again I made the trip myself, but very rarely. I don't suppose I saw her more than three or four times altogether. She'd always keep you on the doorstep, never let you in. Paid up very promptly, though. There and then you would get your cheque and not one of them ever bounced.'

'She was able to handle her finances, then?'

'I'd say she was, certainly. There were always things she wanted posted, envelopes she would give to the boy. Payments for water and rates and so on, I should think.' Mr Trelease began to laugh. 'She always rewarded him with a five pence piece. A shilling, see, for the messenger boy. That would have been a generous gratuity in her day, and I suppose she still thought it the right thing to do, poor old soul. Oh, we did laugh about Miss Penhale and her five pence tip.'

Yes, I thought, how interesting, and at the same time how odd. Genevra was not so addled that she couldn't manage money. She knew the importance of paying her bills on time. She knew the present-day cost of living – and yet thought it proper to give the 'errand boy' a shilling tip. Meanness? I suspected not. More likely this was simply where a mental schism showed, a confusion between today and a long-gone yesterday.

'Sounds as if it was kindly meant,' I said.

'Oh yes, and for all her strangeness, you knew she was a real lady.'

'I take it she wasn't keen on the idea of having a dog?'

'No,' sighed Mr Trelease. 'It would have been good for her, too, some proper companionship. A damned sight better than imaginary friends.'

I'd been stashing the cat food away in my shopping bag. Halting, I stared at him.

'What?'

'Well, she seemed to think she had company.'

'Company?' I repeated. 'What sort of company?'

'A manfriend.'

'She said so?'

'In a way . . . I mean, it wasn't an outright statement, more a case of something she once or twice let slip.'

I passed him a note for the cat food, not even noticing whether it was ten or twenty.

'How do you mean, let slip?'

'It was when she rang her orders in. I didn't always have exactly what she wanted, so I would suggest an alternative.

103

Several times I heard her say: "No, David doesn't care for those," or words to that effect.'

A kind of thrill went through me, shock and excitement combined.

'She was thinking aloud, you could tell by her tone,' continued Mr Trelease. 'Then she would choose something else instead and we would go on with the list.'

'Did you never ask her who David was?'

'Once. "My friend," was all she said. I did try to press for a few more details, but then she became very brisk and changed the subject. That was always her way of letting you know that she had no wish to discuss a thing further. It was the same with the dog.'

My mouth had gone dry, though I hadn't collected my thoughts well enough to know quite why. Trying to hide my disquiet, I shrugged. 'Well, isn't it possible she did have someone? A regular caller, perhaps? Not necessarily from Polvean.'

'Possible, yes,' allowed Mr Trelease, 'but I really don't think so. I mean to say, where was he after she died? I heard there wasn't a soul at the funeral. I'd have attended it myself if she hadn't been dead and buried before I even knew. If there really was somebody, he can't have been much of a friend, that's all I can say. And she never left her house to him, did she? Went to the Government, that did.'

'Yes, I know.'

The old man wrinkled up his nose. 'There wasn't any David, dear. I'd stake a week's takings on that.'

'The grocery orders,' I said slowly, 'were there supplies enough for two?'

'I suppose so, at a push. Only barely, though. Mind you, I don't think she ate much herself. My boy always used to remark how thin she was. All the same, I just don't believe she had someone there with her all those years, someone nobody else ever saw. She was touched, that's all. Very sad, but there it is.'

He gave me my change and again I didn't even look at it. A thought had crossed my mind, and I asked, 'Did you know anything of Miss Penhale's young days?'

'Can't say I did. I'm not native to Polvean. Came here from Launceston twenty years ago.'

Yes, a Cornishman, but in one way as much an outsider as any of the yachting types. Obviously, the name David held not the slightest significance for Mr Trelease. Thanking him, I left the shop.

Company? A friend called David, whose likes and dislikes Genevra considered when ordering her groceries? I wasn't sure of the implications, but certainly didn't like the sound of that.

Preoccupied, trying to sort out my thoughts, I must have walked about twenty yards before I realised I was going in the wrong direction, away from the spot where I'd parked the car. Turning back, I headed for the quay.

Several boats were tied up alongside and one of them was *Thomasina*. Jack had not been there when I arrived, but now he was leaning against the railings, looking towards the road which came down the hill, and glancing at his watch. He probably had a fishing party booked for the day.

After my talk with Mr Trelease, I already had quite enough on my mind, but there was no way to pass by without being seen. Anyway, I had to take the opportunity to say something.

When he saw me crossing the road towards him, his face took on an expression I had often seen before in men who felt they had been cruelly discarded – a blend of reserve and dignified injury. He let me be the first to speak, and didn't return my smile.

'Hello, Jack.'

'Morning, Christine.'

'Expecting customers?'

'A Birmingham couple.' With another glance up the hill, he added: 'They're late. Won't be worth going if they don't show up soon.'

'Are you doing good business, on the whole?'

'Pretty fair. And how's yours?'

'Fine.'

Now a silence, strained and embarrassing. Is there anything worse than making small talk with someone to whom you've been close? Someone who is now offended, wonders how you

105

have the nerve to speak to him at all, and whether this might represent a climbdown.

'Look . . .' I said clumsily, 'no hard feelings, are there? I mean, I hope we can still be . . .'

'What?' His expression was carefully neutral.

What indeed? Of course, I had meant to say 'friends'. Most hackneyed and hopeless old cliché of all. It never worked that way, not with men like Jack. Oddly enough, one could remain friends with such as Neville. Worldly and not the emotional type, Neville was good at 'civilised' breakups because he never really got hurt. Jack was another matter altogether, and this, of course, was not the first time he had been let down by a woman. Trust erodes and cynicism mounts as wounds and betrayals accumulate. Despite his awful wife, he had been ready for a second try. What a pity his choice had been me, I thought remorsefully.

'I hope we can always remain on good terms.'

A shrug. 'Don't see why not. No war's been declared.'

'I didn't mean to be hurtful, Jack.'

'That's understood. We're different, that's all. You take things more casually than I do.'

I could have given him an argument about that, but to what end?

I forced a smile, though it felt pretty saggy. 'Anyway, I'm glad to have seen you, now that we've both had a chance to cool down. You left so abruptly that morning, and the matter's been bothering me.'

'Well, don't you lose any more sleep over it. "The matter" is water under the bridge now, Christine.'

It chilled me, that emphasis. It was the first time I'd ever heard him sound even remotely sarcastic. Routed, I muttered, 'Yes, well, must be off, then.'

Turning away, I heard him say, 'Goodbye, Chris,' with something slightly different in the tone. Regret, disappointment? I wasn't quite sure.

Then, recollecting the footsteps, I spun around, asking awkwardly: 'Oh, you haven't, by any chance, been out to Trenarwyn at all in the last week or two?'

He blinked. 'Why would I do that? In any case, you would know if I had.'

I lacked the nerve to ask if he might have been hiding outside in the dark one evening not long ago.

'I only wondered if, perhaps, you might have called when I was out.'

The lie sounded lame. He was looking uncertainly at me now, possibly wondering if this was some kind of approach or oblique invitation. Quickly, I said, 'Just a notion. Forget it. I'll see you around.'

I walked on over to the quay. A maroon-coloured car had just drawn up next to mine and a middle-aged couple were getting out. Jack's clients, I supposed. The man was beefy, clad in slacks and a safari shirt. The woman was a bottle-blonde, dressed up in sugar-pink shorts and, of all things, three-inch heels. Putting my groceries in the boot, I watched them go over to where Jack was waiting, saw the man shake him by the hand and introduce his wife. As I unlocked my driver door, I glanced that way again. Jack had taken the blonde by the arm to steady her as she tottered down the steps to board the boat. Just for a moment he looked intently back at me, his face unreadable.

# Fourteen

On the third Saturday of June I went to another craft fair, then spent an evening at the cinema before driving home.

It must have been about eleven o'clock when I got in. Sales had not been good that day, nor had the film been very special, so I felt a mite dispirited and very tired, ready for a nice hot bath and bed.

By the time I had unloaded the car and fed Lucinda, it was getting on for twelve. Pouring myself a whisky and ginger, I took it upstairs and turned the water on. Going to my bedroom, I fetched my dressing gown and opened a tallboy drawer in search of a clean nightdress.

It was then, as I sorted through my things, that I noticed a strange smoky smell. It was in the air of the room and also, I fancied, among my clothes, wafting out of the drawer as the scent of mothballs does. Finding a nightdress, I sniffed it and . . . yes, it lingered about the fabric, faint but definitely there. It wasn't unpleasant, just odd, and I couldn't think where it came from. A scorched smell, that was the best description, something very similar to the odour which rises from linen if the iron is too hot.

I couldn't account for it at all, and only felt mildly curious anyway. Taking the nightdress, I padded next door to the bathroom, undressed and climbed into the tub.

Lying there amid the steam, eyes closed, I almost fell asleep at once. Certainly, I dozed a while, barely conscious of the swish and creak of trees outside. The hot tap wasn't quite turned off and its slow, steady drip bounced a hollow echo off the bathroom tiles.

After a time, I stirred in the warm soapy water and reached

for the sponge. A thin steam hung in the air and dewdrops of moisture clung to the light fitting overhead. The window was of thick and bubbly frosted glass, so I never troubled to draw the curtain. Beyond it, the darkness was tempered by the chilly beams of the moon. They splintered into a radiance splashed across the glass, creating a starburst pattern in silver and black.

With thoughtful eyes I studied it, always alert for good effects to incorporate into my textiles. Nature was a fertile source of inspiration. The coloured flecks in a pebble or the mottling on a leaf, even the hues on the skins of over-ripe fruit; from all such things I derived ideas. Cats' fur and birds' feathers, burning wood in the open grate – they all had their harmonies, from which I borrowed. The moonlight on the window suggested to me a design and I mused on it, absently dipping the sponge and squeezing water out over my shoulders.

Shadows danced across the glass as the branches outside whipped back and forth in the wind. Glistening beads of condensation slid down the knobbly surface, leaving shiny wet tracks. Perhaps I should get something down on paper before I went to bed, I thought. A sketch would do, just to capture the pattern while it was still fresh in my mind.

On the corner of the bath beside my head stood the tumbler of Scotch. I reached for it, took a sip and then a proper gulp. The ice had nearly melted away and I shook the remaining bits round and round, watching them swirl in the golden liquid.

It was as I moved to replace the glass that my glance lifted once again to the window and something made me catch my breath.

A shadow, man-shaped, motionless.

Before I knew it, a scream escaped me. The tumbler fell from my hand and cracked on the edge of the bath. For a second my gaze was pulled from the window by the tinkle of breaking glass and the feel of it sliding down through the water by my thigh. A confusion of dangers seized me, a panic divided between the threat outside and that of being badly cut. I froze, heart thumping, and then . . .

There was nothing, no one, there, only moonlight and the tossing shadows of the trees.

For minutes on end, I don't know how long, I sat just staring at the window and thinking about the balcony outside.

Surely nobody could get up there?

No, certainly they couldn't, I decided finally. There was no means to climb up. The only access to the balcony was from inside the house, and no one could be in the house because the doors and the windows were locked.

Weren't they?

All of them?

Come to think of it, I wasn't entirely sure – but only because I couldn't actually remember doing it. Of course, I would have done it automatically, today like every other day. It just bothered me that I couldn't remember going through the process.

Anyway, if there were an intruder, why would he want to go out and prowl about on the balcony? Why, if he had already gained entrance to the house? Why come to this window and risk being seen?

Unless that was exactly what he wanted . . .

Then the pattern of light on the window was changing again, receding, giving way to a crescent of darkness, and I realised that a passing cloud must have partially covered the moon. Perhaps something similar had happened just now, creating the illusion that a man was standing there. I was eager to think so and breathed a bit easier. Nevertheless, for another ten minutes I scarcely moved, fixedly watching the shadows shift and waver on the glass, waiting to see if that same shape would appear again.

However, it did not come back and after a while the cooling water began to chill me. Cautiously, I felt around for the bits of shattered glass and retrieved the biggest ones before carefully climbing out of the bath. Towelling dry, I dressed, then looked uneasily at the door.

I hadn't locked it. Well . . . why would I?

Again my heart began to thud when I thought about going out on the landing, into the house.

If there should be someone there . . .

But I couldn't – wouldn't – spend the night in here. Summoning my nerve, I opened the door, looked out and listened.

No one in sight and not a sound.

Padding next door to my bedroom, I peeped inside. Nobody there, as far as I could see. Creeping across to the wardrobe, I flung back the door, but discovered no burglar within. Next, with a pounce to the carpet, I sought for a prowler under the bed and was hugely relieved not to find one. The window was securely locked, but with trepidation I opened it, poked my head out and peered along the balcony.

A silvery strip of emptiness in the moonlight. Thank God – no figure skulking in the shadows at either end. No dark form crouching on the roof of the bay window.

Pulling my head in, I locked the window, then spent some minutes checking all the other bedrooms. So far so good, I thought, coming out of the last one. However, to satisfy myself I would have to tour the whole house. The dark pit of the stairwell made me hesitate, but finally I mustered the courage and stole downstairs. From the sitting room fireplace, I picked up a poker for self-protection and went around inspecting every ground-floor room until I was certain that nobody lurked anywhere.

At last I poured myself another large whisky and went up to bed. I was still far from happy, however. Propped against my pillows, sipping, I pondered again on that smell I had noticed, that faint whiff suggestive of burning. The air of my room no longer bore any hint of it. Nevertheless, it had started to play on my mind. A small thing by itself, it seemed more significant when added to the other things which were worrying me. My thoughts returned to the man-shape I had seen on the marble seat. They brooded fearfully on the footsteps, and lastly on my conversation with Mr Trelease.

Yes, that especially. I could still hear his voice in my head, and one phrase echoing over and over: '. . . *she seemed to think she had company.*'

Unless I was going completely mad, something new appeared to be going on around Trenarwyn, and I didn't care for it one bit. Had it not been for that very large whisky, I wouldn't have slept a wink that night.

Once you're rattled, every little thing can take on sinister significance. You find the gate unlatched and torment yourself with wondering if it was you or somebody else who left it that way. You find a flowerpot overturned, a couple of broken branches in the shrubbery. Did the wind do that, or someone lurking? A room feels cold, there's a sudden sharp draught – is something unearthly about?

Try as I might to keep a sense of proportion, I found myself growing increasingly jittery during the days that followed. If Lucinda was in of an evening, I kept an edgy watch on her behaviour, alert for any sign that she was aware of somebody outside. Occasionally, certainly, she would sit up and stare at the window or door, appearing . . . not frightened, just attentive. And then she would settle down again, relaxed, as if nothing had happened. It gave me the shivers just the same.

I remember one night in particular when I was in the kitchen, feeding her. In the cranky manner of cats, she liked to be served her meals on top of the fridge. If left on the floor, her dish would be ignored, so I always put it where her ladyship preferred. That evening, late, I was pouring some milk into her saucer when she suddenly sat back from her food and stared hard at the back door.

My own gaze went straight to the doorknob and a sick feeling rushed right through me. Any minute, I expected to see that handle slyly turn. The door was of stout wood and bore a sturdy old lock with a large iron key which I always hung on a hook nearby. There were no glass panels, yet at moments like this the barrier seemed inadequate. With breath sucked in, I waited to see that handle move . . .

Thankfully, it didn't even twitch.

Lucinda, however, was shifting on her backside and craning her neck, as if she could see through the curtains to something passing by the window. She looked first left, then slowly right, turning all the time, apparently tracking the movements of something circling the house.

I strained to listen, but heard not a thing, not even the wind in the trees, and after a moment the cat returned, unworried, to her food.

It was probably silly to take so much notice. It did occur to me that there must be harmless creatures like foxes and badgers about all the time. Hadn't I seen the tracks myself? And wouldn't the woods behind be the very place for them? A comforting thought, and one to explain Lucinda's odd demeanour from time to time.

But not the sound of footsteps. I knew I'd heard those, all right, that other night. Just once, for certain. There had been occasions since when I fancied they came again, but could not be sure.

Part of the problem was that, having genuinely seen and heard a thing or two, I was doubly prey to my imagination, which could all too easily conjure up repeats. Beyond a doubt, there were plenty of times when I badly frightened myself over nothing at all. One evening close to the end of the month, I gave myself a dreadful scare. Thinking I'd heard a stealthy tread, I went to the bay window and peeped through the curtains towards the porch – then recoiled with a gasp of shock at the sight of a figure, tall and white, with arms outstretched. For several seconds I thought my heart would burst out of my throat.

Then, furious at myself, I realised what it was: only the climbing jasmine fanned out on the trellis, newly burst into clouds of sweet, white flowers.

Whether the causes were fancy or actual peril, the effects on me were pretty much the same. My nerves were beginning to fray, and that by itself was alarming enough.

# Fifteen

S trange to tell, a night arrived when I did see something truly uncanny – and wasn't frightened at all. The experience was vivid, overwhelming, but not in the slightest bit threatening.

It happened within the house at about two o'clock in the morning.

I was woken by music. Dance music, jazzy and dated – and faint, as if it came from a neighbouring house.

I remember turning over in bed with a half-conscious sense of annoyance, thinking I was still in London and someone was holding a noisy party across the street. It must have been several minutes before the reality filtered through to me, the memory of where I was and the sudden shock of knowing that there weren't any other houses out here, not for a mile around.

I opened my eyes to the darkness, rigid now and straining to listen – because the music was in fact coming from downstairs. It had the fidgety, tin-pan quality of the 1920s. The lively brass was punctuated by jokey little spatterings of percussion. Good-time music, Charleston-type.

I had no such stuff in my collection, and even from here I was aware of a thin sort of tone, poor reproduction by the standards of today.

Very old records made that sound: heavy, breakable records played on wind-up gramophones with fluted horns, and needles which had to be constantly changed.

I lay not knowing what to do, and conscious now of something peculiar in the air, a kind of levity, a silly mood, as if the house were full of tipsy, giggly people, their gaiety almost a tangible thing.

Yet I heard no voices, no thump of dancing feet or rattle of glasses, no opening and closing of doors, no tread of anyone going from room to room. There was just the music and that charged-up atmosphere.

The alarm which had gripped me on waking had largely passed, and although I knew that something unutterably strange was going on, I was overcome by a great desire to see, to know.

Pulling back the covers, I crept out of bed and padded across to the door, sneaking like a burglar in my own house, anxious not to shatter the spell and send the phantoms fleeing. I felt I was confronted with something delicate and volatile, rather like one of those coloured soap bubbles I used to blow from a ring when I was a child. It seemed to me that a gossamer bubble of human emotion had somehow expanded in my house, but a cough or a step on a creaking floorboard would instantly destroy it. So I opened my door, moved out on the landing and down the stairs, all at a snail's pace, almost afraid to breathe and terrified of being caught out by a sneeze.

The music was coming from the sitting room, yet it sounded no louder as I progressed downstairs, still appearing distant even as I reached the door and laid my hand upon the knob. Only the tempo had changed; the tune was smoother now, much more melodic. Far-away music, removed in time, with the quality of an echo, a memory.

There was, I noticed, no sliver of light from under the door. Whoever heard of a party in the dark?

Very softly, very slowly, I turned the handle and pushed the door back.

I was mesmerised by what I saw.

A figure, a young woman, whirling and gliding all by herself in her own strange light. She was smiling and her arms were raised as if she were being held by a dancing partner. Her frock was shimmering pink and silver, a silky dress with a dropped waist and a fringe at the hem. Caught up in a knot at the back, her black hair was bound by a spangled headband which circled her brow. She wore glass beads and white silk stockings with two-toned T-strap shoes.

I was not at all scared, not then. I was enthralled – and

115

enchanted, because she was strikingly beautiful and looked so happy. Lovely features, perfect skin, a nose that was straight and elegant, fine dark eyes with winging brows. A face straight out of a *Picture Show* annual.

She was neither misty nor solid. Instead there was a magic lantern quality about her. I was reminded of a projector show we once had in the assembly hall when I was a child at school. The screen, badly rigged, had collapsed, but for several minutes the film had run on, so that watery-coloured wraiths capered upon the piano, the podium and the wall behind. That was very much how she looked: like a film projected without a screen to receive it.

I watched her sway and turn about the room with her unseen partner. For her, my furniture just wasn't there. For her, I guessed, there was a varnished wooden floor with the rugs rolled back, different décor, different furnishings and, some-where in the room, the latest thing in wind-up gramophones.

Where was everyone else, the rest of the party? Gone into time. I could see only her. Genevra's image alone had somehow revived from that long-ago night, yet I felt I was seeing her dance among a crowd of friends, at her own party, here in her own house.

Genevra – the crazy, pitied, solitary Miss Penhale – had once been beautiful, surrounded by admirers.

I don't know what, if anything, I did to drive her away, but suddenly the music ceased and she faded, exactly like daylight turning to night, except that it took only seconds. With her went the fervid atmosphere, and before I knew it the house was perfectly silent again, dark and devoid of any presence save my own.

For the rest of the night there was no sleep for me. When dawn came, it found me huddled on my bedroom window seat. I'd been there a couple of hours and had grown very cold, although I was only vaguely aware of discomfort. I watched the sun rise and the tide come in, and tried to square this latest apparition with the others, with my theories, with what Mr Trelease had said.

It was difficult. To judge by the style of dress she was

wearing, I'd seen an image from the early twenties. To all appearances, she wasn't grieving for David at that time. Quite the contrary, she seemed to be enjoying a frivolous life. Had something put a stop to that? Or was there, perhaps, no party at all? I could have been wrong in assuming there was. Had she become deluded while still in her youth? The unseen partner – was he ever really there? With whom, if anyone, had she been dancing?

In the end I became so confused I could have screamed from sheer frustration. Giving up, I went into the bathroom. From the mirror, a pinched face and dark-circled eyes looked back at me, posing even more worrying questions.

What was I going to do? Could I live with this? There was nothing sinister in what I had seen, yet it was so desperately abnormal. Apart from which, there was the other . . . presence. By now, I was all but convinced there was something – someone – else, a 'he', whose nature was different from that of poor, harmless Genevra.

I felt defensive and defiant. My weaving business was going pretty well, I was succeeding. And Trenarwyn was *mine*, the first home of which I could truly say that. I had lived with my parents, I'd rented flats, I'd moved into the houses of successive menfriends. But Trenarwyn was financially mine and aesthetically mine, decorated to my taste and arranged to my liking. Why should I be driven out? It was *my* domain . . .

Ah, but no, it wasn't, was it? Like it or not, I was sharing again.

Wearily, I blinked at myself in the mirror and raked back my hair. Before I made the move down here, I had tried to anticipate every possible problem. But this was one for which I simply hadn't bargained.

The matter depressed me for most of the week and I went into Truro that Saturday, for no other reason than to have a day out. I'd read in the local paper that there was to be some sort of charity festival with street entertainments.

The day was sunny, and a sense of well-being expanded in me as I drove down the country roads. A smoky blue haze hung

117

over the fields of wheat and barley in the distance, the sign that this weather had settled in for some time to come. Hedges and roadside verges were thick with honeysuckle and briar roses, white drifts of yarrow and cherry-pink sprays of red campion. Shadows and golden light flickered around me as I sped through belts of trees which overhung the road. I drove with my window right down, soothed by the steady flap of the wind and roar of the engine.

I wasn't going to think about ghosts and presences today. I was taking a holiday from them. They could have the house to themselves and do as they pleased, I didn't care. Like Scarlett O'Hara, I'd worry about things tomorrow. Odd how one always imagined one would be more 'up to it' tomorrow.

The town was always bustling on a Saturday, and even more so this particular day. The shopping centre streets had been taken over by Morris dancers, clog dancers, jugglers, fire-eaters, mime artists and a Caribbean steel band, each performing amid a circle of spectators. The city's hanging baskets were a riot of petunias, lobelia and trailing geraniums. Above the heads of the milling crowds, they hung from their poles like giant pompons.

I drifted around, enjoying the freedom of having no errands whatever to perform. This air of relaxation seemed to lie over everyone today. The streets were closed to traffic and nobody appeared to be in any hurry. The music and fair-day atmosphere made me happy and I wished I had brought a camera. Had I been an artist, I could have sketched and painted a host of colourful images that morning. A policeman with his sleeves rolled up, eating an ice cream cornet. A lad selling silver balloons outside the library – and a toddler in tears as hers was pulled from her grip by a gust of wind. A busker, young and very down-at-heel. A town crier in eighteenth-century dress, bantering with two old women. A flock of pigeons swooping round the cathedral spires.

A day in Christine Elford's life, splendid but fleeting, doomed to dissolve like the wake behind a boat. Impossible to preserve it, or ever to live it again. Although, perhaps, as some believed, no experience, nothing that happened, ever

118

passed away. It all remained somehow imprinted, somewhere. All of history, my day out . . .

Genevra's story . . .

Firmly, I stopped myself. I wasn't going to think about her. For distraction, I went and bought some sandwiches and a tin of fruit squash, and wandered across to the park beneath the railway viaduct.

A jazz quartet was playing in the bandstand. Pretty good they were, too. I'd been to New Orleans and hadn't heard anything much better there. All the same, I wanted quiet and shade for a while, so I sought out the picnic benches underneath the trees. There I sat and ate my lunch, entertained by a couple of frisking grey squirrels. The jumpy sounds of the jazz wafted down on the summer air, removed and faint.

Just like the music which woke me a few nights ago . . .

Even on a day like this, I couldn't quite leave my problem behind.

Stubbornly, I focused on the afternoon and what I was going to do. Look around the museum, perhaps, and then the cathedral.

I finished the food and drained the fruit squash. High over the park, on the railway bridge, a train rolled by with slow thunder, approaching the station. I wondered if it had come from London, and remembered the first time I crossed that bridge on the Penzance express the previous summer. From the window, I had seen this park below. Tree-tops, sloping lawns, the pagoda-like roof of the bandstand. And then the sandy-coloured town with its sharply limned cathedral sitting in the middle. That was the day I arrived here to begin my quest for a house. One week later I had discovered Trenarwyn.

Leaving the park, I walked back towards the town centre, stopping halfway to spend an hour in the County Museum.

It was past three o'clock when I reached the cathedral. In the cobbled square outside, a young man in a silver costume was mimicking the jerky, jointed movements of a robot. People were clapping and throwing coins into a hat. Skirting the crowd, I went inside. Shade again, echoes, and motionless air with the scent of stale incense. Completed in 1910, this

119

cathedral, Gothic-style with soaring vaults and arches. A few other people were moving around with hushed voices and slow, processional walks. Strange the effect great churches have, even on the non-religious. The sheer scale of the building creates an impression of listening and watching from overhead. One feels observed.

In a quiet corner, I found a bench with a velvet cushion. It faced a row of stained-glass windows – saints and disciples in jewel colours – lit from outside by the afternoon sun. I sat and studied them for a while, wondering if it would be too ambitious to try and create pictorial designs along similar lines – for cushion covers, say. I'd noticed the cathedral had a shop attached, selling gifts to raise money to maintain the building. However, I feared the work would be too intricate, not cost-effective.

I was pondering this, when suddenly a tall figure clothed in a long red clerical gown appeared before me.

'You look troubled,' said a voice.

Looking up, I met the smile of an elderly white-haired man.

'Do I? People are always telling me that when I'm deep in thought. Actually, I was admiring the windows.'

'Ah.' The smile grew broader. 'Are you a visitor?'

Meaning, was I a tourist? With a spark of satisfaction, I was able to say: 'No, I live near Polvean.'

'How fortunate. A lovely spot.'

'Yes,' I said, then added: 'I'm not a churchgoer, but I like this cathedral. It's pleasant, friendly. They're not all like that. Some of the old ones are rather bleak, there's almost a brutal feel about them.'

A chuckle. 'Hm, the medieval aura.'

'That's it,' I said.

'You must be sure to come here again at harvest festival, my dear. We have such decorations, such a display.'

'I'll try,' I said, and meant it.

He bid me good day and turned away. Like the cathedral, he was congenial, I thought, as I watched him walk off. The sort of person who . . . invited confidences. Somebody to talk to, someone unconnected with Polvean. After months of hugging this thing to myself, I needed a sympathetic ear.

Quickly, I was on my feet. I called out: 'Wait! Excuse me . . .'

He spun around, stood still.

'Could you spare a few minutes, do you think? There's something I'd like to talk to you about.'

He came back. I sat down again and he perched on the bench beside me.

'You have some problem after all?'

'I'm afraid I do. I hope you won't think me dotty. For various reasons, I've been loath to mention this to anybody else.'

'Indeed? Well, spit it out and let's examine it.'

I plunged in. 'I told you I live near Polvean, but the fact is I haven't been there very long – only since last autumn. I live alone and the problem is the house, or rather, something in the house.'

His brows lifted slightly, his eyes were attentive. 'Something?'

A splutter of nervous laughter escaped me. I blurted: 'It has a ghost.'

There, it was out, and what a relief.

Blinking slowly, he considered. 'Are you certain?'

'Completely. In fact, there may be more than one. I can't quite make it out. I've seen her, or them, several times. The last appearance was just a few days ago and put the matter beyond any doubt.'

Frowning, he thoughtfully tapped a finger against his lower lip.

'Can you describe for me what you've seen?'

I spent some minutes talking. His eyes were on me all the while.

'Well,' he murmured at last, 'it sounds as though you have at least one revenant, all right. And you think you know who it is?'

'I believe I do. It's a Miss Penhale, who lived in the house all her life. I've learned a certain amount about her from local people, but I haven't been able to piece together the whole story.'

He mused on this. 'Do you think she wants you to?'

'Oh no, I'm convinced she wants nothing from me. It's not

the sort of haunting that you read about in stories. It's not an attempt to get in touch.'

'You don't imagine there's some task she wishes you to perform?'

'Absolutely not. She's just there, on occasion, like a mirage.'

'Does she frighten you?'

'Not in herself. She isn't menacing at all, but she saddens me. What little I know about her life suggests a tragedy.'

The old man sat and scratched his chin. 'Interesting,' he said. 'Doesn't sound too ominous, though. Rather like one of those apparitions which frequent old pubs and stately homes. They're seen from time to time, but they do no harm. You used the word "mirage". I'm inclined to believe they are something of that order – something reflected out of time – and that physics will be able to explain them one day soon.'

I looked at him, surprised.

He smiled. 'Being religious doesn't make one a simpleton.'

'No,' I said, flushing, 'of course.'

'Anyway, is she getting you down very much? Making life unbearable?'

'I wouldn't say that. Naturally, it's disturbing but I'm not afraid of her. Only . . .'

I knew it would grow more difficult now to express what bothered me, or at least to present it as credible, for I could point to nothing very much as evidence.

'Only?' he prompted.

Taking a deep breath, I said: 'I suspect there's someone else, a male, and he does frighten me. Unlike her, he takes an interest in me.'

The clergyman moistened his lips. He looked a mite uneasy now.

'On what do you base this notion?'

'Not much, I have to confess. Shapes I've seen – though none too clearly. Often, after dark, I get a sense that someone's prowling round the house. I opened the door one night and looked. I had the most horrible feeling of being watched.'

'That's all?'

'I've heard footsteps, I'm sure of it.'

The old man relaxed and smiled. 'Doesn't sound exactly supernatural to me.'

'It felt malign when I was standing on that step. I went cold and my skin crawled.'

He pulled a wry face and his forehead wrinkled. 'The nervous system can respond in very unpleasant ways, even when danger is merely imaginary. You might, however, be well advised to get yourself a guard dog. Have you been to the police?'

'They'd laugh at me.'

He sighed, admitting, 'Yes, you'd need something more concrete to interest the law, I'm afraid.' He patted my hand. 'But you know, it seems to me that this sketchy knowledge of Miss Penhale has left you too much room for speculation and imaginings. It might be a good idea to find out more if you possibly can. To know the full story might set your mind at rest. It may all be far more mundane than you think.'

'I've told you I've seen her ghost. And you accept that?'

'Yes.'

'Is that mundane?'

'Not such a very great wonder, perhaps. The unseen is around us all the time. Most people never pause to consider the possibility that their senses may be designed as much to keep impressions out as to let them in, that they are selective, acting as filters to restrict what we perceive. I doubt we could function, were it not so. Now and again, however, extra signals may slip through, similar to cross-channel interference on the television, and no more sinister.'

'You don't feel there's any need to . . . well . . . try and drive these things away?'

Becoming serious, he said: 'If you're talking of exorcism, that is not something we undertake lightly.'

'And Trenarwyn is not a suitable case for treatment?'

'I would be reluctant. Of course, if this unease continues, a blessing might help to reassure you.'

'A blessing? For the house?'

He nodded. Standing up, he said: 'It's evident you have a problem. I don't think it's dire, but peace of mind is invaluable, not least for the sake of a person's health. If this business goes on troubling you, do talk to your local vicar. It's Mr Peplow, as I recall. George Peplow – excellent man.'

He was kind, and much of what he had said seemed plausible, I thought as I left the cathedral. The idea of having Trenarwyn blessed, however, left me cold. As for keeping a dog – well, I was never fond of them and I knew that Lucinda would promptly leave home. The only attractive suggestion was that of pursuing Genevra's story in the hope that I might learn something to set my mind at rest. Yes, I decided, I could try that, for there did remain one possible source of information. Providing she was still alive, there was Earnestina Toy.

# Sixteen

First thing on Monday morning, I started making telephone calls. I must have rung twenty nursing and retirement homes before I found the right one.

'We do have a Mrs Earnestina Kelland,' said a pleasant voice on the other end. 'If you don't mind waiting, I'll check the records; they'll show her maiden name.'

She was gone a long time. Receiver in hand, I shuffled impatiently from foot to foot, desperate for a positive answer. In the background I could hear the opening and closing of drawers and a rustle of paper.

Finally, footsteps approaching the phone, then the bright voice again.

'You're in luck. Née Toy, it says here.'

'Oh, splendid! Could I come and see her?'

'I expect she'd like that. Mrs Kelland hasn't any living relatives, you see, nobody to visit her.'

So the following afternoon I set out for a home called Chymorna, nearer Launceston than St Austell. The drive took me nearly an hour, but at last I turned in at the gates of a white-painted house with big windows and large, pretty grounds. A good establishment, and yet, to me, it had an air of pathos – perhaps because I was reminded of our monthly visits to Neville's mother at her retirement home in Berkshire. He had chosen a place which was smart and expensive. It took good care of her and Neville scarcely missed the fourteen hundred a month it cost him. Problem solved, Mumsie was in excellent hands. But she had an air of bewilderment and her eyes were always full of sad questions. Where had her time gone? Could none of her children look after her? What was she supposed to do here? It wasn't quite the way she had expected to end her life.

Driving up to Chymorna, I saw a circle of wheelchairs on the front lawn, each containing an elderly person. In the middle stood a young woman, a member of staff. She had a ball and was bouncing it to each of the old folks in turn and they listlessly patted it back. Stopping the car, I rolled down the window. The young woman came across the grass to me and I asked for Mrs Kelland. She pointed me to a path leading round the side of the house and told me to try the gazebo.

Sure enough, I found her there. I had feared she might be deaf or senile. Not a bit of it, however. Although she too was in a wheelchair, she was sitting very straight and reading an Agatha Christie. White-haired and wizened, she was speckled with age spots, but her eyes were bright and astute. Laying her book on her lap, she looked me up and down.

'Mrs Kelland?' I asked.

A nod. 'You must be the lady who rang to enquire about me.'

'That's right. My name's Chris Elford. I hope you don't mind my disturbing you?'

'Not exactly busy, am I?' chuckled Mrs Kelland. A semi-circular bench ran around the gazebo and she made a waving motion with her hand. 'Sit down, dear. My, you're a lovely girl, aren't you?'

'Not so much a girl any more,' I said, taking a seat. 'I'm within sight of forty.'

'Pah! A spring chicken. Wait till you're ninety-four like me.' Gleefully, she patted her knees and another gurgle of laughter shook her.

'I hear you don't have many callers,' I said.

She pulled a wry face. 'No. Never had any children, see, and I've outlasted all my friends. And the old man, of course. He was a builder, my husband. Died twenty years ago.'

'Men are not as durable as we are, on the whole.'

'That's a fact.' She studied me thoughtfully. 'You don't sound local. Come from up-country?'

'London. I moved here last October to set up in trade as a handweaver.'

'Fancy that. Mind you, I've read how the old crafts are coming back. Everything goes full circle, doesn't it? Anyway, what can you want with me?'

'How's your memory, Mrs Kelland?'

'Good,' she said briskly. 'I'm lucky; I'm not addled like some of them here.'

'Then I'm sure you can help me. I'm looking into the history of the village where I live.'

'Where's that?'

'Polvean.'

There was a pause. Then: 'Polvean,' she repeated. 'My Lord, it's a long, long time since I was there. Must be nearly sixty years.' For a moment her gaze wandered absently round the gazebo. The trellis walls of it were twined with clematis and roses, and shadows danced upon the old lady as the creepers moved in the wind. 'I don't think I'm any authority on the village, dear,' she shrugged. 'I don't quite understand why you've sought me out.'

'To be truthful, it's not so much the village, it's my house. I bought a place out by the bay and I'm told you used to work there.'

Uneasily, softly, she said: 'Trenarwyn?'

'Yes.'

Drawing a long breath, she murmured an apprehensive 'Oh'. Then, shaking herself, she half-smiled. 'I'm sorry, dear, it's just not a happy recollection. All right, what can I tell you?'

'You were in service there, to the Penhale family?'

'I was, as a housemaid. I went to work for them in . . . 1912, I think. Yes, that's right, I was nearly thirteen. They were good employers, kind to their staff by the standards of the time.'

'Did you stay with them long?'

'Nearly twenty-five years.'

'You say they were kind, yet it's not a happy recollection. Why is that?'

'The family suffered certain misfortunes. It was very upsetting. Such nice people, they didn't deserve so much trouble. But then, hardly anyone ever does, and of course it was all the result of the war . . .'

Breaking off, she fell to musing, briefly forgetful of me.

'You were fond of them?'

'Yes, I was, especially the daughter of the house.'

'Genevra?'

At that, Mrs Kelland eyed me keenly. 'You already know a little, I see.'

'Only of her later years. I want to hear about her youth, and that's where you come in.'

A slight frown gathered between her brows. 'So it's not really the house which interests you, or the rest of the family? Just her? May I ask why?'

I thought it best to come clean at once. 'I've been having odd experiences.'

Mrs Kelland sat back and cocked her head.

'I'm certain it's all to do with Genevra. I mean, she causes it.'

There followed a strung-out silence. Then: 'How can that be? She died more than ten years ago,' said Mrs Kelland. 'I read about it in the *Cornish Guardian*.'

'I know,' I said. 'She died, but she hasn't entirely gone.'

The old woman's stare grew fixed. 'What?' came the faint question.

'I've seen her, Mrs Kelland. It can't be anyone else. All my instincts and all the facts I've gleaned about her convince me it's Genevra, but I don't know enough to understand why it's happening.'

Her hand crept up to her throat. She whispered, 'What exactly have you seen?'

Recognition, clear and painful – I could see it in her eyes as I related what had happened. She said not a word, just let me talk, but it was obvious whenever something stirred a vivid memory. Emotions flickered and changed on her face, especially when I mentioned the necklace of pearls and the pink beaded dress. Mrs Kelland knew, all right, what this was all about.

'This is all familiar, isn't it?' I said at last.

Nodding, she licked her lips and breathed: 'Oh dear God. Oh my Lord, my poor dear . . .'

I grasped at once that her sympathy wasn't for me. Her eyes

were brimming and tremors of agitation had seized her hands. They jerked and fidgeted, clasping and stroking each other.

I began to feel quite guilty – and anxious too, lest she had some kind of attack.

'I'm sorry,' I said, as a dry sob escaped her. 'Perhaps it was wrong of me to come. I didn't dream you'd be so distressed. There's no need to go on, Mrs Kelland, if you'd rather not.'

But she calmed herself and said, 'Forgive me. It all came rushing back, you see, and what you've told me comes as quite a shock.' Pulling a handkerchief out of her pocket, she blew her nose and spent a silent moment, thinking. Finally, she sighed. 'I was relieved, you know, when I read that Genevra had died, for I knew she would never have any peace in life. The thought of her lingering even after death is just too awful.'

'I don't think she's an actual presence, Mrs Kelland, more of an after-image, if that's any comfort.'

'I hope and pray you're right.' Sniffing, she dabbed her nose again. 'Whatever she is, it must be pretty unnerving for you, so the least I can do is answer your questions, seeing you've come all this way.'

'Sure you want to?'

'Yes,' she said stoutly, 'if only to assure you that there's nothing to fear from her. She was unfortunate. Fate was merciless, so was her conscience. Between them, they destroyed her.' Mrs Kelland smoothed her skirts and folded her hands, which were no longer trembling. 'However, I mustn't ramble. Let's start at the beginning.' Gazing past me, she thoughtfully sucked her lower lip. 'How old was Genevra when I first went to Trenarwyn? Just a year or two older than I was. Oh, and so lovely, such a face – a beautiful girl, and high-spirited too, with the merriest laugh. A bit scatterbrained, as young women often are – at least, the sort who have an easy life. Everyone loved her, although she was given to sudden changes of mood. Giggly at one moment, glum the next, always up and down, but I think that was just her age. Fifteen and passionate about everything.'

'Was she an only child?'

'Yes, but never lonely. Plenty of friends, including boys. She was so affectionate, such good fun – and generous, always giving little presents. She used to tell me jokes sometimes and bits of gossip. Of course, I was always mindful of the class difference between us, but she was never haughty in her manner. Oh, I liked her enormously. She was very popular, always going to parties.'

Mrs Kelland stopped, reflected, then went on more gravely: 'There was one particular lad she saw a lot. David – one of the Lanyon family.'

I felt my heart skip. I hadn't mentioned David, nothing at all about a man, deeming it best to see if he came up in conversation.

'From the time they were toddlers, she and David had always been close,' Mrs Kelland went on. 'She spent more time with him than with anyone else. He was Genevra's special friend and you could tell he simply worshipped her. They used to sit talking for hours on a little marble seat in the bluebell dell at the back of the house. It was their favourite place. I would often look out of the kitchen window when I was working at the sink, and I'd see them up there together under the trees. I expect it's still there, isn't it, that little bench?'

'Yes,' I murmured, 'it certainly is. So that was a bluebell dell? I thought there might have been a garden.'

'Not really, no, it never was. There were a few shrubs and the gardener kept back the undergrowth, but it was always just a glade. Anyway,' resumed Mrs Kelland, 'everyone thought Genevra and David would marry eventually. Like her, he was lovely to look at – a gentle, humorous face and a beautiful head of hair, dark brown and curly.'

The description caused me to frown. A gentle, humorous face did not sit well with the feeling I had about 'the man'.

The old lady seemed not to notice my look and continued. 'David was an ideal complement to Genevra, because he was quiet and steady. Her parents certainly thought so, and David's father too. His mother, though, was another matter. Mrs Lanyon didn't care for Genevra, not one little bit. Whenever you saw them together you could tell.' Knowingly, Mrs Kelland added: 'But then, she was jealous, you see. He was her only son, her darling boy. She'd have resented any girl he loved, believe you me. Not a nice woman at all. Mrs Penhale was sweet, but Iris Lanyon, well, I was always wary of her, I can tell you.

'Nevertheless, in spite of her, it was generally expected that Genevra and David would soon become engaged. But then, when she was about sixteen and he was twenty, the Great War broke out.'

Mrs Kelland's face grew sombre and she started to toy absent-mindedly with a strand of her hair.

'By God,' she said quietly, 'no one had any idea what was coming, what it was going to be like. The whole country was in a fever, spoiling for a fight. We were the great British Empire and we were going to show them. We'd win this one just as we had won so many others. It was going to be another grand and glorious adventure. We'd lick the Hun with ease and it wouldn't take long. The press were bellowing for it. The photos in the papers showed excited crowds outside Buckingham Palace, young men cheering and throwing their hats in the air, young girls hanging on their arms, admiring the boys. Everyone was mad for war, every class from top to bottom. Working men suddenly saw a way out of the mine or the factory, even a chance to go abroad.' Mrs Kelland snorted. 'A uniform, glamour. It seems unbelievable now, but people in those days weren't as cynical or knowing as they are today. They respected politicians and we all looked up to our so-called betters. God help us, we trusted them, thought they knew best.' She made a spitting sound. 'Oh, and I remember all the posters and the slogans. Sentimental, noble-sounding stuff. Crude and corny, but nearly everybody fell for it.' Glancing at me, she added: 'I don't say the war didn't need to be fought. I can't be any judge of that. But the way it was presented as a wonderful chance for manly exploits, the way it was greeted with such eagerness – quite insane. Of course, it's easy to be wise after the event, but I still can't think about it without tremendous anger.'

'Did you lose someone yourself, Mrs Kelland?'

'No dear, I didn't, thank the Lord. But you see, it was that mood, that crazy attitude, which started off the trouble between David and Genevra, made her do and say things she regretted ever after.' Sighing, the old lady shook her head. 'If Genevra had been a man, she would have been the first one down at the recruiting office. The war, the war – like nearly everybody else, she was full of it. Patriotism, king and country, poor little Belgium. The girl was on fire, believed all she read. And that was where the tragedy began, because David, you see, had more sense than most. He didn't want to go. I don't think it was cowardice; it was distaste. He didn't fall for the propaganda. He had plans to study law, and resented being asked to put them aside.

' "Let the politicians fight," he used to say. "There wouldn't be half so much trouble if they had to roll up their sleeves and settle their differences personally." '

Mrs Kelland clicked her tongue. 'His was a lone voice, unfortunately. All the other lads who came to the house were keen as mustard. All Genevra's admirers were joining up. By Christmas of 1914 they had all gone, except for David.'

'And Genevra took that badly?'

The old lady threw a glance heavenwards. 'I should say. She was dismayed at first, and then she was furious. Genevra had waded into war work up to her neck, knitting, fundraising and all the rest of it. Khaki colour became a fashion for women, a way of showing their support for the war effort, and she went about wearing it all the time. Her skirts, her blouses, her frocks – all khaki. It was the first time she'd ever looked drab. Oh, she had quickly become a real zealot, and faced with David's stubbornness, she started to treat him unkindly.'

For a moment, Mrs Kelland's fingers drummed in agitation on the cover of her book. Then she said earnestly, leaning forward: 'You must understand that this was not like her. It was foreign to her nature, utterly. It was just that she was so soaked in the atmosphere and all the war talk, under the spell of it, not herself at all.'

A comparison came to mind and I said, 'The young are vulnerable that way. Look at the ones today who get involved with weird religious cults and turn against their families.'

The old lady sat back. 'A similar thing, perhaps,' she agreed. 'They're . . . what's the word, my dear?'

'Indoctrinated?'

'Yes, and they become fanatics.'

'Quite. I understand.'

'Well,' continued Mrs Kelland, 'she nagged him and lectured him, told him off and he bore it patiently. He tried to reason with her, all to no effect. Oh, I simply lost count of the times I heard them arguing. I used to wonder how he stood it, how he could keep on coming around to the house. But then, he adored her and I would guess he was hoping the war would soon be over and she would snap out of it. The newspapers didn't tell you the truth, you see, not in those early stages. They painted a rosy picture, claimed the fight was going well. It wasn't until much later that the public began to hear of the horrors and learn the true cost.'

For a while she drifted away on the memories, till finally I prompted her: 'So he stood his ground and he wouldn't go. What then?'

'What then?' murmured Mrs Kelland. 'Genevra's patience, what she had of it, gave out, and she did a terrible thing. Her birthday fell in the middle of May and there was a bit of a party. Now, this was 1915, just one week after the *Lusitania* was sunk. The mood of the country was ferocious, everyone wanted revenge and "shirkers" came in for even more abuse. Well, as I say, Genevra had a birthday party. Everyone had a nice tea and they played the gramophone all evening. A lot of her female friends were there, her parents and various Polvean neighbours. All the men were middle-aged or older, too old for the services. All but David, and some young chap who'd been sent home with a shoulder wound.'

As if for comfort, the old woman pressed a hand to her cheek. 'Genevra behaved very badly to David that evening. She pointedly ignored him, while she made a great fuss of the soldier. She couldn't even be bothered to open the present he brought her. I have to add that some of the guests were pretty cold towards him, too, but it was only Genevra he cared about. She was the only one who could really hurt him, and she did.

'It must have been about eight o'clock when she suddenly went to the gramophone and took the needle off the record.

I'd just come in to clear the food and plates away. A silence fell as the music stopped. I looked up from what I was doing and she was standing there with something in her hand – a long, flat box. She thanked them all for their birthday gifts and then she said, "I have a presentation to make myself, as a matter of fact. A decoration, well deserved, for one of my guests tonight." '

Absently, Mrs Kelland flicked at the pages of her book as she recalled: 'The look on her face, a hard sort of humour – I didn't like it. There was a kind of simmering about her, and her mouth was a straight line, tight. I had a sudden awful feeling I knew what she was going to do. Sure enough, she opened the box, took out a long white feather and a pin. In front of everyone, she walked across that room and pinned it on David's lapel.' Briefly, the cracked old voice dropped almost to a whisper. 'The silence was ghastly, everyone staring. Some of them smirked and looked satisfied. Others were appalled, embarrassed. Me – I felt ashamed for her. As for David . . . His face, his eyes – I've never seen such pain.

'Then Genevra stepped back and said: "There, that suits you admirably." And she calmly returned to the gramophone to put another record on. Everyone else just stood there, rooted, till David suddenly tore the feather from his jacket, stalked from the room and slammed the door.

'It was dreadful, dreadful, because he loved her, and she had loved him. Always, ever since they were children. Now she despised him enough to humiliate him in front of everyone. I don't think he would have cared at all if it had been one of those hateful women who went around with trays of white feathers accosting men in the street. For Genevra to do it was quite something else.

'Later that evening,' went on Mrs Kelland, 'I went upstairs to brush Genevra's hair before bed as usual. I took his present and put it down on the dressing table in front of her. She glanced at the box and then pushed it aside.

' "I don't want it, Earnestina," she told me. "It's yours."

' "Won't you even look at it, Miss?" I asked, but she just sniffed and said she wasn't interested.

'Well, I went on brushing her hair for a while. She didn't chat that night and her face was set, cold and beautiful, almost severe. She was watching me in the mirror and at length she said: "You think I did wrong, don't you, Earnestina? You think me harsh."

'I had to be honest. "It was unworthy of you, miss," I told her.

' "He's shirking his duty. You surely don't approve of that?"

' "If it were someone close to me," I said, "I hope I'd care more for his feelings than anything else."

'That got across to her, I could tell,' said Mrs Kelland. 'Her face was always very readable and she couldn't hide much. I saw her gaze go wavering about and she looked very young again, unhappy. After a pause she reached out for the box and slowly unwrapped his gift. It was a string of pearls. Splendid pearls; I've never seen finer.'

Pearls. A chill went down my spine.

The old lady was talking on. 'The following evening, we heard that David had gone and joined up, so Genevra had her way at last, but I don't think she felt very jubilant. Guilty, you see. Cruelty was out of character.'

For a moment I pondered on this. 'Still,' I said, 'David wasn't killed in the war, was he? He died afterwards, drowned in the bay.'

'How did you know that?'

'Someone in the village told me several people had drowned out there, and his name was mentioned. So it wasn't merely a case of a young man enlisting to please his girl and then losing his life at the front.'

'That's so. It was rather less simple and I'll come to that. First things first, however. David came home twice on leave and Genevra was all over him. She was proud of him again and keen to make up for her past behaviour.' Sucking her teeth, Mrs Kelland recalled: 'He was quiet the first time and didn't talk much. I remember Genevra pestering him with questions, wanting to know all about the action. His answers were vague, just fobbing her off. There seemed to be a barrier between him and everyone at home. It was like that for a lot of soldiers. We were living in different worlds and they were angered by all the optimism and jingoism back here.

'Then, let's see, it must have been about eight months later when he came home the second time. My dear, he looked like a man who'd seen hell, which of course was the truth of it. He brooded constantly and Genevra could hardly get a word out of him. Once or twice he became very irritable and snapped at her. He was a changed man, terribly changed, and when he went back that second time Genevra cried for a week.'

A scornful twist pulled at Mrs Kelland's mouth. 'For certain, the truth was filtering through to the public by now,' she said. 'It could scarcely be hidden any longer with such tremendous casualty lists and so many mutilated men returning home to tell the tale. Everyone knew what was really going on across the Channel. Genevra fretted over David endlessly and couldn't forgive herself for the way she had insulted him and pushed him to go and join up.'

I interrupted her. 'But they brought in conscription in 1916. He'd have had to go in any case.'

'Indeed so, dear,' Mrs Kelland agreed. 'What happened to David during the war was not Genevra's fault, if the truth be told. He would, as you say, have been called up eventually. Her conscience troubled her just the same, because of the way she had treated him, because she'd been so wrong about it all, and because she had pushed him into it before he had to go. Remorse had its way with her even then, but it was what happened after the war which really turned her mind.

'In late October of 1917, David was reported killed. He was caught up in that dreadful carnage at Passchendaele. One evening, close to dusk, one of his men saw him shot, then some shells came down close by and he disappeared from sight amid all the rain and mud. That night, when things went quiet for a while, a couple of soldiers crept out to search for him.' Mrs Kelland shuddered. 'They found bodies, and parts of bodies – corpses blown to bits, impossible to identify. The ground was so terribly churned up by the shelling that they were no longer even certain of the spot where he had been hit. But no one was left alive out there and David was listed among the dead.

'Genevra was distraught and so was David's mother. Now, Iris Lanyon was always the sort to lash out when she was in pain. She came around to Trenarwyn and went for Genevra like a tigress. You can well imagine the sort of things she said. "I hope you're satisfied? Sacrifice enough for you? You and your cause and your noble talk!" That kind of thing. Iris had to vent her feelings; Genevra was the perfect target and, being the way she was, the girl took it all to heart. She grieved and mourned and blamed herself. It went on for month after month after month. She was utterly lost and full of self-recrimination. All of us wondered how long it was going to continue. Her father was fearful she might lose her mind.'

Beyond the gazebo, the song of a blackbird thrilled in the summer air. There were distant voices, too, from somewhere in the grounds. Briefly, a faint burst of laughter called me back to present-day surroundings. Then Mrs Kelland was talking on.

'But at last, in the late spring of 1918, she began to recover, for somebody new came along. Well . . . not new. She'd known him all her life, but he hadn't been anything special to her in the past. His name was Joey Praed. He was a nice-looking lad and his family were fairly well-off, as I recall.' Mrs Kelland drew a long breath. 'Poor Joey had lost his sight. The flash from a shell had done it, the army doctors said.' The old woman's words became slow and thoughtful. 'Now, Iris Lanyon sneered that Genevra was trying to make a gesture of atonement, doing something to purge her soul, when she took up with a blind man. I didn't believe that and I still don't. It wouldn't be fair to say he was just a sop for her conscience. Genevra became very fond of him, she always enjoyed his company. In fact, I'd say that he did as much for her spirits as she did for his. It was mutual support and comfort. Joey could talk sense into her when no one else could. Perhaps it was because he was a soldier, I don't know. Anyway, he loved Genevra very much and in the autumn they got engaged. Over ten months had passed since David disappeared, nothing more had been heard of him, and she wasn't clinging on to any hope that he might come back. Her own life remained to be lived, so Genevra was going to devote herself to Joey and make him happy. They planned to have children. Everyone at Trenarwyn was so relieved that she had "snapped out of it". If her parents had misgivings about Joey's blindness, they didn't voice them. It was what Genevra wanted and they weren't going to stand in her way. She was like a new person, even had her hair bobbed . . .'

'What?'

'She had her hair bobbed,' repeated Mrs Kelland. 'A lot of girls did around that time.'

The girl in the tide, her hair chopped off short. Another piece of the jigsaw fell into place.

'She let it grow long again afterwards,' continued Mrs Kelland. 'After . . .' Her voice trailed away and she pondered. 'Do you believe in evil destiny, Miss Elford?' she asked me softly. 'Do you believe that some are ill-fated, cursed, or is it all just random, do you think?'

'That's a deep one, Mrs Kelland. All the religious men and philosophers with their creeds and theories – they're only guessing, aren't they?'

'I fear they are,' she sighed. 'So – as I say – Genevra had plans, a future before her. And then, just before the Armistice, a letter arrived via the Red Cross. It was from David. It seems that on the day he went missing, he had been shot through the thigh and so shocked by the shellbursts that he had staggered off in the wrong direction in the dark. He ended up some way away from his own lines and within an area under German control. The next day, a party of Germans found him unconscious in a farm outhouse. He was lucky they didn't simply shoot him on the spot. Instead, they took him back with them for questioning, but no one could get a word out of him, not even his name. He just sat staring at them, too dazed to take in where he was or what they said to him. No doubt they recognised a bad case of shell-shock and before too long they gave it up and packed him off to a prisoner of war camp in Karlsruhe, where he stayed till the end of the war. During the journey, infection set into the leg and nearly made an end of him, but the treatment he received was good enough to save both his life and the limb. In that respect, he was fortunate; his leg healed faster than his mind. The war was nearly over by the time he recovered his wits enough to write home, and he was still subject to melancholy and lapses of reason.'

The old lady cocked an eyebrow and looked at me. 'However, he was alive. So imagine Genevra's predicament. In her position, what would you do?'

'God knows,' I said.

'Hm. On the one side there was Joey and he didn't want to let her go, that's for sure. On the other, her David, soon to come home, for it was certain now that Germany had lost the war. She felt responsible to both of them. Quite a plight, in fact a mess, for a girl of twenty. But there, a choice had to be made, and after a lot of weeping and agonising she made what she thought was the honourable one – to stick with Joey Praed. After all, he was her fiancé. She and David had never actually become engaged. Moreover, since his leg had mended, David wasn't physically handicapped. All in all, he needed her less, that was Genevra's reasoning, I think.

'Well, David came home at the start of December of 1918, came home and found her promised to this other chap. She hadn't written back to him, preferring to tell him her decision face to face.' Moistening her lips, Mrs Kelland went on. 'I remember that evening all too clearly. They were in the sitting room together with the door shut for nearly an hour. I passed in the hallway several times. There wasn't any shouting, just a murmur of voices, but when he came out at last . . . well, I can't tell you how grim and miserable he looked. Wretched, absolutely wretched, took it very badly. He pushed past me, went out of the front door and . . .' Mrs Kelland shook her head. 'That was the last time I saw him alive, my dear. A few days before Christmas, he walked out there on the sands and kept walking far, far out as the tide was on the turn.'

A hush fell in the cool green light of the gazebo. Mrs Kelland blinked to clear her eyes, then shrugged. 'Some people said it was the shell-shock, that he probably had a bout and didn't know what he was doing. By all accounts, there were times when he was seized by panic and confusion. I did hear of an incident one day just before he died. He was in Polvean, walking down the street, when a car backfired. People said he dived to the ground, squirmed on his belly into a shop doorway and crouched there with his arms thrown over his head. They had to send for his father to take him home.'

'If he was prone to attacks like that,' I said, 'it seems a reasonable guess that he had some kind of fit the day he drowned.'

'Perhaps,' conceded Mrs Kelland, 'but I'm not so sure. Genevra was beside herself, convinced he had committed suicide. He didn't leave any note, but I've often wondered if he might have said something to her that evening, made some threat to take his life. She never could bear to talk about that conversation. His family certainly believed that he had drowned himself and, as you might expect, Genevra took the full blast from his mother.

' "This time you truly have killed him," Iris Lanyon told her. "You can't blame the war or anyone else for this. He came home to you and you didn't want him. You killed him. You're evil. Do you hear me? Evil! You don't deserve any life after this. You don't deserve to be happy. Not ever! Never!"

'Oh, she went on and on like that, screaming and sobbing. It was fearful. She cursed the poor girl – literally, I mean. Invoked misfortune, called it down upon her head.' Leaning forward, Mrs Kelland fixed me with a fervid stare. 'And just as if her ill-wish was working, straight away more trouble struck. In the wake of the war came the Spanish flu. It killed Genevra's mother and Joey Praed within a fortnight of each other.'

Sitting back, the old woman wearily lifted then dropped her hands. 'Naturally, being the way she was, Genevra took their deaths as a further judgement on her. She had made the wrong choice in Joey and so he'd been taken away. That put the tin lid on it, Miss Elford, unbalanced her beyond recall. She simply cracked, as I'm sure many people would in similar circumstances. She felt she was wicked and couldn't make anyone happy. She believed she was destined to be alone and she didn't want to live.'

I had a feeling I knew what was coming next.

'That was why, one winter morning, she tried to kill herself,' sighed Mrs Kelland. 'The notion possessed her of following David, I think.'

140

I already knew, but I wanted to hear. 'Tell me, please.'

'She didn't appear for breakfast one morning. Everyone thought she was still in bed – until the parlour maid happened to look from the sitting room window down to the beach. There was Genevra, stark naked, up to her midriff in the tide! Naked! In those days, a lady would faint at the very idea. The maid nearly did. But instead she went scurrying into the dining room to summon Mr Penhale from his breakfast and he rushed outside to fetch Genevra back. He saw her head go under and he plunged in, fully clothed himself, to pull her out. Genevra couldn't swim, you see, not so much as a stroke. She fought him – there was quite a struggle – but finally he dragged her up on to the sand and wrapped his jacket round her. She'd swallowed a lot of water but was otherwise all right. He carried her in and I put her to bed. She had gone out there wearing nothing except the string of pearls which David had given her the night of that awful party.'

Wryly, Mrs Kelland smiled. 'That little incident was firmly hushed up. We were all ordered to keep our mouths shut on pain of dismissal. It was never known in the village what she had done. To be fair to the staff, none of us wanted to gossip about it. All of us were fond of her and everyone was fearful for her, especially Mr Penhale. She was all he had left, and he was afraid she was going mad. For many months afterwards she was given sedatives and kept under close watch all the time.'

Musing, I said, 'Do you think, if Joey Praed had lived, she might have got over David eventually?'

'Yes and no. I believe it would always have tortured her, but a husband and children would at least have kept her sane and given her healthy purpose. When Joey died, the safety net was cut away, the abyss opened up and down she fell. That was what I meant, Miss Elford, when I said that fate was merciless. Human beings, especially sensitive ones, can only take so much.'

'So, from what, twenty or twenty-one, she just withdrew from life?'

Thoughtfully, the old woman tapped a finger against her mouth.

141

'Not exactly. Oddly enough, there was a time when she appeared to rally. They gradually stopped the medication and Genevra began to seem her old self again, every bit as bright and lively as she had been before the war. She declared one day that life must go on and she was putting it all behind her. Everybody was delighted. The twenties were dawning, and Genevra threw herself into a round of parties and car-rides and tennis games with all her old friends, a whirl of silliness which lasted for nearly five years. There were get-togethers at Trenarwyn all the time, people staying at weekends, the gramophone always playing and everyone dancing. Her father didn't mind a bit. He was thankful she was pitching into life once more. She seemed to be having a high old time, but . . .' Mrs Kelland shook her head again.

'It was just a desperate effort to forget?'

'Yes,' said the old lady softly. 'Desperate is the word, a desperate gaiety. And in the end it didn't work. I think it grew harder and harder for her to pretend. The memories wouldn't leave her, but the friends eventually did. They all got married or drifted away. By 1926 she was alone again, save for her father. It's significant, don't you think, that for all her flirting and busy social life she never took up with another man? To me, that spoke volumes.'

Mrs Kelland pursed her mouth, nodding to herself. Beyond the tracery of cane and flowered climbers, there were still far-off voices and birdsong, but within the gazebo she and I were enclosed in a world composed of her memories and the images I fashioned from her words.

'As the years went by she grew strange – more and more so,' continued Mrs Kelland. 'She would stand by the garden gate for hours, looking out to sea. Or sometimes by the bottom wall, just watching the tide come in.'

'As I saw her.'

'Yes. Once, when it was drizzling, cold, I went down and begged her to come in. "What are you waiting for, miss?" I asked her. "What are you looking at?" She didn't answer me, but I guessed. She was watching for him, for David.'

'But she knew he had drowned.'

'Indeed, she never questioned that, even though his body wasn't found.'

'Well then, isn't it much more likely she was just remembering?'

Mrs Kelland eyed me keenly. 'Do you recall what you told me, Miss Elford, that you saw her in a 1930s' frock, but with her hair right down her back and loose?'

I nodded.

'Before she became disordered, Genevra had always kept her appearance up-to-date. But by the thirties when the shorter hairstyles came in, she had ceased to bother with things like that. Now and again she bought a frock, or rather, her father would order one for her, but she wouldn't put on make-up or change her hair.'

'Because there seemed no point in bothering?' I suggested.

'Oh no, my dear.' A faint and rueful smile touched the old lady's lips. 'Oh no. She told me it was because David liked her best that way. He liked her natural. I said to her once, "But, miss, he's gone. He can't know how you look." And she turned to me with a smile so confident, and whispered: "He does, Earnestina, he knows, he approves, and I want to please him. It's all that matters." '

Shifting in her chair, Mrs Kelland helplessly spread her hands, confounded.

'Just as if she were seeing him, talking with him every day! I was appalled, I tell you straight. I went to her father and told him she ought to be seen by a doctor again, but he wouldn't have it. I was ordered to mind my own business and not to talk about it. He was afraid they would lock her up, I suppose. That was around 1932, of course, and mental institutions were still pretty grim places, so I can't say I altogether blame him. Genevra was harmless enough, you understand. She simply had this notion in her head that David was still around.'

For a while the old lady fell silent, allowing me to digest all of this. Distressing though the story was, it certainly chimed with my experiences. Perhaps too well. I didn't like the sound of that last bit at all.

However, pushing that aside, I asked, 'The night I saw her dancing? That must have been . . . ?'

143

'One of her parties. I remember she had such a dress. It was pink silk, sewn all over with silver glass beads. She looked so lovely in it. Dear God, what a waste . . .' As if she had a headache coming, Mrs Kelland stroked her temples. 'The whole thing upset me so much. In the end I couldn't bear it any more – remembering how she used to be before the war and seeing what had since become of her. I couldn't stand it. I left the Penhales' employ in 1936, and I haven't been near Polvean in all these years.'

'I don't know when her father died,' I said, 'but it seems that she lived alone at Trenarwyn for the rest of her life. The place went to rack and ruin, by all accounts.'

'Yes, I was the last of the servants. I know Mr Penhale didn't plan to hire anyone in my place because he feared gossip about Genevra. He knew he could trust me, but someone new might have a busy tongue.' Again, the tears welled up in Mrs Kelland's eyes and this time they spilt freely down the wrinkled cheeks. 'She didn't deserve it, you know,' she said brokenly. 'Genevra was silly and mistaken at the start about the war, and of course it was cruel of her, that business with the white feather, but she was always trying to do the best thing, the right thing – especially when she chose to stay with Joey. Her motives were always good, even when she was misguided. On the other hand, what David did . . .' The old woman clenched a fist. 'If it was deliberate, that was wicked. Wicked! He had a life in front of him, he could have found another girl. Indeed, if he hadn't drowned, he might have married Genevra after all when poor Joey died. I hope I'm wrong, but in all honesty it's my guess that he destroyed himself, and in doing so he meant to hang such a weight of guilt on Genevra that she could never be happy. They were old, old friends and he must have known how she would react. Suicides often do that, don't they? "You'll be sorry when I'm gone", that's the reasoning. If David wanted her to blame herself, if he wanted to blight her life, then he succeeded beyond his wildest dreams. I don't say he wasn't in an anguished state of mind when he did it – he must have been. But it wasn't all despair; I'm very much afraid he was taking revenge as well.'

144

Considering, I murmured, 'Lapses of reason – you used the phrase yourself. Wouldn't you be happier if you gave him the benefit of the doubt?'

'Would I?' pondered Mrs Kelland. 'I don't know. Which would be worse, Miss Elford: to think his death intentional, or else to believe that she wasted her life over what was, in truth, a simple accident? Is either one less cruel?'

I had no answer, and feared I had done Mrs Kelland no kindness in dredging up all those memories. She seemed composed when I finally left her, but as I walked off I turned once and looked back. She was slumped in the wheelchair, her head in her hands, and her shoulders were shaking.

So now I knew, but not everything; and nothing I'd heard had allayed my unease regarding a second presence at Trenarwyn. Quite the reverse. Echoes of Mrs Kelland's words kept returning to worry me.

*'Just as if she were seeing him, talking with him every day . . . She had this notion in her head that David was still around.'*

For which reason, everyone thought Genevra was crazy.

Or was she, too, haunted, I wondered nervously.

# Seventeen

It was twenty past seven when I reached home. Parking the car, I walked down the few yards to the beach. Such a beautiful summer evening, everything bathed in golden light, seabirds cruising across the sky. A peaceful scene, but deeply melancholy too, now that I understood the things I had seen and dreamed, the how and why of a tragedy greater than I had guessed. Strange that I only felt it – really felt it – now. Talking with Mrs Kelland had been an exercise in detective work, just eliciting facts. While driving home I had calmly assessed her tale and found it a good, coherent explanation. But now, standing here, I truly felt the pathos of those doomed and wasted lives.

And still there remained many questions. Coming home in the car I had done a few calculations in my head. Mrs Kelland had left Trenarwyn in 1936. Genevra had died in 1982. What of the forty-six years in between, her life here alone and her death?

Turning, I went up the lane to the house and in through the gate. Pausing a moment, I looked at Trenarwyn. This house, my house. It happened here, behind this same façade, in the rooms I knew so well. But not as well as she who was born here, lived and died here. Eighty-four years beneath this roof. The place was saturated with the memory and knowledge of Genevra.

I walked up the path and let myself in, went to the sitting room and stood for a while in the doorway.

My workroom, and my place of relaxation too. There on the table stood my loom. There, my racks and baskets of coloured yarns. Books, records, tapes, knick-knacks. Brightly patterned cushions and throws. All my cheerful clutter.

My much-loved sitting room. But now I saw it with the

mind's eye, saw, as if through a misty tunnel, a girl in a khaki-coloured dress, face to face with a tall young man, pinning a white feather on his lapel. Figures, blurred, stood all around – other people, watching – but only the central couple were clear to me.

In this very room. She had done it here. Here, too, a few years later, she had told him that after all he'd been through, she couldn't marry him because of Joey Praed.

Overcome by the need for a comforting drink and some food, I turned away and headed for the kitchen.

That was when I noticed the smell.

Stopping halfway down the passage, I sniffed the air, detecting a hot, rich odour. I knew it at once, recalling that night when I had such a fright in the bath. The smell had been in my bedroom then, and among my clothes. Now it was here in the hallway and hanging about the staircase.

I ran to the kitchen to check the stove, but found it burning clean and clear; there were no escaping fumes. Troubled, I put a saucepan of water on to boil, then went upstairs. Sure enough, the scent was there again, and I fancied now that there was something new in it, something extra, a kind of sweetness, warm and spicy. It made me think of sunburnt skin.

A woman's perfume?

No, more like an aftershave, but nothing to which I could put a name.

What else, then? Something to do with tobacco, possibly?

Or something no longer in use today? What did macassar oil smell like, I wondered uneasily. Perhaps I should have asked Earnestina Kelland if David ever wore any sort of cologne . . .

Imagination was running away with me, I told myself firmly. No call for alarm. Perhaps the kitchen chimney needed sweeping, perhaps now and then the soot smouldered. Or there might be a tiny crack in the flue and a few puffs of smoke wafted back into the house when the wind blew from certain directions. It couldn't be a man's cologne. What man would wish to smell like a dying bonfire?

I opened some windows, and after a while the smell had gone. Going downstairs, I dropped some pasta into the boiling water

147

and heated up mushroom sauce to go with it. Waiting for the food to cook, I washed the dishes left from breakfast and lunch. Drying them off, I glanced from the window and . . .

Up on the slope was the marble seat. Mrs Kelland's words came back to me.

*'They used to sit talking for hours . . . their favourite place.'*

With troubled eyes on the little bench, I slowly turned the teacloth round and round inside a cup. Was it a man I had seen sitting there, in . . .

*'. . . their favourite place.'*

A fierce bubbling noise from the stove interrupted and told me to pull the sauce off the heat. Dishing up my makeshift meal, I took it outside on the front terrace, where I'd set up a table and chair. These days I had breakfast al fresco whenever the weather was nice, sometimes lunch and supper too. Washing down my food with a couple of glasses of wine, I sat for a while mulling over again the things Mrs Kelland had told me.

Parties. She said there had been many parties and 'desperate gaiety'.

It precisely described what I'd felt that night when I saw Genevra dancing. A frantic jollity, as if having a good time were a matter of life and death. Certainly, for her, a matter of sanity. An attempt to escape, or hold at bay, the misery poised to engulf her.

But in the end, as the old lady said, the guilt and remorse had closed in. There are some who can shrug things off, forgive themselves their sins and errors and just get on with life. Genevra wasn't one of those. It was her misfortune to have an unappeasable conscience.

I thought again about the pearls. David's gift, all Genevra had worn when she tried to drown herself. Ah yes, presents. How poignant they were and what a power of reproach they had once the giver was gone. Whether the item was cheap or costly wasn't too important. What mattered was that the loving eyes saw it in a shop window, the hands picked it up and gave over money, brought it home and wrapped it up for you. The heart hoped you would like it. Presents. I understood all too well, because of a doll my mother gave me. After she died, I put it away for years, unable to look at it without breaking down.

The sun was setting. I thought about going inside, but delayed moving. It was pleasant out here. Tones of sapphire and cobalt and purple filled my garden – delphiniums, honesty, clematis, veronica. As the light began to fail, they fused into a dusky haze, mysterious as only blues can be. I wished I had some music on – the Moonlight Sonata, say.

Did I feel any better for talking to Mrs Kelland? Yes and no. The story was sad, as I had expected and I had never feared Genevra anyway. But one thing truly did disturb me – the idea that Genevra was not quite as crazy as everyone thought. For if I saw shades of her, why should it not be true that she saw David, as she claimed? If so, what kind of presence was he? Sorrowful, desolate, as a suicide might well be? Or angry, vengeful, menacing?

Looking around the garden in the twilight, I suddenly felt once more a creeping of nerves and a prickling of hair. Had David, or something of David, hung around Genevra while she lived? And now that she was dead and I was the lone woman here, had that something attached itself to me instead? Was that why I sensed on occasion that somebody prowled outside at night?

The notion chilled me, sent me hurriedly indoors.

All those years alone at Trenarwyn. I pondered on that in the days that followed, tried to imagine it. No friends and no relations left, no outings, no contacts made through any sort of work. Ladies of Genevra's background and era never worked. I don't suppose it would even have crossed her mind. Nothing, absolutely nothing, had intervened to save her from her solitude.

What was she like in her middle years, when her looks began to fade and every day that passed was just like the one before? Although she was aging, there must have been a sense of timelessness. After less than a year at Trenarwyn, I already understood that feeling very well. Life had hardly any structure. Friday was my one commitment, my day at Good Harvest. The rest of the week was a free-floating round of pleasing myself. I worked when the spirit moved me, sometimes half the night.

Quite often I slept in the day and lost all track of time. Peacefully separated from human schedules, I no longer troubled even to wind up the clock. The sun rose and set, the shadows changed on the walls and I guessed at the hour. I knew when to eat, because I felt hungry, slept when mind and body told me to. There was something dreamlike in the way day melted into day. For me, it was a novelty and a relief. For Genevra's mental health, it must have been pernicious.

Was she aware of her life slipping by? Were there times of despair and times when her fantasy failed her, if such it was?

The answer to that came one night shortly after. The answer, as well, to the little mystery left from New Year's Eve.

That day, in a fever of enthusiasm for a new design, I had worked from early morning until very late. When at last I slipped the final piece off the loom, I was exhausted.

Pouring myself a nightcap, I sat down on the settee with it, meaning to go up to bed as soon as I had finished my drink. Fatigue and whisky combined to knock me out before I knew it. In a matter of minutes my eyes were closing, and climbing up the stairs began to seem like too much trouble. I remember turning off the lamp, tucking my feet up and easing down into the cushions, then nothing more.

Until . . . it must have been the middle of the night. I woke, I think, because I was cold without a cover over me. I opened my eyes and . . .

The room was not dark, as it should have been. From the corner of my eye, I could see a bright point of light by the window. Beside it stood something shadowy, a female figure.

Very slowly I raised my head, looked, and saw that the light was a taper she held in her hand. Before her, on the windowsill, stood a candle in a plain brass holder, and even as I watched, she touched the fire to the wick and a wavering teardrop of flame sprang up. The taper light vanished at once, as if she had blown it out. The candle now burned steadily and she stood before it, motionless. Again she seemed to me quite solid, a stately figure at the window, illuminated on one side by the candlelight. She stood there staring out over the bay, and seemed to be waiting for something, or someone.

150

Trying to be stealthy, soundless, I laid a hand on the back of the sofa and pulled myself up to a sitting position. The rustle of the cushions seemed not to disturb her. Again, I was convinced that she was not aware of me at all, not aware of the living world or the present time. She existed still in her own familiar surroundings, where I was a thing of the unformed future.

God only knows how long we remained there in our frozen stances, she gazing out of the window and I staring fixedly across the room at her. Five minutes, perhaps, or it could have been ten.

Her clothing, I noticed, was different again. The dress, of a printed crêpe fabric, was early 1940s' style, but her hair was still waist-length, unbound, and therefore out of keeping with the fashion of those days. There were shadows about her feet and I couldn't see what kind of shoes she wore. Indeed, she seemed to emanate from the darkness of the floor like a genie risen from a bottle.

Then, at last, a movement. Her shoulders dropped, her head bowed sadly, she turned away from the window and I had a momentary clear sight of her face.

It had aged. The bloom had gone, and the youthful verve. Instead there was hopelessness and a hint of anguish. The face of a woman in her forties, one for whom life had gone terribly wrong. It was still the dancing flapper's face, but stricken now with grief. It was on the way to becoming the face of the old woman out by the gate.

I knew now what light it was I had seen in the window on New Year's Eve. A guiding light, a kindly light, a beacon for the drowned. How many nights of her life had she carried out this . . . ritual? How many nights had this scene been replayed while I was asleep upstairs?

The candle flame suddenly seemed to grow sickly, turning from yellow to white. The glow became ever more weak and wan, and as it was dying I saw her hands lift. She buried her face in them just as the candle went out.

By all that was natural, I should have been afraid, but I knew instinctively that she had gone. Quite calmly, I reached out and switched on the lamp.

Everything perfectly normal – including the fact that the curtains were drawn.

Not for a second had it crossed my mind while I sat watching her, but now it hit me forcefully. I had pulled the curtains that evening in the usual way, and so they remained. Yet hadn't I seen her, just minutes ago, staring out into the night?

'. . . *something reflected out of time* . . .' the old clergyman had said. Something similar to a mirage. I felt very strongly now that he was right.

Going to the window, I pulled the curtain aside. Beyond the glass, the beach was a great pale scythe in the moonlight and the sea a shield of lustrous gunmetal grey. What had she been hoping to see? A figure coming across the sand? Yes, David coming home. Glancing down at the windowsill, I ran my fingers over the wood. No candle, of course, no drips of wax.

Of all my glimpses into her life, this was the saddest by far. Genevra had known despair, all right, that of keeping vigil and waiting in vain. And yes, there were times when no comfort was found; her lover didn't always deign to appear when she wanted him.

# Eighteen

It can't have been more than a week later that I took it in my head to visit Polvean churchyard. I wanted to see Genevra's grave, and I took along a bunch of flowers from the garden.

Grey granite with a low, square tower, St Martin's church was the stuff of picture postcards, and its graveyard one of the kind which lent a charm even to death. There seemed to be nothing dreadful in the prospect of lying for ever beneath those waving grasses and wild flowers. I had always felt a deep aversion to manicured cemeteries; God, like all artists and crazy inventors, is cheerfully untidy, and I felt more comfortable with burial grounds which testified to that. Polvean churchyard was the sort of place I would wish to be buried. Wild grasses grew high and their feathery seed-heads stroked the ancient tombstones in the breeze. Buttercups, mallow and lady's smock crowded in company with rose-bay willow-herb and yarrow. Nobody ran over this wild garden every week with a noisy mower.

It didn't take me very long to locate the Penhale family. They occupied a sizeable portion of the graveyard in the south-west corner. The earliest of their stones was dated 1630 and almost black with age, its legend nearly worn away by wind and rain. Only the name, more deeply incised, could still be read, and only just: 'John Bosketh Penhale'. Wandering between the slabs, I read all the inscriptions. Husbands, wives, mothers, fathers, together with children and infants who had failed to survive many years or even days. A host of probably unremarkable Penhales who had lived and worked and passed on their genes and died without causing much stir in the world. Whatever their joys and misfortunes and struggles, no echo of those passions now remained. They had quit the world cleanly and gone. None left behind so much as a fading whisper. None but Genevra, the last of them.

Her parents' gravestone still looked fairly fresh, free of lichen and only faintly weathered. Mr Penhale had been buried with his wife and I saw that he had followed her in 1947.

A quick mental sum told me that Genevra had therefore lived alone in that house for thirty-five years. Alone with her great obsession.

Finally, I spotted her memorial, a dark grey polished stone.

GENEVRA PENHALE
Died 1982, Aged 84

There was also, unexpectedly, a verse:

'To-morrow, love, to-morrow,
And that's an age away.'
Blaze upon her window, sun,
And honour all the day.

Tennyson. I recognised it and sensed that it was apt. I was moved, and puzzled too. Since Genevra had no living kin, no friends, who had known her well enough to choose a verse for her? Who else had known her story?

For a long time I stood staring down at the grave, trying to absorb the fact that here in this ground lay the woman I saw about my house, the bent old woman, the black-haired girl in the snow, the laughing, dancing flapper, the sorrowing figure at the window lighting her candle and waiting, waiting. Here she was, at my very feet, her poor remains, her bones.

A sharp wind swiped through the trees and I shivered in my summer frock. A mean gust of wind for the time of year and it seemed to me almost as if I were being shooed off. Laying my posy down, I turned and walked off along the path to the church and went inside.

The bang of the door behind me echoed down the aisles. Again, as in Truro cathedral, a smell of old incense. Sunlight

154

slanted in through the stained glass windows, falling in dusty slices on hard, dark-varnished pews. The roof was quite low and the central pillars massive. Behind the altar, gilded organ-pipes filled the whole wall. To one side the pulpit stood high, its lectern ornamented by a great brass eagle.

Was Genevra baptised here, confirmed here? Almost certainly. She would have been married here too, and had her own babies christened in this church, if life had been kind to her. Did she come here to pray through the years of the war? Most probably. And when her loved ones died, and afterwards . . . ?

No. I suspected not. By then, I would guess she had given up on God, or thought He had turned his back on her. Not until countless years later had she returned here, just the once, laid in a box before the altar with no one but the vicar in attendance.

Wandering round the deserted church, I read all the plaques of brass and marble set into the walls. They commemorated dignitaries, benefactors, heroes. Laid in the floor at intervals along the aisles were slabs which celebrated important local families. I paced along slowly, scanning them as I went. An eighteenth-century farmer by the name of Tallack was represented by a tablet of pink granite and the list of his descendants was three feet long. A family named Nankervis merited a big green square of serpentine. There were also the Trelievers, who had produced two members of parliament in the nineteenth century, the Lanyons, the Praeds, and . . .

Naturally, the Penhales. Again, the original patriarch and a list of descendants. But she who was the last of them, Genevra, had not been added, although there was plenty of room for her name.

No one left to see to such matters. And yet . . .

I thought again about the verse. The vicar, I thought, must surely know who had arranged for it.

The vicarage was right next door. I went round and knocked but received no reply, so I walked down the lane at the side to see if anyone was in the garden.

There, sure enough, I found the Reverend Peplow and his wife. Mr Peplow was wandering round the garden, hands in pockets, inspecting his roses. Over among the soft fruit canes,

155

Mrs Peplow had her back turned. She was wearing old trousers and wellington boots, and snipping at a currant bush. I thought for a moment of going away. They were enjoying their relaxation, of which they probably had little enough, being like doctors, forever on call. However, Mr Peplow saw me at the gate and beckoned me in.

'Miss Elford, isn't it?' he said, coming over the grass.

'That's right.'

'How's the weaving business?'

I looked at him, surprised.

'Oh, I hear everything, you know, all the village gossip.'

'It's going pretty well.'

'Good. Excellent.' He beamed at me and his knobbly face was pleasantly florid under its thatch of grey hair. I imagined him the sort of parson who, in Cornwall's lawless past, would have appreciated a keg of smuggled brandy. 'Well now, just passing, were you, or is there something I can do for you?'

I felt guilty at taking up his time, seeing I never came to church, but he didn't seem the sort of vicar to take umbrage if you didn't join the club. So I said, 'I'd like to ask you a few questions, if you don't mind.'

'Oh?'

'About the Penhales. Well, mostly about Genevra.'

'Ah.' The smile faded a little. 'In that case you really should talk to my wife. She knew the poor lady much better than I did. To be truthful, I didn't know Miss Penhale at all.'

'Was it your wife, by any chance, who chose the verse for her headstone?'

'Indeed it was. May I ask why you are interested? I'm aware that you live in the Penhales' old house, but . . .'

Had I been so inclined, it would have been the perfect time to confide and talk about a blessing, but the thought of 'mumbo-jumbo' rather embarrassed me. Shrugging, I said, 'People have told me all sorts of things about her: that she was eccentric, strange. The whole business strikes me as terribly sad, so I brought some flowers for her grave today. I was intrigued when I saw that someone had put a little poem on her stone.'

'Mm, yes. Well, my wife used to visit her now and then, tried

156

to keep an eye on the poor old thing.' Lifting his head, he called across to the woman in the fruit garden. 'Kate!'

Mrs Peplow looked round and then put down her shears. Threading her way between the gooseberries and raspberries, she came towards us, wiping her hands on the seat of her trousers. She was wearing a battered old canvas sunhat. The face beneath it possessed a crinkled prettiness and was framed by fading blonde hair. I judged her somewhere in her middle fifties.

'This is Miss Elford, Kate,' Mr Peplow said. 'She's living at Trenarwyn, you know.'

'Ah yes! The lady from London. Settled in all right?'

'Thank you, yes.'

'Miss Elford should have a chat with you, Kate. Wants to know a thing or two about old Miss Penhale.'

'Really?' Her face became sober.

'Perhaps I'm morbid and nosy,' I said, 'but she fascinates me – what I've heard of her, that is. I gather you knew her in her final years?'

A gentle sigh escaped the vicar's wife. 'I suppose I did. I made it my business to visit her, help her out in a few small ways. It was little enough, I can tell you. She wouldn't allow very much, wouldn't be . . . taken in hand. But I did what I could. I'm sure she only tolerated me because she needed the odd errand run.'

'Leave you to it, then?' suggested Mr Peplow, plainly keen to make his escape.

'Yes, yes.' She waved him away. 'He wants to spray his roses this morning,' she murmured to me as he hurried off. 'Let's walk, shall we? I'll show you my stream garden. This way.'

We went through an old brick archway in the garden wall and down to a dell where a rivulet pooled in a rocky hollow. It was planted round with astilbes, hydrangeas and water irises, and was lightly shaded by overhanging branches. We sat on flat stones by the water's edge.

I said, 'It must have taken years of work to get your gardens in such good order.'

She laughed. 'It has – and requires endless labour to keep them this way. But it's our pastime; George and I, we love to

157

grub around out here and we never go far from home for long.'

'Peplow doesn't sound like a Cornish name.'

'It's not. We came here . . . let's see . . . in 1978. Yes, sixteen years ago.'

'So you must have known Genevra Penhale the last four years before she died?'

'Yes . . .' The sound was sibilant, regretful. 'I knew her far too late – although, to be realistic, I doubt I could have made much difference to her life, given even twenty years. She was . . . doomed from youth – if that's not too dramatic.' She looked at me. 'Do you know about her, what happened when she was young, I mean?'

To repeat Mrs Kelland's story would have taken an hour or more, and I wanted fresh information now, given without such distractions. Rather guiltily, I muttered, 'Just the gist of it.'

'Mm.' Mrs Peplow gazed at the water rippling over the stones in the pool. 'I'm not too well informed about the exact events myself. Most of what I know, I pieced together from talking to Genevra. I gather she lost a young man, that he drowned out there in the bay and it was believed to have been suicide – for which she blamed herself. Whatever the actual facts and details, it certainly turned her mind and robbed her of her life.' Picking a stem of grass, Mrs Peplow nibbled the end for a moment, then started twirling it round between finger and thumb. 'She became a recluse, as you've probably heard. No marriage, no children, no career. She shut herself up in that house all her days to keep faith with a man long dead.'

'She told you that?'

'Not in so many words, but it soon became clear to me.'

'What was she like as a person?' I asked.

'Very odd, as you might expect, but not incapable or senile. Oh dear, no. You might have gained the impression from local gossip that she was ga-ga. That's not so. She had some peculiar ideas, it's true, delusions about her young man, but she wasn't a babbling idiot. You could have an interesting conversation with her about the old days. Nothing much else, mind you, because she'd withdrawn from the world for so long, but she could talk about the old days very lucidly. She'd been well educated; still read the classics and sometimes played good music on an old 1940s' gramophone.'

I was briefly amazed. It sounded quite normal. Of course, I had never before paused to wonder what Genevra did with all her time. I realised now that she couldn't have spent her whole life staring out at the bay. Because I had seen her that way, those were virtually the only images I had of her, but she must, naturally, have done ordinary things as well. Strange how much it surprised me.

Kate Peplow carried on: 'She was sharp in many respects. Always checked her bills to make sure the addition was right, and she certainly wasn't the sort of old lady who'd let anyone trick their way into her house. No, Genevra wasn't unhinged in any gibbering, helpless way. She just had that one set of notions about her lost lover. Also, of course, she looked dreadful, and so did Trenarwyn, which all conspired to give her a weird reputation hereabouts. You see, she wore her hair long and dressed as she had when she was young. On a woman of eighty – well, you can imagine the sort of figure she presented.'

'The house,' I asked, 'was it really as dilapidated as I've been told?'

'Heavens, yes!' exclaimed Kate Peplow. 'I don't think the place had received a lick of paint or had even the smallest repair carried out since her father died. Not in thirty years or more, my dear. You should have seen it. The paintwork was filthy and flaking, the wood was full of worm and rot.'

'Inside and out?'

'Well, outside certainly, and that was all I knew at the time. She seldom asked me in, and then only into the big sitting room, no farther. The place was a tip, of course, absolute chaos, and the dust was inches thick. But then, some people live like that, especially old widowers or bachelors. I've seen many such homes. That sort of messiness is less common in women but certainly not unheard of.' Mrs Peplow laughed. 'She brought me some tea, I recall, and pretty dreadful it was, completely stewed, but she drank some herself and seemed to enjoy it. Offered me biscuits, too, fresh out of a packet. I felt that she coped in her own muddled way – at least to her own satisfaction.' Unhappily, Mrs Peplow bowed her head. 'Of course, I didn't see the rest of the house, how bad it was, and that was quite some time before the end, when she fell ill.'

There was something different in her face and voice when she said that, a real distress, but I let it pass for the time being, remarking instead: 'I noticed from the gravestone that her father died in 1947. Between then and the time you met her, she must have been left entirely to herself.'

'Very nearly,' sighed Mrs Peplow. 'I think the old villagers avoided her because she was reputed to be "touched", and it has to be admitted that she never welcomed visitors. Anyway, all through the sixties and seventies, Polvean was being taken over by the yachting types, strangers who knew little or nothing about local history, least of all about a peculiar old woman living alone out there by the bay. Wouldn't know she existed, most of them. Of course, people have their own lives, their own concerns. I happen to be a clergyman's wife, so it falls within my province to go around visiting parishioners – to be a bit of a busybody, if you like. I'm sure Miss Penhale considered me just that. She put up with me and sometimes I came in handy, but she didn't want too much to do with me, and nothing at all to do with anyone else. She had cut herself off from the rest of the world, never left Trenarwyn and only used the telephone to order her groceries from Mr Trelease.'

'Yes, I had a chat with him. It sounds as if she wasn't poor.'

'No, not in the least. I think her father left her quite well-off, but to look at the house you would think she was destitute. Didn't care about anything, my dear, except her young man. Always called him "my David", ' added Mrs Peplow softly. 'Poor Genevra, she spoke the name with so much love and a shine would come to her eyes.'

Briefly, the tinkle and splash of the stream replaced her voice as she chewed on the blade of grass, remembering.

After a moment, I asked: 'Did she talk about him much?'

'Not a great deal, no, but what she did say was astonishing. It was when she got on to the subject of David that her dottiness really showed through. Genevra believed that he visited her, she truly did.'

160

'She thought she saw him?'

'Without a doubt. Quite matter-of-fact about it she was, too. "I'm not alone, I have my David," she would say. "He'll never leave me. We've been together since we were children. When it pleases him, he comes to keep me company. That's why I have to be here all the time. I must wait for him, just as I should have done during the war. He mustn't come and find I'm not here, he mustn't find me with anyone else as he did before. Everything is all right now, I'm faithful and so is he, but if ever he came and found me missing, he might go away for ever." '

Mrs Peplow shrugged. 'I didn't understand all of that, but her suggestion clearly was that he haunted her.'

'Always waiting for David,' I murmured. 'That was how she spent her life.'

'Yes, and when I picked out the little verse for her headstone, I felt it expressed that endless patience and fidelity. Today, tomorrow and all the other tomorrows after it. Waiting for David, pledged to be there whenever he might decide to appear. If not today, then perhaps tomorrow. When it pleased him, as she said.'

It wasn't comforting to know that Genevra had to wait on David's whim. If he had been an illusion of her own making, could she not have summoned him at any time? The question troubled me a lot. Mrs Peplow might think him a figment of Genevra's imagination, but I had reason to fear that he had an existence of his own.

Bitterly, Mrs Peplow muttered: 'If only something wonderful could have happened to shatter the spell, some great breaking-in of light to rescue her from her seclusion while she still had a life to live. But of course, nothing ever did.'

'Did you never think of calling the social services in?'

The vicar's wife glanced at me sideways. There was guilt in the look, but defensiveness too.

'I thought about it, certainly. But as I've said, she was hardly the docile sort who'd accept being taken in hand. She was peculiar, no question of that, but I felt it would do more harm than good. What might they have done – committed her? Taken her away from Trenarwyn and put her in some sort of institu-

161

tion? I really believe that it would have killed her; that she would have pined away and died. It was far too late for any cure, her life had all gone by. And if she could have been brought back to reality, what would she have had to face? The waste of sixty years. Her fantasy was all she had, her lover and Trenarwyn. The two went together; you couldn't take her away from that place without severing her from him. As long as she was in reasonable health and could do for herself, I felt it would be kinder to leave her in peace. A bad decision, possibly, but I thought it the best at the time. Later, when the end came, it did give me cause for regret. Those last few months before she died . . .' Rubbing a hand across her forehead, Mrs Peplow emitted a soft, dry chuckle. 'That was when she badly needed my help, and the very time when I wasn't there to give it. I had an accident, you see, in the summer of 1982; I fell off a ladder. George and I were decorating. I was quite high up when I slipped and came off – broke my leg and had to be put in plaster. After I came out of hospital, I was laid up for weeks and weeks. To my shame, I didn't give much thought to Genevra in all that time. I did remember her once and asked a friend of mine, Mrs Blunt, to call and see her. It seems that Genevra was very curt and sent her packing. Mrs Blunt came home in a huff, so I didn't push her to go again.'

Mrs Peplow drew a long breath. 'It was late November before I was able to go myself, and what I found . . .' She broke off, shaking her head in distress. 'I knocked and couldn't get an answer, so I tried the door, found it open and just walked in. The house was terribly cold. It hit me straight away. You know how, sometimes, it can be colder indoors than out?'

I nodded.

'That's how it was. The place was like a fridge. I called out but she didn't answer, and so I started going from room to room. I saw it all, then, the rest of the house. Worse by far than I'd ever imagined. That messy sitting room was the best of it, the cleanest and the driest of it. Everywhere else was wet . . .' Mrs Peplow began to wring her hands '. . . and mouldy and dark. Oh, terrible! Not fit for man or beast. The walls were so damp, the paper was peeling off, hanging in folds. Half the ceiling plaster was down in the dining room. A great chunk of it lay in pieces across what had once been a beautiful walnut table. Trenarwyn was full of antiques, you know, lovely old things, elegant furniture, but all of it was dreadfully damaged by moisture and worm. There was plenty of food in the kitchen cupboards, most of the packets still unopened, but the place was a shambles, alive with mice and cockroaches.

'I thought she must have died,' said Mrs Peplow in a whisper. 'When I started up the stairs, I braced myself to find a corpse. Those stairs, they were full of holes. There was carpet, threadbare in places, and I felt it sink beneath my feet where the wood underneath it had crumbled away. I went up very carefully, and as my head came level with the landing, I saw the photograph.'

She paused for a moment, musing.

'Photograph?'

'It was hanging on the wall which faced the top of the stairs. A head and shoulders portrait in a gilded frame. I knew who it was, I guessed at once. Her David. Really quite handsome, with curly hair. He was wearing the sort of stiff collar and tightly buttoned coat that were stylish before the Great War. Lovely eyes, arresting eyes, gentle and intelligent. A very attractive young man.' With significance, Mrs Peplow glanced at me. 'It was clean and polished, that photograph. No dust round the frame, no smears on the glass. Everything else was neglected, but not his picture. There were other photos on the landing, rows of them, half obscured by dirt. Friends and family, I dare say, and Genevra herself when she was young. But his was the only image she kept clean and fresh.

'Well, I called out again, because it occurred to me that if she had died there would surely be a smell, and there was none except that of dry rot and general mustiness. However, still no reply. I looked in the front bedrooms – nothing there but more decay. Stucco crumbling from the friezes, dead flies on the window ledges, a fluffy grey coating of dust and cobwebs which made the furniture look as if it were draped in gauze. I don't think she ever set foot in those rooms, you know. For some odd reason, she slept in the one at the back above the kitchen.

'That's where I found her, finally, in that back room. Miss

Elford, the walls were running with water. The carpet was so wet it squelched underfoot. There was a lamp on the bedside table and half the insulation had crumbled off the flex, which was lying across that soggy carpet. I'd never thought about it before, but I suddenly realised that all the wiring must surely be in a parlous state. The house was a positive death-trap, and heaven only knows how there had never been a fire.

'Genevra was in the bed in a heavy sleep. She had gone downhill in the most appalling way since I had last seen her. She seemed to me like a doll or a puppet, a thing made of papier mâché and wire. You hear of people described as husks and take it as figurative, but in Genevra's case it was virtually true. I woke her and she looked up at me, so bewildered at first. Then she smiled, and she asked: "Where's David?"

' "You're very ill, I told her. I'm fetching the doctor straight away." Do you know what she said?

' "There isn't any need. David's taking care of me. He'll be here soon, he'll bring my tea."

'I guessed, then, what had happened. She'd stopped eating, simply didn't feed herself. She had finally lost all grip on reality. She was starving to death, tended by a phantom lover who brought her phantom meals.'

Mrs Peplow began to cry. 'I looked around that awful room and it broke my heart. That was the closest I've ever come to losing my faith. It was touch and go, I tell you truly. She kept smiling at me, so confident, content, and it was more than I could bear.'

Wiping her eyes, Mrs Peplow went on. 'Anyway, I decided to bypass the doctor. I went downstairs, dialled 999 and asked for an ambulance. By the time it came, Genevra had drifted back into a stupor and I don't think she knew a thing about it when they carried her downstairs and the front door shut behind her for the last time. She died in the hospital four hours later without coming round. There was nothing more I could do after that, except arrange her funeral and find a fitting epitaph.

'She hadn't made a will and had no kin, so Trenarwyn went to the Crown. It was quite a while before it was put on the market and during that time the decay continued apace. When I heard that someone had bought it to renovate, I thought he must be a very brave and optimistic man. It seemed to me less of a challenge to demolish the place and rebuild. Indeed . . .' Kate Peplow sucked her lip '. . . I would have preferred it at the time. I'd have liked to see Trenarwyn gone. The memories attached to it were painful for me and I also felt – it's hard to explain – but I thought that the site needed cleansing, for want of a better word; that everything should be bulldozed and made all new. While it remained in its original form, the sorrow connected with the house would never be erased, there would always be . . . an atmosphere. You'll think me fanciful, no doubt, even superstitious. Perhaps I am – goes with the job. Can't be a vicar's wife without a sense of the spiritual.'

'You say that,' I pointed out, 'but you don't accept that David haunted her?'

'That's a good point, I suppose,' conceded Mrs Peplow. 'But honestly, no, I just didn't believe it. The poor chap drowned and that was that. I gave the matter a lot of thought and it's still my opinion that Genevra was simply deluded. It was the piteousness of her life and the manner of her death which made me hate Trenarwyn as the scene of it. I really wished the place had been pulled down – until the Deans moved in and started work.'

'Did you know them well?'

'I wouldn't say that. Paid a few calls, certainly, in hopes they'd come to church, but they weren't the type.'

'What sort were they?'

'Noisy,' chuckled Mrs Peplow. 'Young, boisterous and noisy. The parents were in their thirties and they had a couple of teenage sons. I could always hear the Deans as I came down the lane, before the house was even in sight. There was always hammering or sawing or drilling, and pop music pumping out through the windows. The younger son rode a motorbike. He was forever taking it to bits, tinkering round with the engine and revving the thing. They were nice enough people in their way, but you wouldn't want them living beside you, not if you like a quiet life. What's the expression – the neighbours from hell? The Deans were a bit like that.'

I had to grin, remembering how I sometimes played my music loud enough to shake the rafters.

'Not the sensitive sort, then?' I said. 'Not the kind to be troubled by any . . . atmosphere – as you put it?'

'Dear Lord, no! They weren't the kind to notice, much too rowdy. Still, I have to hand it to Mr Dean, he and the eldest boy transformed that house. It took two years, but when they'd finished, well, it was bright and cheerful and sound, really a lovely home. It felt entirely different and I quite changed my mind about it. The Deans were exactly what it needed to expunge the past.'

If only they had, I thought, but refrained from saying so.

Later, I returned to the grave for one more look and Mrs Peplow walked with me.

'How good of you to bring flowers,' she said, as we stood before the stone.

'Someone should. I'll come again. I'll make it regular.'

She smiled, her face pink and kindly beneath her canvas hat. 'Ah well, Genevra's at peace now, thank the Lord. It's a nice little churchyard, this, don't you think? Comforting somehow. Needs a bit of trimming, though. An old chap with a scythe comes up from the village now and then, but only when matters are getting really out of hand. I must give him a ring.' Then, hesitantly, she asked: 'Do you think I did wrong, Miss Elford, to let her be?'

'I suspect that it just had to be that way. You said it yourself, she was doomed from youth. Have you ever read *Moby Dick*, Mrs Peplow? Remember the line: "This whole act's immutably decreed"?'

'She had her role, you mean, and played it to the hilt?'

'Perhaps we all do and we simply don't know it.'

'I think you're just trying to make me feel better,' she said ruefully.

# Nineteen

I had gone to the church on foot, and as I walked home through the summery woods I could picture very clearly now Genevra's long, long years alone. Life at a standstill, while yet growing old. The rest of us measure our lives by events, but for her there were none after David. We add all the time to our store of memories and milestones – new crises, fresh excitements, disappointments, followed by more plans, more people, more places. Not so Genevra; the clock in her mind had stopped with David's death. Only the relentless timer of the body had ticked on as the dawns and sunsets came and went, the seasons and the years. She and the house had decayed together, weeds and brambles covering the garden as lines began to crease the lovely face, slates blowing off the roof in winter gales as grey crept through the long dark hair, worm and rot invading the woodwork as firm flesh melted off her frame, which began itself to bend and shrink.

What had she done when the rain came in? Probably placed a few buckets and pans which filled and overflowed. Had she tried to keep any sort of order? Perhaps at first; less and less so the older she grew, until the only thing she did with regularity, with conscientious care, was light that candle in the window after dark.

Reaching home, I looked at Trenarwyn again and tried to beat down my unease. A poor, pathetic woman had lived and died here, that was all. No violence, no murder had occurred. The only brutality was that of fate, of Iris Lanyon's tongue, of what Genevra had done to herself. Nevertheless, it had been enough to leave echoes and the occasional sense of unwelcome company.

167

Unlocking the door, I pushed it back with rather a bang, announcing my return. The New Owner was home. Going through to the kitchen, I made coffee with much noisy rattling of crockery, a mortal, possessive and heavy-handed, determined to exercise her rights.

But what did spirits care who owned the deeds? I sat in the bay window drinking my coffee and brooded on my talk with Mrs Peplow.

Genevra's belief that David was with her had lasted to the very end. Her lifelong companion, albeit capricious, appearing when it suited him.

How did she perceive him? How did he look to her? Did she see him as I saw her, sometimes almost flesh and blood, sometimes insubstantial? Did she truly see him at all, or merely sense a presence? Was he a shadow she glimpsed in the trees, a dark shape at a window, a male scent in the air . . . ?

That smell of warm skin, scorched linen, that smell which made me think of fire and sunburn.

What did she hear? Was there breathing, were there whispers? Soft, soft footsteps?

What did she feel – his anger, sadness, reproach, forgiveness, love?

Or just a watchfulness? Was there a knowledge that she was observed, her movements followed?

A mind deranged could fashion such things for itself, experience them as real, and certainly everyone dismissed Genevra as disturbed.

But *I* was not, yet I too had that sense of someone there with me. And it wasn't Genevra but someone less forthcoming, far more cautious.

Almost sly. Not nice at all . . .

Yet his appearances had made Genevra happy, especially towards the end.

'David's taking care of me,' she had told the horrified Mrs Peplow.

To her, he must have seemed benign. By contrast, my reaction was one of crawling unease. Could it be that I was resented? Perhaps I wasn't welcome at Trenarwyn.

An unpleasant thought. Anxious to push it away, I tried to share Kate Peplow's scepticism.

I had seen Genevra, yes, poor creature. But David? What was he? A trick of shadows, a thump and a creak on a windy night, a whiff of charred wood from the kitchen stove, a host of explicable, mundane things. The way Mrs Kelland described him, and Mrs Peplow too, as a quiet young man with gentle eyes – how could he ever become a malevolent spirit? It didn't fit. If sometimes I felt edgy . . . well, wasn't it natural for a woman living alone and far from any neighbour? Wasn't it just the chill which creeps around everyone with leisure and solitude enough to ponder on life and death and fate, to think too much? The causes of mood with all its attendant fancies could be very simple. Melancholy came with lowering fog, or cheer with sunshine. A sad adagio could bring depression, or a spritely waltz could make me dance and sing. A shift of hormones was all it took to change the world from grey to golden and back again. We, all of us, constantly sway to these forces like corn in the breeze, half the time not realising why. It might be that even the colours with which I was working on any particular day could affect my temper and render me sombre or merry. No need to postulate unfriendly phantoms, no need at all.

Anyway, I was entitled to be at Trenarwyn. I would not be persecuted, driven out by spooks, genuine or otherwise. Everything else had gone so smoothly, there had to be some sort of challenge to face, I supposed, and this was it. Moreover, moving away was not a simple option. Selling property just then was difficult, a process taking many months, or even years if one held out for a decent price. The only way to get a quick deal would be to take a heavy loss. Needless to say, if I were silly enough to let anyone know why the house was on the market, I might not find a buyer at all. Financially trapped and loath to feel cowardly, I had to stand my ground. To cut and run would cost me both money and self-respect.

As if to test my resolve, shortly afterwards I was offered an avenue of escape. It came in the form of a visit from the last person I expected to see. One morning, just before midday, I answered a knock at the door and there on the step was Neville.

No one could say he had dressed for the country. He was wearing the usual sharply cut suit and tasteful tie. The smell of male cologne was about him, as always, and flashes of gold – his tie-pin, watch and cufflinks – relieved the sombre tone of his clothes. A perfect clean shave, not a hair out of place. Smooth, immaculate Neville, fair-haired and grey-eyed. At forty-five he had the good but faintly worn features of a male model just past his best.

I was speechless with surprise. When he set eyes on me, he burst out laughing.

'Oh my God, it's Gypsy Esmeralda! Where in hell did you get those clothes? Been on a trek to Katmandu?'

I had on a calico blouse and a long skirt of Indian cotton with a flounce around the hem. Hippy stuff, yes, but comfortable. I enjoyed the swish of the skirt as I walked and the billowing looseness of the top, always felt greatly relaxed and at home in such garments. Their very cheapness and scruffiness made them a kind of inverted luxury. I was free now of suits and tights, high heels and make-up. But here was Neville, uninvited, poking fun at me. I glared at him.

'Chris, my dear girl, whatever next? Not thinking of having your nose pierced, I trust?'

'Why are you here?' I demanded.

'To see you, of course.'

'You've made a special trip?'

'Got a few days off, thought I'd spend them on you and see how you were doing.'

'A bit of advance notice would have been nice.'

He gave his nose a little scratch, half-concealing a smile. 'Sorry. Not intruding on anything, am I?'

'I'm rushing to finish an order, that's all.'

'Oh – getting some work, then?'

'All I can handle.'

There was no hiding his surprise. He had never taken my plans seriously. Make a living out of homespun textiles? A thing of the past, a peasant's trade. He couldn't imagine it succeeding. As for the money, it would seem to Neville not worth

170

having. What I made for two days' work, he could charge for one hour of his time.

'Not starving, then?' His eyes ran over me, and once again mirth overcame him. 'No, I see you've put on a few pounds – or is it just that enormous skirt?'

'Off to a great start, aren't we?'

'Sorry,' he said again, straightening his face. 'Well, may I come in?'

I stood back and he stepped past me, looking round him. I gestured towards the sitting room.

'Go on in.'

Following behind, I heard him say: 'Good Lord!' as he went inside and surveyed all my clutter. Turning, he eyed me from under his brows. 'Bit of a tip, isn't it, darling? You used to keep the flat so beautiful for me – for us, I mean.'

He coloured a bit at the slip he had made and I smirked. 'Right the first time. For you.'

'This is the way you prefer to live?'

'It is. Anyway, sit down.'

He chose an armchair and flopped into it, looking first amazed then pained as a haze of dust puffed up around him.

'I never use that one myself,' I said.

'I can tell.' He flicked at his clothes with his neatly trimmed fingernails.

'So . . .' Curling up on the sofa, I grinned at him. 'Who's keeping house for you now?'

'No one. You were irreplaceable. My best friend and lover. I've missed you, Chris.'

'Flannel. Have you, by any chance, come here to try and entice me back?'

'I was hoping you'd had enough of this nonsense, yes.'

This nonsense. This tripe about a life outside the city – to him the only conceivable habitat for a civilised person – a life of my own where his needs didn't figure, where my interests were paramount. And, ultimate insanity, a life without much money.

'These days I enjoy my work. I couldn't say that before.'

'Novelty hasn't worn off yet?'

'It isn't going to.'

171

'Saw one of the partners from your old firm the other day. They'd love to have you back. The new girl just can't fill your shoes, she isn't bringing in the business.'

'Tough, but not my problem. You know, there was an occasion some years ago when they passed me over for promotion to Southern Area Manager – brought in an outsider instead. So much for loyalty. She was no good either, I might add. Still, it all worked out for the best, made it that much easier for me to pack it in.'

Heavily, Neville sighed. Then: 'I take it I can stay?'

'I have spare rooms.'

He gave me a look.

'I'm not going to sleep with you, Neville. It's finished, remember?'

'Amicably. Surely for old times' sake . . . ?'

'I didn't ask you here! My God, what cheek!'

'Oh, now, Chris . . .' He put on his bloodhound face, the nearest he could get to looking hurt.

'No.'

Wryly, he sniffed. 'Found somebody else, I expect?'

Fleetingly, I thought of Jack, and Neville saw it in my face.

'Bit of local rough?'

'There's no one. I can't be bothered with men just now.'

'Living celibate in the wilds. Horrendous fate for a girl like you. I suppose you exist on pilchard pie and saffron buns?'

'Wholefoods, actually. In fact, I have a part-time job in a health-food shop.'

'Bought the complete, hideous package, eh? Be picking up the accent soon, and sounding like Long John Silver.'

'If you're going to do nothing but mock you can leave right now.'

He made a pacifying gesture, holding up both palms. 'Ah well, at least you invested in a good house. Could be very nice, this, if you furnished it properly.'

'I like my old stuff, it has character.'

'Not to mention woodworm.'

I had to admit he was right about that.

172

Pulling his earlobe, he smiled quizzically. 'Is that your old rollerskate out in the lane?'

'My car? It is.'

'I should think you're dicing with death every time you go out on the road. Honestly, Chris, I don't understand. You were used to the best of everything.'

'I was accustomed to paying through the nose for things I didn't really need and thinking it made me someone special.'

Thoughtfully, Neville considered that. I expected him to argue, but he didn't, probably deeming it pointless.

'What an odd girl you are,' was all he said.

'Would you like me to show you around?'

A grunt. 'Yes, I might as well size up my rival.'

'It isn't just Trenarwyn, Neville, it's the whole way of life.'

He shook his head. 'You were never firmly decided, Chris, until you found this place. Without it, you might have abandoned the whole idea.'

Something in that observation struck home, and for a moment I was disconcerted. Was it true that Trenarwyn had tipped the balance? Quite possibly. After all, it had fitted so perfectly into my vision of this new life, almost as if to assure me that I was Doing The Right Thing. Perceptive old Neville perhaps had a point – but I wasn't about to admit it.

'If it hadn't been this house, I would have found another.'

'So you say.'

Refusing to dispute any further, I took him around all the rooms. Although he didn't say much, I could feel his disapproval at the lack of central heating, fitted carpets, double glazing. He looked at my precious wood-burning stove as if it were a museum piece. He didn't actually call it barbarous, but I guessed he wanted to.

Coming in from the back yard, Lucinda seemed to remember him and was plainly annoyed to find him there in the kitchen. Unmistakable pique crossed her face and she stalked straight out again.

'Still got the moggy, I see,' Neville observed with distaste.

'Of course.'

173

'Thought she might have wandered off. They sometimes do when people move.'

'Try not to sound so wishful.'

Neville chuckled despite himself. After a while he went out to fetch his overnight bag from his car. I could see its roof over the hedge, large, dark blue and gleaming. Parked in front of it, dented and mud-spattered, was my vehicle. No wonder he had laughed at it. Just for a moment I lovingly recalled the chic little red car I had sold before leaving London. Then I remembered the first-year depreciation, the hefty insurance premium, and felt reassured of my wisdom.

I gave Neville the spare bedroom above the sitting room.

'Lovely view,' he admitted, standing at the window, hands in pockets. 'Splendid view. But Chris . . .' He swung round, eyebrows cocked. 'This is a bloody lonely place. I'm serious now – do you feel safe?'

Knowing he would ask, I was ready for him. The reply was swift and firm. 'Completely.'

Neville, though, had a nose for lies. 'That sounded just a bit too hearty, sweetie. Over-confident.'

'I'm no less secure than I would be in the city,' I said stoutly. 'Polvean doesn't even have a policeman, you know, because it doesn't need one.'

'Shangri-la,' he murmured, drawling. 'You don't feel nervous, then, at night? Not ever?'

I hadn't the slightest desire to confide in him. To talk to Neville about David and Genevra would be impossible. He would cut the whole business to pieces with mockery. He would say I was already going potty, believing local stories and thinking I saw things which really weren't there. If I owned up to feeling threatened, Neville would seize on that as proof that he was right. Whether there was a genuine hazard or I was merely imagining things, either way he'd triumphantly say that living alone here was bad for me. He would plague me to sell up and go back to London and . . .

Might I weaken? He had come like the Tempter at a time when I was in a vulnerable state, and I hated the thought of retiring in defeat. Fiercely wishing he'd left me alone, I said

174

testily, 'I like having the house to myself. I trust you won't be stopping more than a day or two? I shan't have much time to entertain you and I certainly don't cook regular meals any more. I don't know what you'll find to do with yourself, I'm sure.'

'And you used to be such a good hostess,' he said mournfully.

'Yes, but you know what? I rarely enjoyed it. A professional obligation, that's all it was.'

Subdued, he asked: 'Would you rather I left straight away?'

I couldn't be as hard as that. He must have been driving since dawn.

'Stay and have a few days on the beach,' I said. 'Just don't nag me about going back. Or going to bed. Agreed?'

Pulling a face forlorn, he started to unpack.

# Twenty

I half expected him to come tapping on my door that night and was ready to repulse any such attempt. However, he left me in peace. Next morning at breakfast, though, he was reproachful. Neville was good at silent reproach, he didn't have to say a thing. He'd perfected a hangdog, how-could-you expression. Once upon a time, I used to fall for it.

He looked utterly out of place at my kitchen table in his red silk dressing-gown. Remembering poor Jack sitting there, I realised just how well he had blended in.

Neville's preference was smoked haddock for breakfast, but he had to be content with a poached egg on wholemeal toast. To his anguish, I served up instant coffee with it. Instead of having his normal second cup, he smoked an extra cigarette.

I had been up since six o'clock and had a load of washing ready to go on the line. After breakfast I made him carry the basket out and hand me the pegs as I went along. He stood around looking lost and silly, in the same way that men always do while waiting for their wives in dress shops. At the flat, of course, we had always dried everything in the machine. Hey presto! Clean dry laundry without all this primitive labour. He never wanted to see or hear the processes that went into making life comfortable – the cleaning, vacuuming and so on. Ideally, he would have liked it all done overnight by a squad of magic elves.

Beside the woodshed I had the beginnings of a compost heap, mostly comprised of kitchen waste. Neville eyed it with repugnance.

'That's rotting down for the garden,' I said brightly. 'Lovely

176

stuff. See how much ground I have. Nearly an acre, mine all mine.'

'The forest primeval,' he said gloomily, looking up over the slope to the woods.

'I'm going to grow herbs and dyestuffs,' I told him.

'Of course,' came the leaden reply. 'I suppose in time you'll have chickens too? Perhaps a goat?'

'What a nice idea. If I had all my trees cut down, I could set up a tidy little smallholding here, keep all sorts of stock.'

'Pigshit and gumboots,' he muttered darkly.

'There, there, I was only joking.'

Lucinda had left a dead rat in the yard as a present for me. Neville watched, revolted, while I fetched a shovel, scooped it up and flipped it on to the compost heap.

'I don't know how you can,' he said, following me back inside.

'There are rats and rats,' I sniffed. 'Some of my colleagues and clients were much more offensive than that little thing.'

That made him smile, and he offered no argument. I guessed he was thinking of some of the people he knew.

'Going to spend the day on the beach, then?' I asked.

He looked hopeful. 'If you'll come with me.'

'Sorry, no, I want to weed the front garden. Go for a swim, it'll do you good. The tide will be high very soon.'

'Won't be any fun on my own.'

'You invited yourself, don't forget. I can't help it if you're bored.'

'Oh, all right, all right.'

He went off upstairs to change, while I put on my gardening gloves and sallied forth to tend my flower beds. After a while the front door opened and Neville emerged with a rolled-up towel under his arm. He was wearing shorts, and a loose shirt with his cigarettes and lighter tucked in the pocket. Despite all the years I had lived with him, I'd never noticed when he was naked, but he did have comical legs. It was all I could do to keep a straight face.

'Have a nice time,' I said as he passed me on the path.

He went through the gate and down to the beach. The day

was warm but windy, with quite a strong surf running. By mid-morning the tide was right up and I could see Neville performing an elegant crawl stroke about ten yards out. He was not a bad swimmer at all and I fancied he was enjoying it, now he'd gone in. When I looked again, I saw him standing up, towelling himself. Later, he was lying on his stomach and seemed asleep.

The morning flew by and I worked on, but around one o'clock I began to feel hungry. The tide had started to ebb again and Neville still lay on the sand. He too would be ready for something to eat, I assumed.

Going indoors, I made ham salad for us both. But when I came out with a plate in each hand and opened my mouth to call out to him, Neville had gone.

I squinted across the beach. He was nowhere in sight. The tide had dropped several yards, leaving behind it a strip of wet sand. Neville's towel lay crumpled on the spot where he had been dozing not half an hour before.

Anxiety seized me at once, but I clamped it down. He was a grown man, and hadn't I warned him about the bay? I had.

Nevertheless, I put the plates on the terrace table and went hurrying down to the beach.

Still no sign of Neville anywhere. I couldn't see any footprints leading out to the water's edge, but the sand below the tideline was still soggy and they might have disappeared.

I shouted: 'Neville?'

No reply.

'Where are you?'

Nothing again.

'Neville, I've made lunch.'

More silence.

'Neville, answer me!'

I gazed to the point where the sloe bushes grew and then to the distant headland on the opposite side of the bay. Not a trace of him.

'Neville!'

I scanned the pinewoods behind the beach. Nothing but shadow and stillness, not a sound. Staring round me, this way, that way, I began to panic.

My dear God, I thought, did he go in again when the tide was falling? Did he swim out too far and get caught by an undertow?

'Neville!'

Now it was a shriek, for dreadful fear had taken hold of me. The breakers boomed, the seabirds screamed and I was frantic. Until, from behind me, a testy voice called.

'What's the matter, Christine?'

I spun around and there he was, coming down over the sand from the trees. I must have looked frenzied, for he stopped in his tracks and stared at me.

'Good Lord, what is it? You're distraught.' Coming forward, he grasped me by the shoulders. 'Calm down, do.'

I grew angry instead. 'Where have you been? Why didn't you answer me?'

His hands dropped away. 'I only went in the woods to sit for a while in the shade and have a smoke.'

'You must have heard me calling!'

'Why should I hurry? Nothing urgent, is there?'

'Damn you, I thought . . .' Breathless, I broke off.

He peered at me. 'What? Why are you so worked up, Christine?'

'I thought you'd drowned!'

'Now, would I be as foolish as that?'

'Other people have. It's dangerous, this bay.'

'Yes, so you told me, and I took heed.' Studying me, he began to look smug and a grin appeared on his face. 'You were concerned about me, Chris. You care.'

'Well, naturally I wouldn't want to see you come to harm. I'd feel responsible.'

'You were nearly hysterical. It was the thought of losing me.'

'No, it wasn't! Well, it was, but not the way you mean.'

'You love me.'

'I do not!'

'You realised it when you thought I'd come to grief. Sweetheart . . .'

Cajoling now, he tried to kiss me and I shoved him away.

'This is all an act, isn't it?' wheedled Neville. 'I understand,

179

you don't like to be seen backing down and letting your true feelings show.'

'I'm furious with you, Neville. You gave me an awful scare. You weren't far off, you could have answered me.'

'I hate to shout, as well you know. Chrissie, darling . . .'

'Spare me the soft soap. Just come and eat your damned lunch.'

Stalking away, I could feel his smirk following me.

I took my salad into the kitchen and left him to eat his alone on the terrace. During the afternoon, I settled myself at the loom to do some work. For a brief while he came in and hovered, watching me.

'How can you bear the monotony, darling?' he asked.

I ignored him, wouldn't talk, so he went and rang his office, then flopped down on the sofa with a book. Every time I caught his eye, he gave me a knowing smile.

Next day was Friday. He drove me into Polvean and dropped me at Good Harvest. Jane was outside, setting up boxes of fruit on display, and he favoured her with his most engaging smile before roaring away. He planned on driving to St Ives to see the Tate, and then to Newlyn for a look at the galleries there. It had been my suggestion; I knew he couldn't amuse himself for a whole day alone at Trenarwyn.

'Who was that?' asked Jane, over-awed. 'Smart car – must have cost him forty thousand.'

'My friend from London.'

'The one you were living with?'

'Yes, he came down unexpectedly the day before yesterday. He's trying to coax me into going back.'

'I wouldn't blame you if you did. My, he's attractive – I'll bet he has to fight the women off with a club.'

'That's part of the problem, Jane. He doesn't fight hard enough.'

'Oh, I see. Still, you must be very flattered to think he's so keen on you. I mean to say, coming here after you . . .'

'Be that as it may, I'm going to be cruel and heartless and send him packing in a day or two.'

'Such power,' sighed Jane. Then, becoming prim: 'I do hope you won't be sorry, Chris, discarding every man who comes along.'

'Especially at my age, eh? Don't start that again.'

She gave me another worried look, but nothing more was said. I set to work weighing up bags of brown rice, and pondered again on Jane's concern to pair me off. Nothing had really changed so much, had it? The Relationship was still supposed to be central, indispensable. Without it, all else was deemed hollow, even today. The attitude annoyed me and I couldn't help thinking that romance was squarely to blame for Genevra's disastrous life. Of course, she came from a period when there wasn't much for a well-bred woman to do except get married, and if for some reason The One Great Love was lost, then life was blasted. Never mind the world out there with all its wonders. Never mind knowledge and music and travel, jokes and flowers and good food and drink, all of which could be enjoyed, often more intensely, when alone. None of it counted for much because the Great Love had come to naught. It truly was a madness, I thought. People actually killed themselves because they couldn't have a certain person. They entered convents or at least spent the rest of their days in bitter with-drawal, had breakdowns or made life hell for everyone around them. But what often happened if things went smoothly and marriage took place? What all too frequently followed? The humdrum, that was what, the bogging-down. At best, a fond familiarity – and slight boredom. At worst, increasing irrita-tion, finally even hatred and contempt. Certainly not an end-less, delirious love and excitement. Ecstasy couldn't flourish in the soil of everyday trivia. Drama required adversity, pain. The events of Genevra's youth had plunged her into a lifelong, tragic wallow; she had martyred herself, and all on account of the Great Relationship.

A taste for staying single was a boon, in my opinion, but you couldn't tell that to people like Jane, who tutted and worried about you and nagged you to be just like them. Even now, her silent concern could be felt in the air between us.

There was always pressure, I thought resentfully. Right now

there was pressure from Neville, from Jane and, worst of all, from my own nervousness. By themselves, other people's coaxing and opinions would never sway me, but when their arguments were added to my own misgivings, it wasn't easy to be resolute.

Just before closing time, Neville returned. He had bought a painting. It was all wrapped up, but he assured me it was marvellous, so I knew it would be modern and peculiar. The flat in London was full of such works; they went with the furniture.

'Found a nice riverside pub this morning,' he told me on the way home. 'There's a restaurant attached. Quite a decent menu. I'll take you to dinner, Christine. We can have a few drinks and then eat about half past eight.'

He meant Skelley's Brewhouse, a couple of miles up the creek. Despite its rough-sounding name, Skelley's had lawns and shrubberies running right down to the river and looked more like a country hotel. Needless to say, it was very expensive, with a cordon bleu menu much more to Neville's taste than the humble fare which I served up these days. Undoubtedly, too, he wished to remind me of the joys of eating out when money was no object. I wasn't going to fall for the ploy, but the meal would be a treat. What a good job I had kept a couple of smart outfits.

'Quite like old times,' Neville said, when I came downstairs that evening in a black silk dress. 'I was always so proud to be seen with you, Chris. You still look wonderful in that, even though you have filled out a bit.'

'Thank you,' I said dryly, slipping on gold earrings and a bangle.

'Doesn't it feel good, being done up, looking lovely again?'

I said nothing. In fact, it felt quite uncomfortable. The dress was short and I kept wanting to tug it down behind. I'd already lost the habit of wearing high heels. My centre of balance had changed after nearly a year in trainers and flat sandals. I felt unsafe, tilted forward, and hated the sharp clack I heard as I walked. Hard to believe that for almost all of my adult life I had dressed nearly every evening like this, gone traipsing round shops and run up and down stairs quite happily in shoes like these.

I stood at the mirror to comb my hair and the old Christine gazed back at me, fully made up. There in the mirror too was Neville, wearing precisely the right grey suit, pale green shirt and dark green tie. Had it not been for the room around us, I could have believed we were back in London, making ready for a night out on the town.

As if he divined the thought, he said: 'Don't you miss the night-life, Chris? Surely you must. Dear Lord, there's nothing whatever round here.'

'I miss the theatre, that's all. If I were desperate, I could always make the trip to London to see a show.'

'Buried alive,' he said glumly, shaking his head.

'I wish you would stop making comments like that. Believe me, they don't cut any ice. Come on, I'm ready, let's go.'

Skelley's Brewhouse was busy that evening and the bar crowded, so we had our drinks outside at a table beneath an apple tree. The air was warm and the river placid, reminding me of days I had spent on the boat with Jack. We had passed this place but never stopped. It was hardly his type of watering hole.

A waiter brought menus out and we ordered. The prices were extortionate, but the market around here would bear it. This was where wealthy Polvean came to eat. Skelley's was virtually their club. I recognised many of the patrons there that evening, knew pretty well what their houses and boats were worth. Neville felt at home among such people. I would have, too, not long ago. Less so now. I was already starting to feel like a different species. A drop in income transforms us fast.

We had been there about half an hour and were just about to go inside to eat when an awkward encounter occurred. Around the corner of the restaurant came a man in jersey, boots and jeans, carrying a pair of shears. He stopped in his tracks at the sight of me.

It was Jack Roskear. He was obviously doing some work for Skelley's, probably tidying up the shrubbery. I stared at him, embarrassed, and he returned a hard, cool look which took in my dress and my made-up face and my polished companion. Jack's expression told me very clearly what he thought.

Neville, chatting, suddenly noticed me gazing past him, turned and spotted Jack. He glanced between us once or twice and then said softly, 'Chris? Who's that?'

For a moment I didn't answer. Then, turning his back, Jack walked on down over the lawn and vanished among a clump of rhododendrons. Neville was looking at me, waiting.

I muttered, 'Just a chap I know.'

'Seemed a mite put out, didn't he?'

'I brushed him off a while ago.'

'And now you're here with me. Oh dear.'

I shrugged. 'There was nothing in it.'

'Not on your part, perhaps. I'd say he looked positively wounded.'

'Can't help that,' I said, trying to toss it off lightly.

'Toyed with him, then cast him aside? Shame on you, Christine. Fancied a fling with a poor honest son of the soil? Made him fall for you?'

'Stop it, Neville! And for your information, he runs a boat. The gardening's just a sideline. He's a nice man, very decent, and we were good friends for a while.'

He eyed me soberly. 'Yes, I'm sure. Was it serious, then?'

'Would have been, if I hadn't called a halt.'

'Hm. Well, I fear you've left him with a bad case, sweetie. Naughty of you. See what comes of trying to be something you're not? Come on back with me, Christine, before you break any more country hearts.'

Trying weakly to laugh it off, I said, 'You flatter me far too much.'

'Not at all. Just look what you've done to me – I'm a man bereft. Must have been six times worse for that poor devil.'

'Oh, please don't!'

One thing I will say for Neville, he always knew when to stop joking and change the subject.

We went in to eat at half past eight, but though the dinner was superb I was not the best of company. Being seen by Jack

184

had upset me and Neville knew it. He went rather quiet and looked a bit sad.

Next day he decided that he would go home, but not before making a last-ditch attempt to win me over. To my astonishment, he offered to marry me.

It wasn't the most flowery of proposals. I was boiling up dyestuffs in the kitchen, probably looking like one of Shakespeare's midnight hags, when a voice from behind me suggested: 'What if we made it legal? How about that?'

I turned and stared at him. In my hand was the cricket stump, with a skein of steaming wool hanging over the end. It dribbled a puddle on to the floor as I registered what he had said and assured myself that I'd heard him correctly. Hands in pockets, shuffling a bit, Neville eyed me from under his brows.

'Are you talking matrimony, Neville?' I asked finally.

'Um-mmph,' he confirmed. He sounded like a boxer taking a punch.

'This is so sudden.'

'Oh, now don't make fun.'

'I'm sorry. But, Neville, you don't believe in marriage, not for yourself.'

He let out a sigh, enormous, defeated. 'No, but if it's the only way . . . I can't get on with anyone else, Chris. Other women. Can't live with them. I meant it when I said that you were irreplaceable. We made a good couple, you and I, before you were seized with this fad.'

He would never understand. Still, I thought, this was a huge concession for him to make. Really a tremendous compliment. He must indeed have missed me sorely.

Anyway, here was the moment of truth. If I wished to turn and run, the way was not only open but laid with red carpet. I could go back, live with Neville and wait as long as necessary for a good offer on Trenarwyn. Finance didn't have to be an obstacle.

He went on: 'I was thinking, you could still indulge this whim for textiles. You'd be my wife, I'd support you and you could weave to your heart's content. I'm not suggesting you take up your old line of work again. I know you'd grown to hate it.'

A pretty good offer, and did it really matter where I exercised my craft? Wouldn't I, in fact, be better off in the capital, at the very hub of everything, with countless outlets to exploit and helpful contacts to be made? Might I not open my very own shop in due course, employ other people to do the hard work, while I just produced the designs . . . ?

Back to ambition. Oh, get thee behind me, I thought.

Neville, though, could see that I was weighing my options. Glancing down at the kitchen chair, where Lucinda lay with her paws tucked in, he threw in another sweetener. 'I'll even make the moggy welcome,' he said reluctantly.

All I had to do was say yes, and security would be guaranteed. Was it really preferable to stay here alone in a haunted house, living on a meagre income and sometimes feeling quite afraid? Did I love Trenarwyn that much? Was it so important to be brave?

Yes, I did, and yes, it was. Furthermore, I did not love Neville, I'd just be making use of him – as he would continue, however affectionately, to make use of me.

Dropping the cricket stump and the wool back into the saucepan, I dried my hands on my apron and said, 'Neville, I truly appreciate your offer. I'm touched, seriously I am, because I know how legal commitment goes against the grain for you. But you see, old love, I don't care for the notion either. And what difference would a ring and a certificate make to us?'

'A big financial one,' he muttered.

'You know I'm not mercenary. I've never looked on men as meal tickets or a means of acquiring property. There's no going back, old darling, it simply wouldn't work.'

Poor Neville, his trump card had failed and he looked so dejected. I truly did feel sorry for him. Grossly, if charmingly, selfish, he was not accustomed to making sacrifices. The cup was bitter but he was prepared to swallow it. The trouble was that too much else would remain unchanged. I would still have to keep house immaculately, and give dinner parties to entertain his clients and friends. And there would still be 'girlies'. Oh yes, there would, a lot of them. He wouldn't be able to help himself. Whatever problems I had here, I couldn't go back to that.

'Lucinda's happy here,' I said gently, 'and so am I. You'll find some other lady, Neville. You have to give it time, you know. You have to give people a chance. It's less than a year since I left.'

A pause, and then: 'That's your last word, is it?'

'I'm afraid so.'

He tried one more lingering, waifish stare and then gave up. Taking his car keys out of his pocket, he sniffed. 'Ah well, it was worth a try. I shall never get over you, Chris.'

'Bull,' I said cheerfully, and walked with him arm in arm to the garden gate.

He stowed his bag in the boot of his car, then came to the gate and kissed me goodbye.

'Take care, won't you, sweetie?' he said gravely. 'Look after yourself in this godforsaken place.'

'You'd call Eden desolate,' I said, laughing.

'It always sounded deadly dull to me.' Then, with a last, regretful smile: 'Goodbye, Chris. You know where to find me, if you want.'

'Bye, Neville.'

I waved as the car disappeared up the lane. For good or ill, I had made my choice, and it was final. Genevra had spent her whole life alone at Trenarwyn because of a man. I was going to stay because I was determined that I could do without one.

It was on the very next Tuesday that I ran into Jack in Polvean. Coming out of the post office, I met him on his way in. He was going to go past without speaking.

'Jack . . .' I said, catching him by the arm.

He paused. We stood outside and he scowled at me.

'That chap,' I explained, 'he was just an old friend from London on a flying visit – invited himself.'

'Why tell me?' came the huffy retort. 'Nothing to do with me, is it?'

'I know what you must have thought.'

'Care about that, do you?'

'I just want to set the record straight.'

'No need. You don't have to make excuses to me, I'm nobody.'

'Now, look . . .'

'Didn't want to be bothered with men, you said. Had time enough for him, though. Slumming, were you, knocking about with me? Wanted to know what a bit of common was like in bed?'

'Ye Gods! I never heard such tosh!'

'Thought you'd try one out, then dump him? Why didn't you just accept Jennings? He likes it brief and unemotional.'

'Oh, Jack! Don't accuse me of anything so mean! As for Neville . . .'

'Neville, is it? Plenty of money, by the look of him. Just the sort my wife would have gone for.'

'He's well-off, yes, but that makes no difference to me. He's gone, Jack. I sent him packing. I just wanted you to know.'

'Why? At a loose end again, are you? Well, don't look to me.'

With that, he pushed past me and stalked through the post office door. His whole reaction left me staring after him, open-mouthed. Fiercely jealous, he had obviously been brooding for days and had formed an ugly interpretation of what had happened between us. Evidently, Neville was right. He did have a very bad case.

# Twenty-One

The following Sunday morning, I was woken at dawn by the screaming of gulls, and knew at once that the day was going to be too good for work. I didn't realise at the time that this was to be the start of a heatwave, but the signs were there. Even so early, the air was warm and the sky had the delicate lucidity of thin blue glass, promising temperatures in the high eighties later on. A day to be in and out of the water, a day to laze on a towel and snooze away the hours.

I got up and made breakfast, and then a packet of sandwiches to take out with me. A few little chores about the house and minor pottering round the garden whiled the time away till nine, and that was when I set off.

I went out without shoes, straight from my gate down the few yards of lane to the sand. Fine, soft sand, a sensual treat for naked feet. I remember how it lay that morning in little pits and humps arranged by the wind, and how it flew from my tread in tiny sprays. Hitherto disturbed by no one else – my beach, my sand. That was how I thought of it, anyway. In truth, of course, the beach was not my private property, but since I rarely saw a soul out here it was easy to imagine it my own. One time I had noticed a woman out walking a dog along this shore, and once I had spotted a young couple strolling arm in arm, but that was all.

The tide was coming in, but it was still a very long way to the sparkle of blue and white which marked the water's edge. Between lay the plain of wet sand, pocked here and there with shallow pools. It would be a couple of hours before it was high enough for swimming, so I thought in the meantime I would walk to the opposite end of the beach, to the point where the sloe bushes grew.

Neville's visit already seemed slightly unreal, as if I might have dreamed the whole interlude. An emissary from the world outside and that other life, he had come to lure me back and had failed. In fact he had confirmed in me a dogged intention to stay. I only had to look at Neville and mentally I could hear traffic, and telephones ringing, and voices arguing round the conference table. Whatever its drawbacks, this was my world now, and today it was all sapphire water, cream-puff clouds and emerald pines.

I had my swimsuit on and a tie-dyed skirt which flapped about my legs in the breeze. In one of my own woven bags, I carried a towel, my sandwiches and sunglasses. Happily dawdling, I took half an hour to reach the far end of the beach.

For a while I simply sat there enjoying the scent of brine and seaweed, mingled with that of the pine trees. The distant shimmer of the tide slowly widened into a broader band of blue, appearing at first to be creeping forward, pushing its line of surf before it. Then the darkness of the water was stretching out fast, drawing across the sand like a vast spangled cloak of cobalt hue, its leading edge trimmed with ermine.

The screaming gulls had gone away and a dreamy quiet reigned as the sun climbed higher. Within an hour the water had reached to twenty yards from the tideline, so I started to make my way back. I would go for a swim, I thought, and then eat my sandwiches.

It must have been about halfway along that I found the footprints. Just a few, no more than a dozen, left below the tideline where the sand was damp. They were large and without a doubt made by a man. I was certain the tracks had not been there when I crossed the beach earlier on. While I was sitting out at the point, or on my way to it, someone had come down here from the woods and then gone back again – but not before pausing and looking in the direction I had gone. The footprints led down the beach, turned a few paces towards the point, then went up again and disappeared where the sand was dry. The ones facing the point were deeper, clearer than the rest, as if whoever it was had stood for a spell, quite still.

The notion bothered me. It suggested that he had been

watching me as I sat . . . No, as I walked, with my back turned to him. Had I been sitting at the point, I could have looked across the beach at any time and spotted someone standing here. Indeed, I had several times glanced this way and had not seen a soul. But while walking across to the point I hadn't turned to look behind me. Why would I?

For a chilling moment I had the feeling the footprints had been made here not long after I passed by, as if someone were following me.

Nervously, I glanced around. At the top of the beach loomed the clustering pines. Beneath them were heavy shadows, and briefly I was seized with an urge to run. Run and run, back to Trenarwyn, get inside and lock the door.

But just as quickly the feeling passed. The hiss of water broke through to me and I saw that the incoming waves were already erasing the footprints. After all, it was not my beach, I reminded myself. Anyone could come here. So someone was out for a walk in the woods this Sunday morning. So someone had made a small detour down the beach and back. They had a perfect right and I shouldn't let a thing so trivial trouble me.

Going on, I came to a spot about fifty yards from the house, put my bag down, slipped off my skirt and went in for a swim. Turning on my back for a while, I floated, buoyed with little paddling movements of my hands and feet. Trenarwyn seemed to watch me indulgently, friendly sunlight winking off its windows. Anything less like a haunted house it was hard to imagine just then. Slightly overdue for cutting, the grass lay lushly green, while the rose-bed was a froth of salmon and scarlet. Everything so pretty, so inviting. That was how it must have been before the Great War, when friends called all the time and took tea in the garden on days like this. Women in lace dresses, with parasols. Men in blazers and boater hats. Nearly ninety years ago, when Genevra was very young. I could picture her, aged nine or ten, dressed in a pinafore and button boots, playing bat and ball on that lawn with David, a dark-haired boy in knickerbocker trousers.

After a while I began to grow tired and struck in towards the shore, where my bag and skirt were a little pile of brown and purple on the sand. Drying off, I spread out the towel, then sat down and ate up the sandwiches. Already, I had forgotten about the footprints I had seen.

From the angle of the sun, I'd say it was roughly noon when I put my sunglasses on and lay down on my back. I must have dozed for a while, because I don't remember much until something suddenly touched my face. A flutter, a tickle – it made me start and swipe at whatever it was. An insect, I first thought, perhaps a wasp. But then my fingers caught it and I found it was a feather. A white gull's feather, bowling along the beach in the hot south wind.

Rolling over on to my stomach, I took off my sunglasses, looking at the feather, stroking it. Was Genevra down here on the beach one day when she found that other feather and decided to give it to David? Probably. Afterwards, after he died, what must she have felt whenever she saw one of these?

Along came a gusty breeze. I loosened my fingers and let it carry the feather away, then laid my head down, meaning to snooze a while longer and brown my back.

I'd forgotten to put the glasses on again. The glare of the sun came crimson through my lids and soon I felt my right eye start to water. Groping around me, I reached out for the glasses but couldn't locate them, and so looked up.

That was when I saw the figure in the trees.

A sick sensation shot right through me. I blinked and squinted, caught my breath. Someone was crouching just at the treeline, just within the shadows of the overhanging branches. Looking straight in my direction was a sinewy figure, dark and hunched and very still.

How far away? Perhaps sixty feet. I would have sworn that I could see a head and skinny limbs. It seemed a listening, watching posture and I had the strongest sense of unpleasant attention fixed on me. Immediately, my mind returned to the footprints in the sand.

There *was* somebody about, and he'd been watching me all morning, while I walked and swam and slept . . .

Despite the heat of the afternoon sun, I turned stone cold

with fright. Scrabbling around for the sunglasses, I found them at last and thrust them on.

Shielded from the brilliant light, my eyes focused better – and now I wasn't quite so sure what it was squatting there beneath the trees. What I'd thought was an arm had jagged ends, what had seemed like a head was too shapeless . . .

Hesitantly, I stood up and went towards it. Drawing near, I let out a sound that was both relief and exasperation at my own foolishness. My 'prowling man' was a lump of driftwood, a bleached old piece of tree trunk with a couple of broken branches attached and dried seaweed draped about it. It had probably floated down the creek into the bay and been thrown up to the treeline here by one of those winter storms. At any rate, it was nothing sinister after all and I kicked myself for being frightened a second time this day.

Turning, I headed back towards my towel. Yet, something made me glance around for another look at the stump and . . . I thought this time there was a shadow behind the driftwood, much further back in the trees. Man-shaped again.

I stared and stared, but it didn't move.

'Just a play of light,' I muttered finally.

Spinning around, I walked on and refused to look back any more. I had to beat this kind of thing if I was to live here alone. Had to beat it, defy my nerves, or else they would rule my life.

Somehow, though, I couldn't settle on the beach again. Before very long, I picked up my stuff and went back to the house.

The heat grew more intense as the days went by. Tempered at first by winds from the sea, it had not been unpleasant, but when those breezes ceased and sweltering stillness descended, I was glad to stay indoors. Even there the air felt heavy and little was needed to tire me out. I would work for a couple of hours, then stop and rest, carrying on again late in the day.

Mid-morning one Wednesday, I laid down the shuttle and thought about calling a halt until evening. I felt sticky, my arms were aching, and the most attractive thing I could imagine was lying in a tepid bath and drinking iced lemonade. I was on my

193

way upstairs to run that bath when somebody rapped the front door knocker.

Answering it, I found Kate Peplow, looking remarkably fresh in a blue cotton sundress and a straw hat.

'Hello,' she said brightly. 'Thought I'd include you on my round today. Hope I'm not being a pest?'

She was, but I said, 'Not at all. Please come in.'

She stepped in, glancing round her. There was a basket over her arm, containing what looked like a lot of pincushions, needlecases and lavender sachets.

'To tell the truth, I'm on the cadge,' she said. 'I wondered if you might have any bits and pieces for the handicraft stall at the next church fête. Perhaps the odd scarf or cushion cover? It's all in aid of a new hospice.'

'I expect I can find a thing or two. Would you like a nice cool drink?'

'Wouldn't say no.' She ran a glance over me. 'Are you all right? You look a bit harassed.'

'Sweaty and bedraggled, you mean. I can't abide this heat.'

Mrs Peplow laughed. 'Everyone's saying that. Doesn't bother me a bit. But then, of course, George and I spent many years in India and Malaysia when we were young.'

I left her in the sitting room, where my favourite Vaughan Williams tape was playing, and went to fetch a jug of pineapple juice. When I returned, she was fingering the length of goose-eye patterned fabric stretched upon the loom.

'How lovely,' she said. 'You're very skilled, aren't you?'

'Thank you. I'm learning all the time.'

We sat and I poured out two glasses of juice.

'Actually,' Mrs Peplow said, 'I haven't just come begging. I've brought something for you.' Foraging in the depths of her basket, she drew out a large leather-bound book. 'I thought about this when you called at the vicarage, but couldn't remember where I'd put it. Came across it yesterday while I was rummaging around for jumble.'

Laying it upon her knees, she patted the cover gently. I could see now that it wasn't a printed book but a kind of album.

'I bought this at the auction,' she said, 'soon after Genevra

194

died. It took them ages to sell the house, but the contents were disposed of fairly promptly. I thought it quite wrong that this should go to a stranger. I felt it should be kept by someone who remembered her, and so I purchased it. It's Genevra's photograph album. I'm sure you'll be interested to see what she looked like – in youth, that is.'

I smiled at that. If she only knew. The album would hold few surprises for me as far as Genevra was concerned. However . . .

I asked: 'Are there pictures of David?'

'Several,' nodded Mrs Peplow. 'I know I described his portrait last time we met, but there's nothing like seeing for yourself.' Passing me the book, she said: 'It's for you to keep, if you want it. You know her story and I feel it belongs in this house.'

The padded leather cover creaked as I opened it. There, for the first time, I saw her writing, Genevra's own hand.

*This Book Belongs To* . . . was printed in fancy script. Upon the dotted line in large letters she had filled in: *GENEVRA PENHALE, OF TRENARWYN, POLVEAN IN CORN-WALL*. I could see where the old-fashioned nib had opened under the pressure of her hand, creating a double stroke. I could see the break in the 'R' of Cornwall, where she had paused to recharge the pen with ink. *MY FAMILY AND FRIENDS* was added underneath.

Turning the pages, the first thing I found was a formal portrait of a couple. The man had a waxed moustache and the woman was dressed in turn-of-the-century fashion. Both were pleasant-faced and dark. The woman held a baby in her arms.

'Her parents?' I said, holding up the book.

'Almost certainly,' agreed Kate Peplow. 'The man bears a facial resemblance to Genevra.'

So he did. The eyebrows, the nose, the shape of the chin. Her face was indelibly etched on my mind and I saw it reflected in him.

Moving on, I found group photos of small children and parents. Among them again were Mr and Mrs Penhale, and an infant girl whose beauty was already striking at two years of age, perhaps three. Still further on, a trio: Genevra aged somewhere round ten, another girl, just a toddler, and a boy in his early teens. The lad was curly-haired and laughing.

'The boy, that's David,' I said softly.

'Yes, and he didn't change a lot as he grew older. In the photograph at the top of the stairs, he was much more serious, dignified, but it was obviously the same person five years on.'

'Who's the baby girl?' I asked.

'Not sure,' said Mrs Peplow, 'but I've a feeling it's David's sister, Julia. Genevra mentioned her once or twice – said she was a sulky child and grew up nasty.'

'A sister,' I murmured, greatly interested. 'Is she still living?'

'Couldn't tell you. Genevra once said she had married and left the district. Good riddance, she declared – became quite heated!' chuckled Mrs Peplow. 'She did mention Julia's married name, but it's gone from me, I'm afraid.'

I carried on turning the pages. Mostly adolescents now, and parents thickening in face and body with middle age. Among them undoubtedly Praeds and more Lanyons – though it was anybody's guess just who was who. There was Julia, aged about seven, dressed in a party frock but looking somewhat dour. 'An old head on young shoulders' was the impression she gave.

I skipped a few pages with barely a glance at the nameless people staring out. Towards the end, increasingly, were photographs of David with Genevra, no one else, his face taking on the stamp of adulthood, hers retaining something childlike, even though the bones had attained their final lovely form and her hair was pinned up. In character, she had been slow to mature, and it showed.

The very last picture of all was a large one of David, wearing a motoring cap and sporting a small moustache. I gazed at the smiling mouth and the eyes, the warm, dark, shining eyes. How hard it was to credit the miserable end to which he had come. Harder still, almost impossible, to imagine him a sinister presence lingering about this house.

And yet, the man who came home from the war was dreadfully changed. The man who had expected to marry Genevra had suffered an awful disappointment, which he might well have seen as a betrayal.

Abruptly, a word which meant nothing to me interrupted these thoughts.

'Redding!' exclaimed Mrs Peplow. 'Redding, yes, that's it.'

I stared at her. 'What?'

'Julia's married name.'

'Oh, I see.'

'I hate it when I can't remember things, don't you? Bothers me for hours, even days.'

'Hm,' I said vaguely, closing the album. Then: 'Are you sure I may keep this? You really don't mind?'

'Wouldn't have brought it if I did. Fascinating, isn't it? Wasn't she beautiful? What a good thing we don't know what lies in store for us,' Kate Peplow added sadly. She drained her pineapple juice and declined a refill. 'Anyway, did you say you might find an oddment or two . . . ?'

'Of course.' I went off to search through my samples and dug out a set of linen place mats and a little waistcoat. When I returned, Mrs Peplow was gazing out of the window, a far-away look on her face. The Vaughan Williams tape was still playing and she turned to me, remarking, 'How odd that you should like this music.'

'It's a favourite of mine,' I said.

Curiously, she cocked her head. 'The whole tape, do you mean, or just this particular track?'

I listened to what was playing. It was the *Theme by Thomas Tallis*.

'I'm extremely fond of this piece. I play it a lot. What's strange about that?'

'Why, it was Genevra's favourite, too. We talked about music sometimes and on one occasion she made a point of playing this for me. Of course, it was rather an old recording, not nearly such good quality as yours . . .'

I stared at her, not taking in the rest of what she said – for I had remembered straight away that the first time I ever set eyes on Genevra, the stooped old woman out by the gate, I'd just been listening to the Tallis theme.

197

'Is something the matter, dear?' Mrs Peplow came up to me, frowning. 'You've gone almost white.'

'Touch of migraine coming,' I said quickly.

'Oh, poor you!' The crinkled face creased even more with concern.

I handed her the sample pieces. 'Will these do?'

'My, they're lovely! Are you sure . . . ?'

'Discontinued lines, you're welcome to them.'

'Well, thank you very much!' Delighted, she dropped them in her basket. 'I'll be off, then. Should have a lie down in a shady room, if I were you.'

I fibbed: 'Expect I shall. Thank you for the album.'

When she had gone, I sat down on the sofa, staring at the slot on the cassette deck. The tape had finished and silence pressed thickly around me.

Genevra's favourite, the *Theme by Thomas Tallis*, which I played so very often – not every day, but certainly several times each week. Indeed, when I was in the mood, I would run the tape back, listen to it twice or three times in succession.

It seemed far-fetched, yet had I unwittingly conjured those apparitions by playing the music Genevra most loved? Was it merely coincidence or more a case of rapport? We had something in common, she and I. Could that be why I saw her?

Whatever the truth, I thought dismally, this was going to cost me one of my little pleasures, because I would think twice before playing that tape again.

# Twenty-Two

A day or two passed before I looked at the photograph album again. When I did, I found in it much I had failed to notice before. In one of the photographs, for example, three female servants and an old man, probably a gardener, were shown with the family in an informal group. The Penhale household in its entirety, in the year 1912. At one end stood a young girl in a mob cap, black dress and long apron. Eight decades stood between that child and the old lady in the nursing home, but I clearly recognised the features of Earnestina Toy, later Mrs Kelland. In the centre of the picture, like the jewel in the family crown, sat Genevra. Her smile was wide, ingenuous, and I could well believe that she had been friendly towards the servant girl.

Pondering on the likeness of Julia Redding, née Lanyon, I perceived a strong resemblance to a handsome matron in another photograph. Taking the former out of its corners, I compared them side by side and became convinced that the older woman must be Iris Lanyon. The face and demeanour were proud, unapproachable. She was wearing a large, feathered hat, and her stately figure was rigidly moulded by corsets. David's mother, of whom Earnestina was wary, and who, according to Jack's grandad, became a 'real heller' upon the loss of her son. Studying her features here, I doubted it had been any great transformation, merely an intensifying of an already unkind temperament. Her daughter Julia, I noted, tended to wear the same sort of expression, and I concluded that David's mild nature and gentle looks must have come from his father's side.

Could he have changed, I asked myself, altered fundamentally? Could a person's disposition be turned from good to bad? Possibly it could, if given sufficient ill treatment, more blows than it could take. He had been through the war in the trenches, suffered and seen God knew what. He had been let down, as he probably saw it, by the girl he so adored. On top of all that, how much ugly talk had he heard from his mother when he came home? How much venom concerning Genevra? Enough to poison his mind?

I considered his portrait again. It was taken in 1913. There were no more photos of anyone after that. Such a beautiful, happy young man. I felt great sorrow for him – but a tickle of fear as well. What was the devil, after all, but a fallen angel?

Later that day, an idle impulse made me go to the phone book and look for the name of Redding. I hardly expected to find the woman herself, but thought there just might be a son or in-law who could tell me if she was still alive and, if so, where she was.

To my great surprise, I found her straight away. Well, I guessed it was probably her. In fact, it was almost certain, for the entry read: 'J. Redding, Barn Cottage, Roskenwith Estate'.

Roskenwith Estate, the Lanyons' old home. It surely had to be Julia. However it had come about, it seemed she had returned to the family acres to live out her final years.

I drove out there the following day. At the entrance gate was a small wooden hut, where a young man sold tickets for parking spaces and entrance to the house. Jack had said it was not especially interesting, but I thought I might as well look over the place before seeking out Barn Cottage. I paid five pounds at the kiosk, plus an extra eighty pence for a map and leaflet.

Standing outside, looking up at the house, I decided I didn't like it. Elegant though Roskenwith was, it spoke too loudly of snobbery. Even if maternal jealousy and personal dislike were left aside, Iris Lanyon would surely have felt that Genevra was beneath the social level of her son.

Going inside, I found it sparsely furnished. There was a custodian at the door, but visitors were allowed to wander about unescorted, so nothing easily removable or of any great value was left inside. Everything was large-scale and ornate, especially the fireplaces and doorways. As I went from room to lofty room, I tried to imagine the family living here, but somehow could not. Neither was there any sense of emotion; nothing seemed to have permeated these walls. I had thought I might feel David's presence – but no. The place was devoid of psychic echoes, quite neutral, as if the constant flow of strangers had purged it of passions which might otherwise have lingered. It was, as Jack had said, uninteresting, with an odd lack of character and air of stuffy dignity.

Leaving the house, I consulted my map and located Barn Cottage. It looked to be quite a walk. I set off down a wooded path which seemed to go in the right direction. However, the first thing I came to was a signpost: 'Gift Shop and Tea Room'. These I discovered to be a pair of converted cottages. Cream teas were on sale, with home-made cakes. I thought I would have a quick look at the gift shop while I was there.

It was typical National Trust. The cottage, with its slate floor and low ceiling beams, was crammed with jams and Cornish fudge, fancy soaps and gardening books, herbal pillows and pot-pourri.

Browsing around, I was vaguely aware of a woman sitting behind the counter, reading, though she gave no sign that she had noticed me. Looking at the goods on display, I spotted a packet of scented candles which appealed to me, so I picked them up and went to the counter to pay. The woman at last looked up from her book and wished me good morning.

It took me a moment to answer. She must have thought me idiotic, the way I stared at her.

'Two-fifty, please,' she said. The voice was old, hard and educated. It went with the face, which I already knew. Julia Redding was far gone in years, but tough and well preserved. I would say she was in her late eighties, a wiry woman with straight, well-cut grey hair. Dressed in slacks and a loose shirt, she struck me as one of those fit old ladies who keep dogs and take brisk daily walks.

I shook myself. 'I'm sorry, how much?'

'Two-fifty,' she repeated blandly.

Fishing out the money, I put it on the counter and she dropped the candles into a paper bag.

'Thank you.'

She gave me a slight smile, then made to sit down and pick up her book again. There was nothing for it but to plunge straight in.

'It's Mrs Redding, isn't it?'

She straightened up and looked at me. 'Yes – but I don't know you, do I?'

'No, I heard about you from the local vicar's wife.'

'That's odd. I'm not acquainted with the woman.'

'No . . . well she, in turn, heard about you secondhand.'

'From whom?'

I swallowed and saw her eyes follow the flip of my throat. She made me nervous, standing there so upright and unsmiling.

'One of her parishioners, the lady who used to live in my house.'

She waited.

'Trenarwyn,' I supplied.

'Ah.' The tone was knowing, dry. 'That crackpot, Genevra Penhale.'

'I gather you knew her very well.'

'To my everlasting regret.' Suspiciously, she added: 'How did you recognise me?'

'I have a photograph album which used to belong to Miss Penhale.'

'Oh,' said Julia Redding dismissively.

'To be honest,' I said, 'I looked you up in the telephone book and came here today in hopes of meeting you.'

'Indeed? Why?'

'I've been trying to piece her story together. I thought you might fill a few gaps.'

Mrs Redding pulled a face. 'I don't know about that. What I might give you is a different assessment of Genevra Penhale. I'm aware that she was a figure of pity locally. There was far too much sympathy for her, Miss . . .'

'Elford.'

'People seem to think her a tragic victim of fate, Miss Elford.

202

Well, she wasn't. All that befell her was richly deserved. It was scarcely enough, when you think of the damage she did.'

'You're talking about your brother?'

'Among other things. I see you've investigated quite extensively already. A garrulous woman, I take it, the vicar's wife?'

'Informative.'

'Mm.'

'I've also had a good long talk with Earnestina Toy.'

Mrs Redding's eyebrows lifted. 'Who on earth is she?'

'Used to be a servant at Trenarwyn. She remembers all that happened during and after the war.'

'Oh.' The tone was very offhand. 'Oh yes, well, I wouldn't recall her. A good source of gossip, of course, household staff. They see and hear everything, interpret it in their own way, according to their loyalties.'

Loyalty to an employer or loyalty to a brother. It didn't seem to occur to Mrs Redding that she was every bit as partisan. Presumably she thought a servant's bias less valid than her own. However, it would not be well to goad her by saying so, not if I wanted her to talk to me.

At that point, a couple of people came into the shop. Unexpectedly, Mrs Redding lifted the counter flap and motioned me inside. 'You may as well pull up a stool and be comfortable,' she said.

Going in, I discovered that she did indeed have a dog, a golden labrador who greeted me by trotting up to lay his head and a forepaw on my lap as I sat down.

'He's called Barley,' Mrs Redding said. 'Do push him off if he's a nuisance.'

She waited until the people had gone, then took her own chair, facing me. She had a pile of well-thumbed novels behind the counter to help her while away the time here in the shop. There was also a kettle and coffee and milk, but she didn't offer me a cup.

'Well now, what can I tell you, Miss Elford? I detested Genevra Penhale and I'm not ashamed to admit it. Mother and I, we always knew just what she was – a vain and silly creature, a flirt and a troublemaker. If she hadn't turned queer in the head, she would have grown into the sort of woman who breaks up marriages, and goes about causing scenes just for the excitement and the drama. All impulse and emotion, with precious little thought or self-control.'

Despite an intention to keep a bland face, I already felt myself frowning.

'You know what became of her?'

'Yes.'

'And that doesn't move you?'

'It was justice.'

'Self-inflicted,' I pointed out.

'Remorse was in order after what she did to David. She broke his heart, and when he died it broke all of ours. Can you conceive what it was like for us, to have him back and then lose him again in the space of a month? It was ghastly, indescribable.' Leaning forward in her chair, Mrs Redding skewered me with ice-pick eyes. 'I adored my brother, Miss Elford. I was proud of him, looked up to him. There were twelve years between us, but he never treated me as a nuisance, always had time for me. He used to read me bedtime stories and give me piggy-back rides. Of all my family, he was the one I loved most.' Sitting back, she sniffed. 'I was only nine years old when he went away to war. Even so, I understood how miserable she had made him. She couldn't stand the fact that he didn't want to rush off and be a hero for her, like all those other silly lads. She collected boys, you know, played up to everyone to amuse herself and feed her conceit, and none of them ever saw through her. They were all so eager to please her, keen to indulge her every whim. My, it must have rankled when David wouldn't go. How it must have pricked her vanity.'

'You don't believe she really cared about the war, the cause?'

'Pah! All she cared about was getting her own way and having all the men make dashing gestures for her. Well, in the end poor David went – and how was he rewarded? She took up with somebody else,' said Mrs Redding hotly.

'But she thought he was dead. You and your family thought so too.'

'It didn't take her long to get over him, did it? Believing him dead, she hadn't the patience to wait a decent interval before finding somebody else. Imagine our joy to learn that David was alive. For us it was a miracle, for her an inconvenience. She still had her chance to keep faith with David, but did she take it? No.'

'You're saying she should simply have abandoned the other man, but it must have been a dreadful choice to face.'

'Her first commitment was to David,' said Mrs Redding tartly.

'You'd have liked it, then, if she'd married him?'

'I don't say that. Like it, having her for a sister-in-law? I would not. I doubt she would have made a steadfast wife.'

A breathtaking statement, I thought, in view of Genevra's lifelong vigil. An accusation patently unfair.

'But at the time it would have saved him,' went on Mrs Redding. 'He was still so badly shaken by the war, hadn't had a chance to get over it, and her treachery was the last straw. If she had at least kept her promise, he might have been living today. Oh, he would have found her out eventually, but in later years he would not have killed himself on account of her, especially if there were children for consolation.'

Reluctant though I was to provoke this tigress, I had to venture a risky question.

'You're certain it wasn't a kind of revenge?'

She snorted. 'Don't be preposterous! David? Vengeful? He was a lamb, too mild for his own good. Not an ounce of malice in him. Me . . .' A wry smile twitched her mouth. 'I'm a dragon, yes, I know it. Tough, cantankerous and cynical. Hardly lovable qualities, but people like me survive, while people like David do not. See what happens to the gentle and the trusting of this world. They are betrayed, young woman. They are used and short-changed. What is more, the sweeter the nature, the harsher the treatment.'

She made David sound angelic, and it niggled me.

'You don't think it was wicked, what he did? To kill himself and cause such misery for everyone left behind?'

'He was out of his mind with grief! David wasn't thinking like

205

a sane man. He was distraught when he walked out there and drowned himself – couldn't face the pain of seeing her marry someone else.'

'Did he say so? Did he actually say that he wanted to die?'

'Not in so many words.'

'Then don't you even entertain the possibility that David died by accident, that he had some sort of fit brought on by the shell-shock?'

Her nostrils flared, and savagely she muttered: 'No. We knew whose fault it was. I tell you, Miss Elford, that's the sort of effect she had on men, the baneful creature. They lost their poor, silly wits over her. It's lucky for the world at large that her conscience woke and punished her, shut her up at Trenarwyn where she couldn't do any more harm.'

'*We knew . . .*' she had claimed. But they had no way of knowing, could only guess. It had simply pleased them best to blame Genevra.

Julia Redding was talking on. 'It wasn't just David she cost us, you know. Father went to pieces after my brother died. He wasn't the same man at all, he began to mishandle his finances. It seemed as if all his good judgement had died along with his son. We started losing money. Losing, losing, losing, all the time. Why else do you think we were forced to sell our home?'

'I was going to ask.'

'Well now you know. We couldn't afford to keep the place. Quite soon after I got married, Mother and Father had to sell up. The Lanyons had been at Roskenwith for generations and then, in not much more than fifteen years, the whole lot just slipped from our hands. My parents went to live in Truro. My husband and I moved to Wales and we stayed there for fifty-five years.'

Briefly, she fell silent, musing. Then she gave a sigh. 'Mother and Father both died in the forties and gradually I lost contact with all my acquaintances back here. You know how it is when you move away, especially as half a century goes by. Then, in 1989, I was widowed and decided that I would come home for the rest of my days.'

Wryly, she twisted her mouth. 'Of course, I found Polvean to

206

to relieve the sweltering stillness. A heat haze shimmered over the beach, blurring the outline of the distant point where the sloe bushes grew. The tides came and went with unnatural quiet, stealthily creeping in and sliding away again. Trenarwyn was oppressive, stuffy in every room, and the motionless air began to assume for me a presence of its own. It filled the house, a warm, thick pressure, a constant touch on the skin. I tried to weave, but the rhythm of throwing the shuttle and beating and working the levers soon raised a sweat. For a week I let the orders slide and spent much of my time out swimming. At night I slept naked, without even a sheet, and woke up feeling groggy, poorly rested in the mornings.

In the garden, things were wilting and I busied myself with a watering can each evening, reviving whichever plants looked most sorry for themselves. It must have been about the twentieth day of that awful heat when I saw . . . him. Someone. I wasn't sure who, but I had my fears.

It was dusk and I was later in the garden than usual. So many of my flowers were drooping; I'd had to make several extra trips back and forth to the kitchen for water, and by the time I had drenched them all, the deep grey of imminent night lay over everything. I was turning to go in the house when I chanced to look down to the gate and the beach beyond.

A full moon was rising and the tide was very low. Far out from shore the sea shone black, and so did the myriad pools in the flat sand between. And there he stood on that eerie plain of moonlit sand and glassy water. Unmoving, a dark but unmistakable outline, a man stood looking up at the house. Or at me.

I could think of no good reason at all why anyone should be there at this hour, in the failing light. No reason that didn't make me sick with fright.

Bravado told me to shout out, challenge him. If he were flesh and blood he might answer or simply clear off. If not, perhaps sound would somehow cause him to . . . dispel, just fade

However, spellbound, I stayed silent. It must have been a three minutes I stood rooted, staring at him. He remained

be greatly changed. New houses, new people – new money. I enquired all over the village for friends I used to know, but barely a trace of the old society was left. Even Genevra had been dead for seven years by the time I returned.'

'So who told you about her?'

'That man at the grocer's shop.'

'Mr Trelease?'

'I believe that's his name. I must admit I was surprised to hear how she finished up. I hadn't imagined her carrying on those theatrics the whole of her life and to such an extreme conclusion, but . . .' Fixing me with frosty eyes, she ended: 'That is not to say I'm sorry for her.'

A vast distaste rose up in me for the harshness of this woman. She, who had gone away and lived a normal life, felt no pity for the hapless 'enemy' left behind, forever trapped by a tragic yesterday. For a moment I had to look away, and then I changed the subject.

'How do you come to be back at Roskenwith, seeing it's owned by the Trust?'

'They let me rent one of the old workmen's cottages, and I run this shop three days a week. The truth is, I'm not short of money, but this is the only way I can live at Roskenwith now. It gives me something to do – and I feel there should be a Lanyon here for as long as it's possible. If David had lived, it would all have passed down to him and his children. I have no children, so when I die we'll be gone from this place for ever. That is largely Genevra's fault, and I'll never forgive her for it. I'd like to think she was doing penance, living as she did. It was little enough by way of compensation.'

How neat and convenient, I thought, to lay all the Lanyons' misfortunes squarely at Genevra's door. I had a suspicion that the 1930s' depression probably had much to do with the family's reversals, but of course it was always more satisfying to hate a specific person than rage against blind circumstance.

An hour with Mrs Redding left me thankful to return to the car and quit the Roskenwith estate without further ado. To some extent I could pity Julia, old and alone in the world, and feeling dispossessed. But I guessed her tongue had been just as harsh when she was young and still had life before her. I guessed she was exactly like her mother, and if what I had heard was a sample of what Iris Lanyon had drummed into David during those last few days of his life, it might indeed have been enough to warp his mind.

# Twenty-Three

No malice. There was no malice in David, Julia Reddin had insisted. But then, of course, she would be prejudice If, as Genevra believed, he had haunted Trenarwyn, one mi well ask why. For love, or retribution? After all, his 'preser if such it was, had kept her there, caused her to waste he and expire in appalling conditions. It seemed to me that s ghost could only be called malign. For a day or two aft trip to Roskenwith, I pondered a new possibility: tha evra's social whirl of the early twenties had been a recovery, but that 'he' had pulled her back.

Had he, perhaps, held on to her, as if to say: 'Y forget me or put me behind you, I won't let you go. have you marry, bear children, enjoy life. You will this place, abandon me here where I died because

It was a chilling thought. If such a thing were tru tragedy was all the greater and David Lanyo would acquire a cast more sinister than saintly.

Not the sort of presence I would want aroun bering my chat with the nice old clergyman in T I wondered briefly if the blessing might not b

However, nothing much had happened in cause me alarm and I delayed. It was all sp and I knew how silly I would feel inviting sor prayer for my house. An incantation – onl there had been prayers enough for David's died. If they hadn't been effective then, w

The weather grew hotter as August w thirty-one, thirty-two. Then the therm thirty-three and held steady for day afte so uncannily still that he might have been a life-sized cardboard silhouette, were it not for the sense of avid attention I felt from him. It was very unpleasant and rather as if I were being dared, confronted, as if he were saying: 'Well? Look, here I am, right out in the open, and what do you think you can do about me, eh?'

If I had been unnerved before by the reticence and slyness of this other presence at Trenarwyn, I was even more alarmed to see him growing bolder. It made me wonder just how close he was prepared to come.

A sudden sensation, cool and wet, briefly jerked my attention away. My grip on the watering can must have slipped, for the spout had tipped downwards and the last pint of water was dribbling round my sandalled feet.

I dropped it, my gaze snapping back to the beach. The figure remained, still defiantly facing me.

Panicking now, I ran into the house and went around fastening all the windows, locking all the doors. Lucinda was in the sitting room and I scooped her up, hugging her like a nervous infant with a teddy bear. Padding to the window, I pushed the curtain aside, peeped out.

And recoiled as if I'd been burned. He had come to the gate. Just a shape, a shadow. Oh, but he was there . . .

And then he wasn't. I looked a second time and realised it was merely a trick of the dwindling light, an empty space that looked like head and shoulders, limned by the hanging lower branches of the amelanchier. Beyond, the beach was deserted now and the little pools reflected a sky full of stars.

Lucinda looked up at me, mewed and purred. I backed away, letting the curtain fall, sat down on the sofa and listened, just listened intently for what seemed a very long time.

I listened to the house around me, listened to the night outside, and later, in the heavy silence, I thought I heard footsteps again. Quiet, quiet footsteps . . .

But I wasn't sure. Sound asleep, my cat didn't twitch an ear – even when I fancied I heard those steps a second time, and a third.

I went to bed very late that night. The atmosphere felt wrong and strange, both inside the house and out. The sky was clear but there were flashes of sheet lightning. No thunder, though. Not the faintest growl of thunder. I knew for sure, because all night long I lay awake, still alert for every tiny sound.

All through the following day I was edgy, and then came another broken night when I managed only fitful sleep, so that by the time I went into Good Harvest on Friday I was badly wilted. Floppy-haired, with rumpled clothing, I was turned out below even my modest standards, but had simply felt too exhausted to make a better effort.

'Forgive me for saying so, but you look as if you've been on a binge all week,' Trevor said.

'Spot of insomnia,' I muttered.

'Oh? Nothing worrying you, I hope?'

'Not a thing.'

'If ever Jane and I can help, you know we'll be only too pleased.'

'Good of you, thanks, but everything's fine.'

'Sure you're all right? Thing is, Jane and I want to drive up to Exeter today, but if you're not well enough to cope alone . . .'

It was all I could do not to snap. 'Of course I am, Trevor,' I said wearily. 'Just tell me what needs doing and then go.'

They were in a rush, but he left me a list: cheeses to cut up and meats to carve, honey jars to label, saffron to seal in little bags. Plenty to occupy my hands but nothing for the brain. Listlessly, mechanically, I went about the work. The shop was hot and growing hotter as sun streamed in through the plate-glass windows. Soon it became nigh unbearable, so I went and hooked the front door back, leaving it wide open to the quay. Inevitably, wasps and flies came in, and before too long I was in a little rage, swatting and flicking them away from me and from the food.

Tired and tetchy, I hadn't much patience for anyone awkward that day, and none whatever to spare for the bantering pest who turned up at mid-morning for a bag of fruit and nut mix. Around eleven o'clock, a shadow fell across the wooden floor. I looked up, and there in the doorway, grinning broadly, stood Phil Jennings.

'Looking flustered, dear,' he said. 'All hot and bothered?'

'Well, it is sweltering, in case you hadn't noticed.'

My testiness seemed only to amuse him.

'Never seen you quite so tousled. Mind you, I like that. Very attractive. Let me see, how does the poem go – something about disorder in the dress and wantonness?'

He chortled loudly, pleased with himself because he knew a disconnected phrase or two of Herrick.

'What can I get you?' I asked through gritted teeth.

'Pound of that.' He jerked a thumb towards the tub of fruit and nut. 'Serve myself, shall I? Save you the trouble?' He reached for the scoop.

'No,' I said curtly, seizing it from him and flapping open a paper bag.

'Oh well, mind you pick out a few good walnuts for me, and plenty of pineapple pieces.'

I ignored that. If left to serve himself, he would have taken all the walnuts and brazils, not to mention the best of the fruit. Plunging the scoop in, I shovelled up whatever came and dropped it into the pan on the scales. Jennings watched my every move, still grinning.

'Bad tempered today, and a bit bleary-eyed,' he said, teasing. 'Who's been keeping you awake, then, eh?'

'Don't be personal,' I said tartly. 'And mind your own business.'

'Can't be Jack,' continued Jennings, undeterred. 'Heard you finished with poor old Jack. Someone else keeping you company now?'

I looked at him. His eyes were dancing, his whole demeanour suggestive, full of bawdy merriment.

'Got a secret boyfriend out there? I believe you have. Wouldn't be natural if you didn't, nice-looking woman like you. Wonder who it is. Some local chap?'

His voice had dropped low, almost to a whisper. He was leaning slightly across the counter, as if he expected me to confide the answer in the same undertone. His eyes were locked

213

with mine, intent and sparkling. Offended, I drew sharply back and in so doing knocked a pile of sesame crackers to the floor.

Jennings straightened up, tut-tutting. 'You're some nervous, maid.'

Angrily, I grabbed the crackers and slapped them back down in their place. Smirking, Jennings waited while I tipped the fruit and nut mix into a paper bag.

'You're shaking,' he observed – and so I was.

'One pound thirty, please,' I muttered.

He handed the coins across. I had thought he would go now, but still he loitered.

'Heard about old man Roskear?' he asked lightly.

'Who – Jack's grandad?'

'Yes. Died last weekend.' The tone was so breezy, one might almost think it was good news.

I stared at him. 'Oh no! Oh Lord . . .'

'Funeral was yesterday.'

Shaken, I breathed: 'I had no idea.'

'Mm, popped off sudden, he did. Another old Polvean character gone.' Dipping into the paper bag, he tossed a few nuts into his mouth and crunched them cheerfully. 'Expect old Jack will miss him. Always losing people, poor old Jack.'

I wondered how he could be so callous, even if Jack had given him a well-deserved pasting for carrying on with his wife. My fingers twitched. I would have loved to slap him. Jennings seemed to know it, too, and beamed at me again.

'Born unlucky, Jack Roskear. Now me, I'm just the other way. Everything seems to go right for me.'

'Oh come,' I said dryly, 'I'm sure even you must suffer the odd defeat.'

He glanced at me sideways. 'Setbacks, yes, but I never let anything beat me. You, for instance.'

'Is that so?'

Winking, he wagged a finger at me. 'I haven't given up on you. Told you before, didn't I? You're still near the top of my list.'

The cheek was simply astonishing. What was more, he made it sound as if it were some kind of honour.

'One of these days we'll get together. That's a promise, maid.'

Yes, I thought, you gloat because I finished with Jack and you'd love to rub salt in his wounds by stepping in with me yourself.

'I'd rather have a duodenal ulcer,' I said sweetly. 'Now, if you've bought all you came for, you'd better excuse me. I'm busy.'

He swaggered out, still chortling, and coldly I watched him saunter across to the pub. An encounter with him was the last thing I needed today. Bad enough to be persecuted by shadowy figures at home, without being further tormented here by that conceited fool.

I was saddened, as well, to hear about Mr Roskear. Death at such a ripe old age was hardly a tragedy, but it left Jack all on his own again and, as Jennings had said, he was always losing people. What depressed me even more was what the old man must have thought of me. I had sorely disappointed him, no doubt. Just another no-good woman who treated his grandson shabbily. Strange how upsetting it was to think he had died thinking me no better than Jack's wife.

Trevor and Jane were still not back by the time I left the shop at half past five. Locking up, I started across the quay towards the car. Before I had gone very far, however, the sight of a boat coming up the river caused me to pause and wait.

It was *Thomasina*. I could see three men on board: Jack and a couple of brawny types in gaudy Bermuda shorts. The sound of laughter and excited talk came faintly across the water. Drawing near, the boat disappeared beneath the harbour wall and a couple of minutes later the two anglers were coming up the steps. They had a five-foot blue shark, and each took turns to pose with it while the other snapped a photograph. I waited until they trooped off with their trophy, then I drifted over to the railing and looked down.

*Thomasina* was tied up below and Jack was stowing the fishing tackle away. For a moment I stood watching him, wondering what sort of reception I would get if I went down there. After that encounter at the post office, I was very wary.

Nevertheless, his grandad had died and I had to offer my sympathy.

'Jack?'

He looked up and, to my surprise, appeared more embarrassed than hostile. He was coiling up a length of rope and the rhythm of his hands became slow, uncertain, when he saw me.

'Oh,' he muttered awkwardly. 'Hello.'

'I heard this morning about your grandad. I wanted to tell you how sorry I am.'

He half smiled, shrugged. 'No need. Went in his sleep. Best way there is.'

I leaned my forearms on the railing. 'You must miss him, though.'

'House feels funny,' he admitted. 'Still, I'll get used to it.'

'I wish I had known. I would have come to the service.'

He looked a bit sheepish at that. Then, tossing the rope aside, he came up the steps to me. Clearing his throat, he said, 'Look, I think I should apologise, Christine.'

'It's all right, I don't suppose he'd have wanted me there.'

'I don't mean that.'

'What, then?'

'Those things I said to you a few weeks back – there was no call for them.'

'Doesn't matter, Jack.'

'It does. I was insulting and I'm sorry.'

'I don't mind, as long as you understand now – especially my reasons for ending it with you.'

'Yes, well . . .' He scratched his ear. 'To tell the truth, I believe I did all along. Didn't want to accept the situation, that was all. Must confess, it peeved me, though, to see you with what's-his-name.'

'Neville. Yes, he came to try and get me back. I'm sure he expected to find me chastened and ready to throw in the towel.'

Faintly, Jack smiled. 'You gave him his marching orders, then?'

'I did – and I'll have you know he had offered to marry me.'

'Had he, indeed? And you refused. Did he take it graciously?'

'Fairly. That's his way.'

'Behoves me, then, to do no less. Anyway, if you won't have him, you won't have anyone, I suppose.'

'Perhaps I was always meant to be a spinster.'

The grey eyes surveyed me thoughtfully. 'One who spins – or weaves. Well, that's exactly what you are.'

'Yes,' I said slowly, 'literally true, isn't it? How funny. It hadn't occurred to me before.' For a moment I pondered on that. Then: 'Ah well . . .'

I turned to go, but he suddenly caught me by the hand.

'I wonder if you'll always find it so amusing, Chris? The time may come when you won't feel so tough and independent. Certain happenings and milestones have a way of making a person think twice. One day you fall ill and no one's there. One day you hit fifty. One Christmas there doesn't seem much point in cooking. You start to feel a sense of lack . . .'

He was smiling, half joking. But only half. Glad though I was to have made my peace with him, this kind of talk was the last thing I wanted, especially at a time when I was jumpy once again. I tried to sound airy, laughing it off.

'Not in the foreseeable future, as they say.'

'All right,' he said mildly, as I took my leave. But softly, a few more words followed me. 'We shall see.'

# Twenty-Four

August reached its end, September began, and still the scorching weather held. The countryside was looking parched, grasses turning brown or yellow, flowers withering before their time. Despite the man I had seen on the beach, I still went out each evening to water my plants, determined, no matter what, to see them through this dry spell. But I didn't enjoy the job, not any more. What had been a leisurely, pleasant task now became a nervous, hurried exercise. I was always glancing around me, over my shoulder or down to the beach or across to the gate, always pausing, listening, fancying I heard something.

The crunch of a stealthy tread on a bit of loose gravel? Was it?

No.

The swish of feet through the grass behind me?

No again, nothing there.

When I looked, never anything there. Nevertheless, I was always starting, turning sharply round and thinking this time I'd come face to face with who or what was causing the horrible feeling that I was watched. It's a feeling everyone knows; it touches the back of the neck and the shoulderblades, makes the muscles tense and cringe. And sometimes it builds to a jumpy sense that someone is just about to lay hands on you. I felt it every single night when I went out to water my garden, and quite amazed myself with my own willpower, for I never shirked the chore, no matter how sorely tempted, even if I did make a hasty, slopping business of it.

Next day, in the full glare of sunshine, I would often tell myself it was all about nothing. The shivers were all of my own creation, just imagination's teasing. But when evening fell again, such comforting thoughts fled away with the fading light.

Still, I always felt all right as soon as the watering was done and I was back indoors, always felt much better inside the house. As a belt-and-braces gesture, I locked my bedroom door when I went to bed, but on the whole I felt secure within Trenarwyn.

And then one night . . .

It was particularly hot, even through the small hours, and I lay on my bed with the covers stripped back. I felt sticky all over, tossing from side to side and dozing fitfully. The top sash of the window was down a few inches to admit some air, but no breeze wafted in. The curtains hung straight and still and pale, as if their folds were of sculpted stone instead of cotton.

Beside my bed, the luminous digits of the clock showed ten to two when I reached out for my drinking glass and water jug. The moonlight revealed a faint gleam and sparkle of bubbles as I poured. For a while I sat up, sipping it, and pulling the hair away from the back of my neck where it was clinging, thick and clammy. Beyond the window, the sky was marbled black and grey, with a thin cloud cover lit from behind by the moon. The cloud was delicate, like gauze, but still enough to hold in the heat of the day gone by and make this night into a sweat-bath. Down the beach, the tide was sighing, and the whisper seemed to carry a note of lament. The sea at night, with its blackness and vastness, always made me think of death.

After a while I tried again to sleep and managed another short snooze. What woke me . . . well, I just can't say. Even to this day, I don't know. My ears, perhaps, picked up a sound, and the part of the brain which never sleeps knew that something was afoot. At any rate, I suddenly woke with a sense of alarm, darting glances all around the room.

There was nothing to see, but I lay unmoving, listening keenly now.

Nothing, either, to hear, except faintly the tide.

And yet, I had a conviction that all was not as it should be. It must have been fifteen minutes before I found the nerve to stir, to look outside, for it seemed to me that yet again the source of unease was not in the house, but around it. The clock told me it was now twenty to three. Rising, I slipped on a nightdress and padded to the window.

The tide was going out; the shining rim of it had receded a good way from shore. I scanned the beach, but no dark figure stood there on the sand, nor did any troubling shadow linger at the gate. Panning slowly round the moonlit garden, my gaze identified shrubs and trees, the daylight friends I tended, knew intimately. That crouching shape? The weigela, with its pale pink bells. That rounded blob at the edge of the lawn, a choisya. That spidery form, an azalea. That spindly figure, a young rowan tree. All harmless, lovely things, as normal as could be.

But then, what of the sides of the house, the places I couldn't see? What of the back where the woods came down, and the blind spots under my window, beneath the balcony?

Pressing closer to the glass, I misted it with a pent-up breath I could hold no longer, and briefly everything became a blur. With shaky fingers, I wiped the glass, craning my neck and straining to see. I could hear my heart and it sounded like loping footsteps.

For minutes on end I watched and waited, but outside all was still. Finally, deciding it was just my nerves again, I returned to bed, peeled off the nightdress, lay down and closed my eyes . . .

Closed my eyes, but even so, I felt the sudden change in the room's feeble light. Call me fanciful, if you like, but I swear I felt that shadow fall across my bed and over me.

My eyes flew wide and saw . . . the looming shape of some-one at the window. Right outside, right up against the glass and staring squarely in at me. He was only an outline against the night sky, but all in an instant I saw that he was tall, quite muscular. And young. Youth has something in its stance, and a tightness of body tone, recognisable even in silhouette.

The shock of it chills me even now and turns my stomach sick. The memory still has power to make my limbs feel weak. There, that night, I simply froze, as if turned to stone. Throttled off by fear, my voice deserted me.

I may have been physically petrified, but in my head was

tumult. There was I, without a stitch of clothing over me, and he was standing . . . oh, at most, ten feet away. Could he see me back here in the dimness of the room, a pale body upon a white bedsheet? What was he going to do? Did he mean to come in?

I'd have given anything right then to be back with Neville, back in the flat with unflappable Neville. Instead I was here, a lone woman, stark naked, at night, in an isolated house with – what?

'There are burglars, there are rapists, there are headcases everywhere you go,' good old Neville had warned. 'You're begging for trouble, Chris, you really are. A woman like you in a house like this – it's an invitation to creepy characters.'

Creepy characters – or phantoms? How could any mortal man be out on that balcony?

Genevra would welcome that dark figure at the window, open her arms and cry out for a lover come back from the sea. But I was not Genevra, and what could he want with me?

He stood and stood, and stared and stared, till such a charge of terror built up in me that I started to feel light-headed, literally sick with fright. My insides heaved and suddenly I was hanging, head-down and retching, over the side of the bed.

When at last it stopped, I looked up, slowly, apprehensively. The figure at the window had vanished as quietly as it had come. Beyond the glass, there was only the moon to be seen and the dim night sky.

Dragging the sheet with me, wrapping it round me, I dived for the window and shoved the sash up, fastened it tightly and then ripped the curtains across. Scrambling for the light switch, I swiped it down and a comforting blaze of electricity flared about me.

Everything looked so ordinary, so unthreatening now. For a moment I could almost imagine that the whole episode had been a lucid dream.

But the mess on the floor was real enough, and so was the bad taste in my mouth. No mere nightmare could have frightened me to that extent. Only once in my life before had I actually vomited from sheer terror, and that was after narrowly missing a head-on crash with a truck. I threw up then, all right, and the scare tonight had been just as real.

I drank some more water and, just for company, turned my clock radio on. What remained of the night, I spent fully dressed and wide awake in my bedside chair.

It was seven o'clock before I cautiously pulled the curtains back. In came the brilliance and warmth of another fine day. In the garden, the birds were singing, and Lucy was slinking across the grass, trying to sneak up on a butterfly. Normality. Once again that contrast which made the events of the dark hours seem incredible.

From the bathroom, I fetched some hot water and tissues to clean off the carpet. Then at last I went downstairs, forced myself to venture outside and look around the house.

There was no sign of anyone anywhere. No footprints either, nothing disturbed, as far as I could see. Like Genevra, the man seemed to have appeared and disappeared at will. Gazing up at the balcony, I shook my head, baffled. A living person would have to be uncommonly agile to climb up there at all, let alone so silently. Indeed, it seemed impossible to me.

One thing, though, was very clear. I could not go on this way. Last night had been the final straw. Something would have to be done, and without delay.

Late morning found me at the Peplows' house. I remember how Kate stared at me, appalled and fascinated, as I talked. Fresh from conducting a christening, George Peplow was still in his robes, all starched white linen and puffed sleeves which made him look twice his actual size. He was frowning slightly at my story, kept sucking his lip and scratching his chin.

'You don't think it might be simply some effect of stress?' he asked dubiously. 'You've been through a lot of upheaval, and living alone is something new for you.'

'Oh, not you as well! Please don't tell me I'm imagining things.'

'Of course she isn't, George,' his wife said sharply.

'All right, all right. I merely want to get any other possible explanations out of the way. You don't believe that it could be an ordinary prowler?'

'I've thought about it, truly I have, but no one could have got on that balcony unless he brought a ladder with him, and that doesn't seem very likely to me. Nobody would carry a ladder out to Trenarwyn on foot, and I certainly didn't hear a car. Anyway, there's too much else which points to something unnatural. I *have* seen Genevra, just as I've told you. There isn't the slightest doubt about that. I know all about her and everything fits into place. What I've seen makes perfect sense, it chimes with all I've learned about her life.'

'And *she* believed David haunted her,' Mrs Peplow said uncomfortably. 'I never entertained the thought that it might be true. But now . . .'

'Wait a minute, wait a minute.' The vicar became slightly testy. 'I hope it wasn't your prattle, Kate, which put these ideas in Miss Elford's head. It's far too easy to create unfounded—'

'No.' I stopped him short. 'She only helped confirm what I'd already grown to suspect.' Spreading my hands, I conceded: 'Agreed, it's difficult sometimes to sort what's normal from what is not, what's harmful from what is perfectly innocent. Some of the things which have worried me are probably quite innocuous. A few weeks ago, for instance, I felt uneasy because I saw some footprints in the sand. Well, of course, it's a public beach and no doubt I was silly. I fully understand that it's all too easy for fancy to run riot, to build on certain incidents or tales, to start interpreting every little thing in a sinister way. But I knew for sure by last winter that Trenarwyn had a ghost. I had guessed by the spring that there might be two. I had glimpsed the man sitting on that seat. I had sensed something hanging about the house and knew that it wasn't Genevra, but something which gave me an altogether different feeling, a creepy feeling. Now, look, I'm a down-to-earth woman. I am not a mystical Celt, nor have I been influenced by this county's reputation for weird goings-on. I'm not even religious, as you are aware. But I definitely saw Genevra Penhale on five occasions, the same person at five different stages of her life. I saw, if you like, the replays of scenes from her story – most of which I didn't learn until afterwards. I certainly did not imagine her, and I don't believe she imagined David. It's my opinion that he is far more of an actual "presence" than she is. Genevra's just a sort of . . . recording, but he is actually *there*.'

Mr Peplow gave me a long, thoughtful look and then gazed out of the window, considering.

'I wonder . . .' he murmured. 'Supposed to have been a suicide, wasn't he?'

'No one knows for sure.'

'But he could have been. Folklore has it they don't rest easy. Of course, they were always denied consecrated ground, but David Lanyon wasn't even recovered from the sea . . .'

'The thought of it,' muttered Mrs Peplow in distress. 'Poor Genevra, all those years alone in the house with . . . that.' A shudder went through her, she looked at her husband. 'You must do something, George.'

He shrugged. 'By all means, I'll come round, say some prayers and bless the house. Have to warn you, though, if there really is a being there, particularly an unpleasant one, it may not be enough. I'd have to consult and get special permission for anything more.'

I seized the offer. 'That's all right. Let's try the gentle remedy first and see where we go from there.'

The vicar went off to change. Mrs Peplow laid a hand on mine. 'How dreadful, you poor thing,' she said. 'Why have you hugged it to yourself so long? You could have come to us at any time.'

'Genevra didn't frighten me,' I said. 'To see her was intriguing and the story was very sad, but she never truly frightened me. It's only in the last three or four months that I've been growing really nervous, only since I became aware of "him". And at first, for a while, I was far from sure that he existed – thought I might just be mistaken. Lately, though, he seems to be, well, closing in on me, if that's not too dramatic.'

'It's very odd,' said Mrs Peplow, pondering. 'When I recall his portrait, how handsome and agreeable he looked . . .'

'But that was before the war, before everything went so dreadfully wrong. People can become embittered.'

224

'Even vindictive?'

'That's my fear.'

She was silent a moment, and then shook her head. 'I should have called the authorities in,' she said miserably. 'God forgive me, I should have seen to it that Genevra was taken away from that place. I was terribly wrong.'

'You said yourself that it might have killed her. That still holds true.'

'Oh, perhaps,' she said helplessly. 'I don't know.' Then, with a tiny snort, she added: 'On one thing, though, my first instincts were right. Trenarwyn should have been pulled down. Takes more than renovation to restore a house to spiritual health when it's seen so much tragedy.'

As she was speaking, her husband returned, wearing a plain dark suit and dog collar. I had walked to the vicarage, so he said he would drive us both down to Trenarwyn in his car. Mrs Peplow came to the gate with us and instructed me anxiously: 'Remember now, you mustn't suffer in silence any more. If you need to, you can always ring us, even if it's the middle of the night – can't she, George?'

Mr Peplow looked slightly pained, but he managed to smile and agree.

As we drove away, passing the churchyard, I caught a glimpse of the Penhale graves. Were the vicar's prayers about to erase the last vestige and echo of that family? I wanted the male presence gone from my house – but would the shade of Genevra go as well? Did I want that? Who was I, an outsider from London, to wipe out the one remaining trace of an old Cornish line, even though she was a mere will-o'-the-wisp?

Well, I thought, hardening my heart, I would just have to live with the guilt – because I certainly could not live with 'him'. Anyway, it was premature to assume that this would do the trick.

For the better part of half an hour that afternoon, I sat on the sofa in my living room, listening and feeling faintly foolish while the Reverend Peplow went round the house with Bible and prayer book, blessing every corridor and room, not forgetting the balcony. At the end, he said a little one with me –

which he probably thought would do more good than all the others put together.

'House doesn't have a bad atmosphere,' he said as he was leaving. 'Not unsettling at all. No cold spots. That back bedroom above the kitchen is a bit gloomy, but then, it doesn't get much sun.'

'That's the one Genevra used.'

'So I understand from Kate. Doesn't strike me as haunted, though, just dreary. Anyway, for the moment I've done what I can and we'll have to await the results.'

'I'm sorry to have troubled you with this.'

Smiling, he patted my shoulder. 'No trouble, I'm glad you came to me. You say you're not religious, but clearly you credit the Church with certain capabilities.'

The smile turned into a chuckle. I flushed, feeling sillier still.

'You will keep this just between us, I hope? I mean, it's confidential, isn't it?'

'Of course.'

'Everyone poked such fun at me that time I called the coastguard out.'

'I shall mention it to the Bishop, no one else.'

'Thank you,' I said gratefully, showing him out.

He paused on the porch and looked around him, taking in the garden and the view. 'I heard what Kate said about pulling the house down,' he remarked. 'I don't agree with her on that. The Penhale family were happy here for several generations, and that has to count for a lot, despite what happened at the end. The laughter and love Trenarwyn has seen outweighs the pain by far.'

'Strange that you should say that. Before this business started, I always experienced it as welcoming. On the whole, I still do.'

He nodded. 'It's worth hanging on here, Miss Elford. I commend you for not turning tail.'

When he had driven away, I went back inside and stood for a while at the foot of the stairs, waiting for any impression which might come.

Was anything different? Did I sense a change?

No.

Same silence. Same warmth. Dancing dust in a shaft of sunlight, the fading scent of fading roses on the table in the hall, the distant plink of water dripping from a kitchen tap. Everything just the same as always – at least while daylight reigned.

# Twenty-Five

Two days later the weather changed. A fresh wind blew up from the south-west, and plump white clouds came bowling across the sky. I was filled with relief, for more reasons than one. The hot months had created a feeling of trance, the heavy stillness dreamlike and debilitating. Now there were breezes, brisk and bracing, constant movement of sky and choppy sea. The world felt normal again and so did I. Better still, I had shared my trouble, done something about it. Just telling the Peplows appeared to have lessened the burden by half. Peculiar how terrors and speculations flourish when locked up in one person's head. Stranger still how they seem to shrink when confided. Words, of course, are inadequate to express some experiences, and by this very failing are apt to cut them down to size.

As for Mr Peplow's prayers, I felt they must have done the trick. A month went by with no more visitations, and a confident lift in my mood assured me that 'he', at least, had been driven away and no menace remained. Just to be on the safe side, I refrained from playing the Vaughan Williams tape and routinely locked all the windows and doors as before, but otherwise I felt pretty relaxed.

Mid-October brought the anniversary of my arrival at Trenarwyn. A year, and what an eventful one, I thought that evening, pouring myself a Scotch. I had moved in and furnished this house. I had set up my business and so far all was going well with it. I'd had my brief affair with Jack and declined a proposal from Neville. Of course, overshadowing everything else was the matter of my ghosts. Now, with any luck, they were a problem I could put behind me. With fingers crossed, I drank a toast to that.

On a Saturday afternoon late in the month, I took my car to a garage just outside Truro for its yearly check. It failed and the tester said it would need about two hundred pounds' worth of work before he could issue a certificate. Having grown quite attached to the old heap, I gritted my teeth and agreed. He told me he would have to order a part, so I couldn't have her back for a few days. Resigned, I left her there and walked up the road to the nearest stop, where I waited half an hour for a bus to take me home.

It was a dreary day, and cold. I turned my jacket collar up and pushed my hands in the pockets, wishing I had worn some gloves. My jeans were tucked into fur-lined suede boots, but my toes had gone numb by the time the bus came along at half past three. By contrast, it was stuffy inside, and when I got out at the foundry stop some fifty minutes later, I was almost looking forward to the walk home through the woods.

A mist had descended within the past hour, hanging about in the tree-tops and starting to filter down to the ground. The bus, as it sped away, seemed to vanish down a hazy tunnel and fade like a wraith.

Setting off along the road, I searched for the path leading down through the woods to the back of my house. The mist dropped lower as I walked, and I was lucky not to miss the track. Had it not been for the leaning gatepost, I might have passed right by it.

Entering the wood was like stepping into a scene from a fairytale. Not at all what I had expected. My one excursion here twelve months ago had found the place sombre, unpleasant. Autumn, however, was later this year and the trees were still flying its colours. Mist drifted thinly among motionless, red-gold leaves. There was utter silence, the rich scent of earth and a heady mushroom smell. Bunches of berries, brilliant scarlet, hung from the rowan trees. Acorns and hazel husks littered the path, and occasional small pine-cones too. I picked a few up as I went, dropping them into my jacket pockets with the idea of making them into Christmas decorations.

For the first half mile the track was almost level. The rustling of bright fallen leaves underfoot went echoing away into the mist. Now and again I wandered from the pathway, straying to examine a cluster of leprous toadstools, the distorted bole of an oak, or a monstrous, butter-coloured fungus growing on a fallen tree. Wild woodland with its eerie magic. As a child growing up in rural Berkshire, I had always stood in awe of this other-world of slinking creepers and crazy-looking growths, and after all the adult, city years between, it could still fascinate me.

Happy, I dawdled homewards, humming to myself. The tune was something folksy – 'Brigg Fair', I believe. The woods seemed to listen, respectfully quiet and very attentive.

The track was just beginning to dip more steeply when I spotted the oak apples lying on the ground. Three of them, perfect except for a tiny wormhole here and there. Bending, I gathered them up and put them in my pocket. Gilded and threaded on string, they would do for my Christmas tree.

Still murmuring the tune, I squatted down and brushed through the leaves with my hand in hopes of finding more. Instead, I discovered something else and it cut my singing off short. Straightening up, I stared at the impression I had found in the soft brown earth.

A footprint, large and deep, made by someone heavy. A foot almost twice the size of mine, I observed, placing my right boot alongside it for comparison. Kicking the leaves aside, I searched for others and found a trail of them. They stretched for about five yards and then stopped at the base of a large oak tree – as if whoever it was had climbed up into the branches.

Like those footprints on the beach, these marks unsettled me. It was probably irrational, but I didn't like the fact that they were there. The big tree was just a few yards outside the wire fence which bounded my land, so I couldn't say that anyone had been trespassing on my property. Others had a perfect right to come into these woods and look for, say, kindling or nuts. But once again I was disturbed to see evidence that someone had indeed been about. Trenarwyn wasn't very far now. Had the day been clear, I could have glimpsed its white walls down at the foot of the hill through the trees. Glancing up at the oak, I wondered how much of my house a person could see by climbing up. Would there, perhaps, be a glimpse through my kitchen window?

Oh, but I was being silly, I decided. Those footprints must have been there for a week or more, judging by the depth of leaves which had fallen to cover them. Nothing had happened to trouble me, had it? No, nothing at all.

Nevertheless, I walked more briskly the rest of the way. It was nearing five and the light was beginning to go. The smells of the woodland began to seem rank, the shapes of stones and stumps malformed and horrid, rather suggestive of skulking familiars and imps. Sudden primitive superstition made me want my fireside, lamplight, and four stout walls around me.

Dusk was thickening fast as I trotted down over the slope Jimmy Kinsman had cleared, and let myself in by the back door. At a flip of the switch, the harsh light of the neon tube flickered a couple of times, then flooded the kitchen with its steady glare. Taking off my jacket, I peered through the doors of the stove. Nothing but feeble embers. I fed it a couple of logs and turned the draught up full.

The sitting room fire was in a similar state, reduced to little pockets of pinkish light amid a grey bed of ash. Going down to the cellar, I brought up an armful of logs, then spent a while down on my knees by the hearth with the bellows.

Anxious to coax the wood into a blaze, I'd forgotten to draw the curtains, and when I glanced across to the window I saw that the fog had grown denser outside and now pressed thickly against the glass. There were slow, slow, curling movements in it, like currents in soapy water. Mist could be pretty, but heavy fog had always bothered me. It hid things, engulfed things, and sometimes seemed almost possessed of a conscious intent. I pumped with the bellows, growing impatient. I wanted to get up and close the curtains. What was more, my knees were beginning to hurt. I shifted a little, trying to ease them, and heard . . . a creak. The floorboards under the hearthrug, I first thought. But then . . .

Hadn't it sounded more as if it came from overhead?

Pausing, I listened a moment. Then, experimenting, I shuffled my knees again.

231

No sound this time.

I looked up, slowly scanning the ceiling, gaze moving left to right and back again, taking in details hitherto unnoticed. A cobweb in a corner, a little hole above the dado rail, probably occupied by a very large spider. Shadows of accumulated dust on the cornices. Chips in the plaster moulding round the central light pendant. For a minute, hardly daring to breathe, I listened intently and watched that expanse of white plaster for some tiny tremor, the faint vibration of a footfall in the room above.

But nothing came.

No one was up there. Of course not – silly idea. What was more, I was getting a crick in my neck. Annoyed with myself, I shook my head and attended once more to the fire. At last the bark of the log began to spark and fizz, and finally flames sprang up from underneath. Laying the bellows aside, I went and drew the curtains.

Something to eat was the next concern. I had a hankering for a huge plate of mashed potato with lots of butter and pepper, accompanied by a stack of crispy bacon. Returning to the kitchen, I skinned some potatoes, cut them up quite small, then put them on to boil. As soon as they started to bubble, I dropped the bacon into the frying pan.

In answer to a yowl at the back door, I went to let Lucinda in. For once, she hesitated rather strangely on the step, peering past me into the kitchen and twitching her nose.

'Bacon, Lucy,' I said. 'Lovely bacon. Plenty enough for you too.'

She trotted in and sniffed around suspiciously, as if she detected something untoward. I wondered if perhaps there might be a mouse behind one of the cupboards. However, I had left the cellar door half open and she went instead to investigate down there.

Taking a seat, I turned out the pockets of my jacket and spent a while examining the little woodland treasures I had found. The kitchen was warm and filled with the gentle murmur of boiling water, the hiss and splutter of bacon in the pan.

And then, all at once, there was something more. Again, a creak, a tiny thump . . .

This time I could pinpoint exactly where it had come from. I froze and my gaze swivelled upwards again, to the corner of the ceiling above the kitchen door. In that direction lay the staircase and the landing. I had the door pushed almost shut. Down the edge of it showed an inch-wide strip of darkness from the hall beyond.

There was a hesitation, and then a little crick-crick noise which I recognised. That was the sound the banisters made at the top of the stairs when you laid a hand on them. Always, at a bit of pressure, the banisters made that sound.

It felt as if all the blood was draining down through me, all going down to my feet, so that they were too heavy to move and the rest of me was left cold and weak. I sat at that table, petrified, while the pans on the stove, forgotten, steamed busily away.

I would have remained there for God knows how long, just staring at the door, were it not for Lucinda. From the corner of my eye, I saw a movement, and there she was, emerging from the cellar. What she did next was completely unlike her and offered me all the proof I needed of something or someone lurking on the stairs. Her eyes fixed on the kitchen door, she suddenly swelled to twice her size, back arched and every hair standing stiffly on end. A growl rose and fell in her throat, followed by a snarling hiss. Her pretty face became a hellish mask of fangs and glaring eyes.

It snapped me out of that numbing fright, rousing my temper instead. Something, somebody, was out there, and after I'd thought myself free of all that. After the peace of recent weeks, I was enraged to think that it might all be starting again. Whatever had been tormenting me was here in my house once more. It was just beyond that door, and with a bit of courage I could meet it face to face.

Very cautiously, quietly, I got up from the chair. I reached up to the hanging rack, unhooked a copper-bottomed pan and fiercely gripped the handle, swinging it slightly to feel its satisfying weight.

Still rumbling with growls, Lucinda had retreated under the table, which was probably the most sensible course. Part of me

233

wanted to join her, but having mustered bile enough for a confrontation, I wasn't about to cower and hide away now.

Striding to the door, I threw it back and yelled: 'Who's there?'

A silence met me, tense and awful.

'Who is it?' I shouted again. 'Who the bloody hell are you, and why are you here in my house?'

No reply – but there was a sound, a very quiet, brushing sound, like a foot being slid along carpet. The light from the kitchen was all I had, but as my eyes adjusted to the dimness of the hall, I made out a darker shadow halfway down the stairs. Tall and broad, a figure standing there.

All at once I was terrified again, very nearly dropped the pan and fled. There he was, above me, looking down. What would I see if he should come forward into the light from the kitchen door? The face I knew from the photographs? Or features rotted by the sea?

Even something else entirely, someone unexpected?

He didn't move and he seemed so huge. I'd never been so scared in all my life. But still I demanded yet again: 'Who are you? What do you want with me?'

Just for a second, I thought I heard an answer, very sibilant and soft. But then I realised that it was only a breath exhaled.

A very shaky, nervous breath, barely controlled. The living breath of someone who, if possible, was even more scared than I was.

One thing I suddenly knew for sure: it wasn't David Lanyon. Whoever had been plaguing me was flesh and blood, and today I had caught him out. No supernatural entity this, but a live intruder, someone who had undoubtedly taken great pleasure in spying on me, frightening me all the summer long.

Fury and a wild aggression seized me. There were plenty of words for men like that. My favourite was 'creep'. Right then I felt I could beat him senseless, however big he was. More than anything else, however, I wanted to see his face.

Just a few feet away at the foot of the stairs was the light switch. It was halfway between him and me. He must have seen me look towards it, guessed what I was going to do, for as I

234

made a dive at it he suddenly came lunging down the stairs.

It was very much like a rugby tackle and I ended up face-down on the floor. My saucepan went bouncing and clanging down the passage, well out of reach, as the man crouched over me. He was fearfully strong, virtually pinning me flat with one hand. Once more that old familiar scorching smell was in my nose. It mingled now with the odour of burning bacon from the kitchen, but I recognised it just the same and realised that it was coming from his clothes.

Next second, he had his forearm across my throat and he pulled me to my feet as if I weighed next to nothing. We were almost in the kitchen doorway and from the corner of my eye, I saw his arm reach out for the switch, then the light went off. There was time enough to note that he was wearing something navy blue and coarse, like heavy denim, with thick seams and stitching to the sleeve. Some kind of overall – a boiler suit! It had a ragged black and brown discoloration at the cuff.

He hadn't uttered a single word and I guessed he wasn't going to – for fear, perhaps, that I would know his voice. I had the strongest impression that he was panic-stricken, desperate not to be seen, and wanted only to make his escape. He must have been trying to sneak down the stairs and out of the front door when I confronted him. It went through my mind that he had probably expected to hear my car return, never dreaming that I would come home through the woods on foot.

He dragged me into the kitchen, which was now lit only by the glare from the glass doors of the stove. Everything stood out in black relief against the orange glow of flaming logs. By now, a haze of smoke and a choking stink of burnt fat were rising from the frying pan. There came a crash and both of us nearly went sprawling as he tripped over the vegetable rack. I heard the bump-bump-bump of potatoes and turnips bouncing across the floor.

At first I couldn't think what he was going to do with me – but then I heard him throw the cellar door back with a bang.

Lock me down there! To lock me in and leave me was what he intended. I could be there for days – indeed, I could die of thirst before anyone missed me. I had so few callers, and wasn't

235

expected again at Good Harvest for nearly a week. Frenzied at the prospect, I squirmed and reached round, groping for his face, to use my nails. I felt a big jaw, rough with stubble, dug in savagely and ripped. He squealed but kept his grip on me. With the heel of my left boot, I stamped on his instep, but that didn't have much effect, so I twisted my head and sank my teeth in the fleshy pad of his thumb. Yelling out, he tried to swing me bodily through the cellar door and down the steps, but I grabbed the plateboard of the dresser, held on tight and bit down harder. Amazing the pressure that one could apply in desperation. His flesh felt like sinewy steak, and I worried at it like a bulldog, even tasted blood. He shrieked and, just for long enough, released his hold on me. That was when I seized the Churchill teapot from the dresser and swung it at his head with all my might.

Backwards he went through the cellar door and I heard the thud of his body tumbling down the stairs. All I had to do now was lock that door.

But first I had to see. Had to, after all this time. Fumbling around for the light cord, I found it, jerked it hard. A dull yellow glare lit the cellar, and there at the foot of the steps, staring dazedly up at me, was a face I knew full well.

Noel Kinsman.

Strutting, bragging Noel Kinsman. Casanova, as they called him. Noel, who worked at the foundry, tending the furnace and pouring hot metal. At once, I understood about the smell. It was obvious now. Even from here I could see the charred patches on his overalls, the singeing round the cuffs. Of course, the stink of smoke got in his hair. Of course, his clothing smelt of fire. Whenever he came here straight from the foundry, he brought its reek with him.

'You . . . !' I said, or rather spat. 'You – bloody article!'

I'd never seen a man look quite so horrified before. His eyes were frantic and his thoughts not difficult to guess. I had seen him now, and knew what he was. I would tell everyone, I would tell the police. He was lost, unless . . .

After the fall he had taken, I wouldn't have thought he could move so fast, but suddenly he was on his feet and charging up those steps. I only just managed to slam the door in time and turn the key. He hammered on it, bellowing.

'You let me out! You hear me? Let me go!'

'Fat chance,' I said, 'I'm calling the police.'

There followed a brief, thoughtful pause, and then a change of tone. Mocking now, he said: 'Oh yes? You'll accuse me of what? I haven't injured you and I'll say you invited me here. Everybody knows I have a lot of girls. You're just one more of them, having a tantrum because of the others, jealous and making things up.'

'You assaulted me,' I snapped. 'You broke into my house.'

A chuckle, soft and gleeful. 'No, Christine, I've got a key.'

I stared at the door.

'You gave me one, that's what I'll say. Can you prove any different?'

He was grinning, I knew he was, could hear it in his voice. Grinning all over his face and savouring my shock. For a moment he said no more, allowing me to digest the fact that he had been able all these months to let himself into my house at any time of the day or night.

The thought of it turned me faint. Somehow, he must have had a key copied during those days he was working here. Probably the back door key, I thought. I doubt I would have noticed if, say, it had disappeared for an hour when he went to lunch. Or perhaps he had made an impression of it. Something like a lump of putty would serve very well for that.

'You'll only make a fool of yourself, Christine,' the voice went on. 'I'll swear we've been having a secret affair out here in your lonely house. I'll tell them all that I'd had enough, that you were far too old for me. I'll simply say I was dumping you and now you're telling lies for spite. Think of the gossip, just think of the figure you'll cut – a middle-aged woman making hysterical charges against a young man who's grown tired of her. Everybody in Polvean will laugh at you.'

'I'll risk that,' I said.

'Just as they laughed when you called out the coastguard. Remember? Embarrassing, wasn't it, eh? You'll be called neurotic, Christine. You may even get into trouble yourself for making false accusations. Why don't you just let me slip away? I won't bother you again.'

Not quite as brainless as he might appear, I thought mordantly. He did possess a crafty intelligence, normally well concealed by his idiotic manner. However, his slyness was going to backfire, for it made me even more determined to set the law on him.

'You were going to leave me in that cellar,' I said grimly. 'You needn't think you can walk away from that. I'm going to bring charges.'

At that, he exploded, losing control, thumping and kicking the door. It was clear, despite his talk, that he wasn't confident at all of bluffing his way out of trouble. I felt, in fact, that he had a pretty good story with which to make things difficult for me. Yet the thought of police attention evidently panicked him, and I wondered how much else he had to hide.

It was no time, however, for speculation. A series of thuds shook the door. It shuddered in its frame and the wood began to splinter round the lock. He was putting his shoulder to it and I wasn't certain at all that it would hold. Rushing to the opposite end of the dresser, I started to shove it, inch by inch, across the floor. Most of my plates fell down from the board and smashed, but I didn't care. As soon as the dresser was tightly wedged against the cellar door, I ran to the phone and rang for the police.

It was forty minutes before they came, which seemed an eternity. The noise from the cellar went on for a while, but gradually the blows grew weaker. They had stopped by the time I heard the sound of a car pulling up in the lane outside.

# Twenty-Six

Noel put on a pretty good act. When they escorted him away, he was still protesting that he and I had just been having a parting quarrel. I was making it all up, he said, concocting a malicious story because he had tried to finish with me. Prowling around my house and frightening me for months? Ridiculous. Truth was, we had been seeing each other. Nothing wrong with that. Trying to lock me in the cellar? Talk about fanciful. Potty, that was what I was. Deranged. They knew the saying, didn't they, about a woman scorned? He hadn't hurt me – but look what I had done to him! Just look at his head! It was oozing blood! He was lucky I hadn't killed him! He could have broken his neck, falling down those steps!

And so on and on. The two policemen listened, expressionless, glancing all the time from him to me and back again. One of them seemed very interested in the smell which hung about Noel Kinsman. His nostrils twitched, he asked what it was, and received the reply with a thoughtful nod. Kinsman, full of indignant bluster, produced from his pocket the back door key, which he insisted I had given him. More nods. They took him off to the hospital and said they would be back to talk to me.

It was nearly forty-eight hours before I heard from them again, and I spent the time in fear that I would be the one charged with assault. Iniquitous though it was, householders were sometimes prosecuted for injuring intruders. And I wasn't sure they would even accept that he was in my house uninvited.

When a knock at the door came at last, I found myself faced with a balding middle-aged officer who told me his name was Blamey.

'What's happened to Kinsman?' I asked, showing him inside.

'Still being held.' He glanced about him. 'Mind if I look around the house before we talk?'

'What for?'

'Just want to see the layout.'

'Oh. Please do.'

I left him to make the tour by himself and went in the kitchen to brew some tea. At length he came in and sat down at the table.

'You do believe me, I hope?' I said, setting a cup in front of him. 'Truly, there was nothing whatever between Noel and me. He's a frightful liar. Have an affair with an oaf like that? Give him a key? Never in a million years.'

The man helped himself to three teaspoons of sugar and stirred them in. For a moment he thoughtfully studied my face as he turned the spoon round in the cup.

Then: 'You claim he's been bothering you for a long time. So when did it start, Miss Elford?'

Casting my mind back, I said, 'It was round about the beginning of June.'

Just after I finished with Jack, I thought. Right at the time when the trees were felled and Jimmy Kinsman found the marble seat. That was the very first time I saw 'the man'. I could be almost certain now that it was Noel sitting there.

'Nearly five months,' the policeman observed. 'Why didn't you report anything earlier?'

Briefly, I stalled and then muttered: 'I didn't think it was a matter for the law.'

'Indeed? Why not?'

I flushed deep red. 'I had an idea . . . Well, you'll think me mad, I expect, but I thought Trenarwyn must be haunted.'

For an instant, I felt certain he was going to laugh. But his eyes just grew rounder, his face remained straight. 'Haunted,' he repeated levelly. 'You said . . . haunted?'

'Mm.' I squirmed a little with embarrassment. 'It was all so vague, you see, until quite recently. I would think I heard footsteps, think I saw someone, but I was seldom sure. Then again, weeks would pass when nothing untoward occurred. It wasn't as if I was being plagued every day.'

To my surprise, a look of satisfaction crossed his face, as if that fitted in with something he already knew. Encouraged, I pressed on: 'Now and again, when I came home, I would notice that odd, smoky smell in the house, yet there was never any sign of someone breaking in. I'm terribly careful about locking up, so I could only see two ways to account for it – either it was something to do with my wood fires, or something uncanny was going on. Neither would be a good reason to call the police.'

He sipped at his tea. Over the rim of his cup, he kept watching me steadily. Unable to gauge his reaction now, I found myself starting to gabble.

'And when I saw a man's silhouette at my bedroom window one night, I felt that it had to be something . . . well, unnatural – because the only way on to the balcony was from inside the house. It didn't cross my mind that somebody might have a key. There was never any damage, never anything missing, and I couldn't see why any . . . mortal would simply hang around Trenarwyn, just for the sake of it.'

He was finding it harder now to hide his amusement. Putting down his cup, he passed a hand across his mouth, but a sparkle of mirth was in his eyes.

'There!' I exclaimed. 'You're laughing, don't pretend you're not. That's what I would have expected if I had reported it. It wouldn't have been the first time I'd been met with ridicule for saying I'd seen something odd.'

'Oh? May I ask what else?'

Sheepishly, I told him of the time I called the coastguard out.

'Now perhaps that really was a ghost,' he said, teasing me.

There was a momentary temptation, but I deemed it unwise to tell him about Genevra. Her story was a thing entrusted, her appearances almost a confidence between us, certainly not a sensational titbit for public consumption and derision. I imagined the men hooting over it at the police station, imagined myself being questioned about it in court. All other considerations aside, I guessed it wouldn't do a thing for my credibility.

'I suppose I just made a mistake,' I muttered. 'Anyway, I was made to feel like an idiot on account of it. Everybody ragged me for weeks afterwards. One of your men suggested I might have a drink problem, or bad eyesight or some such thing. That sort of experience doesn't exactly encourage one to ask for help a second time.'

'No,' he said, serious now. 'I do take your point.'

'Anyway, what could you have done?'

'Not a great deal,' he agreed. 'We don't have the manpower to keep a watch on people's houses, especially when the complaints are vague and the incidents infrequent. However . . .' A pause, a reproachful look. 'We wouldn't have been as sceptical as you imagine.'

Hope began to rise in me. 'You do believe me, then? You don't accept what Noel Kinsman says?'

'Well,' he said with a sly little smile, 'it's by no means unknown for a lady to enjoy a fling with a mindless muscle-bound type. I must admit, I would have had grave doubts about your story, were it not for the others.'

'Others?' I said, frowning. 'Other what?'

'Victims.'

I blinked.

'You thought your experience unique? Oh no, you're not the only one, Miss Elford. If you had come to us before, we could have told you so.'

I stared at him, astonished.

Folding his hands on the table, he went on. 'We know of at least three other women who've been troubled in similar ways: a shadowy figure in the garden, footsteps round the house at night, someone peeping in through windows, doorknobs being tried, a mysterious burnt smell in some of the rooms. All pretty much the same complaints, and all of them from lone women living in relatively isolated houses. They're all within a thirty-mile radius of here: one in Newquay, another up near Bodmin until recently, the third on the outskirts of St Austell. The only difference in your case is that, unlike the other ladies, you failed to report the annoyance promptly. Ironically, you may have suffered the most, being right on Noel's doorstep. Just a short walk along the road, then down through the woods to the back of your house.'

For a moment I couldn't quite take it in, but then the happy implications hit me. There were others. I wasn't alone; it wouldn't be merely my word against his. This time I was not disbelieved. I wasn't going to be blamed for anything and, with any luck, Noel Kinsman was in a lot of trouble.

'Has he admitted it, then?' I asked eagerly.

'Wasn't hard to break him down, once we found . . .' Blamey hesitated. 'Well, there's something more, but I'll come to that.'

Initially, all I felt was relief, but puzzlement soon took over.

'I don't quite understand. I mean, why does he do such things?'

'Oh, it's Noel's secret hobby, you might say. He enjoys prowling round and spying on women, having access to their homes, going through their belongings, unnerving them. Noel gets a thrill from that – same way some men do from pinching ladies' underwear off washing lines. He's in the same pathetic league as the ones who expose themselves or make dirty anonymous phone calls.'

'But he's the village Lothario, always out with different girls! To be blunt, he can't want for sex.'

Another grin. 'Ask any of those girls, they'll tell you he's not up to much when it really comes down to business. There's a lot of talk and show with Noel, but that's about all it is. Actual contact, serious contact, is not what they want, those types. Noel's just a swaggering great fraud who finds far more excitement in creeping round solitary ladies' homes and making them afraid. That's not to take him lightly, of course. Frightening people is never harmless. Mental anguish hurts as much as physical assault. That poor woman in Newquay ended up with a nervous breakdown. The one up at Bodmin sold her home at a huge loss, just to escape.'

For a minute I mulled this over. 'You're certain it was him in every case?'

'We're satisfied of it. Once we got hold of him, it wasn't difficult to piece things together. Within the past two years, Jennings' foundry had installed or repaired a stove in every one of those houses. Then there's that smoky odour he leaves behind him. Two of the women kept mentioning that. Seeing there was never any sign of a break-in, we suggested they got their locks changed just in case someone had keys. This morning we managed to find the place where Noel got those keys cut. He used the same locksmith each time and the man remembered him, recognised a photo of him.'

I thought about that and about the foundry, and something occurred to me.

'His boss, Mr Jennings – do you think he had any idea about Noel and his pastime?'

A sniff, dismissive. 'No, I don't. Cocky individual, Jennings, not very likeable, but there's nothing odd or crooked about him and I don't think for a moment he would have condoned or turned a blind eye to any of this.'

'He's a womaniser himself,' I said.

'And with Jennings it's no pretence. Reprehensible, perhaps, but entirely normal. I should think he'd have total contempt for Noel, in view of what's now come to light.'

'What about Noel's brother?'

'Jimmy? Nothing wrong with Jimmy, perfectly decent chap. Poor devil, it's going to be hard on him when this gets out.'

I muttered, 'You just wouldn't credit that Noel could be so crafty. He seems such a bonehead.'

'And therefore people don't take him seriously.'

'Quite. But see how he plans things. While they were here fitting the stove, he took the opportunity for a damned good scout around. It did cross my mind at the time that he might be light-fingered, but never that he was learning his way about. He must have got on to my balcony through the spare front bedroom up above the sitting room. I think he was out there one night while I was having a bath. It gave me the most awful shock, actually made me scream. He must have enjoyed that no end.'

'Mm. Exciting game for him, no fun for you.'

'Yes, I'm sure he was there,' I went on, 'because now I come to think of it, that was the first time I noticed the funny smell. He had been in my bedroom, he'd been through the drawers where I keep my underwear. Now, I'd been in Truro all that day. You know, it was always when I had been out somewhere that the burnt smell was apt to occur. Of course, the cottages and foundry are on the Truro road, so it's likely he saw me drive by on occasion and knew I was going to be gone for a while.'

Blamey gave a snort. 'Oh, I'm willing to bet he was here more often than you realise. He wouldn't have to notice you driving by. He could see from that tree if your car was in the lane or gone. What's more, Noel doesn't always wear his overalls at work. He doesn't tend the furnace every day. They take turns at the various jobs. I dare say he sometimes changed and had a bath before coming down here or visiting one of those other unfortunate women – in which case you wouldn't know he had been in the house.'

'Several of us,' I said, musing. 'So he had to divide his time. When I had a few weeks' peace, it meant he was off bothering somebody else.'

'More than likely. Seems he also took a three-week holiday last month; went off to Scotland – which must have given you a lengthy respite.'

'Yes,' I said, half smiling, 'yes, it did.' So much for having the house blessed.

'Will it be simple to prosecute him, do you think?'

Mr Blamey pursed his mouth. 'Normally, it wouldn't be easy to punish what he does. There are minor charges, but nothing that carries much of a penalty. There is a move towards legislation against this kind of thing – tormenting women – but nothing's been enacted yet. He did, of course, lay hands on you – but you haven't any injuries to show,' he ended ruefully.

'Pity he didn't knock me about, eh? Or try to throttle me?'

'Hm. Where you're concerned, I'm afraid a good solicitor could make his offences look very questionable – trifling, at most. However . . .' A slight smile lifted his face. 'Luckily for us, Noel made one very bad mistake.'

I waited, and the smile became a beam.

'It happens that one of the women, the one in St Austell, is quite well-to-do. Lovely big house on the outskirts of town, full of valuable stuff. Now, the very first time she came to us, it was not to report a prowler, but a possible theft. Subsequently she did return with complaints of someone hanging round her property, but initially she came to us on account of a loss.

A watch had gone missing – her evening watch, an exclusive piece with a diamond-studded face. Five and a half thousand pounds' worth.'

A malicious glee took hold of me. 'You think perhaps Noel took it?'

'We know he did. When we checked and compared dates, we found that the watch had disappeared just three weeks after Jennings' firm installed a stove for her. So first thing yesterday we went and searched Kinsman's house. We found it in a tobacco tin under Noel's mattress, and for that, Miss Elford, we can certainly put him away. Not for as long as you would probably like, but he will pay a price.' Glancing at me hopefully, he added: 'You're certain you haven't missed anything yourself?'

'Afraid not. I've nothing much really worth stealing.'

'Hm. It's a pity in a way that Noel only succumbed to that kind of temptation the once. But of course, he's basically just a peeping Tom, a pest, not a regular felon. Still, he couldn't resist the watch and that'll be enough to nail him. By the way, how will you feel about going to court and facing him?'

'No qualms whatever.'

'Quite a tough customer, aren't you, Miss Elford? You know, they had to put stitches in Noel's thumb, and he has a fine black and blue lump on his head.'

'Good,' I said pugnaciously, and Mr Blamey chuckled.

'I expect you'll be relieved, though, when this is all over, eh?'

'As far as I'm concerned, it's over already,' I said.

In a vital way, for me, it was. Seeing Noel receive his comeuppance was merely incidental. What really mattered was finally knowing that no restless spirit of poor David Lanyon was shadowing me or my house.

# Twenty-Seven

News of Noel Kinsman's arrest soon got around the village, thanks to Jennings. People kept asking me about it, which quickly became very tiresome, so I stayed at home as much as possible for the next few weeks. Mrs Peplow came rushing over the moment the story reached her. How perfectly ghastly, she declared. Just as bad, in her opinion, as having an unfriendly spectre about the place. Peculiar, though, wasn't it, how everything had gone so quiet after her husband's visit and his prayers? I had to tell her gently of Noel's weeks away – whereupon she roared with laughter, and said that George would be frightfully disappointed.

An agreeably tranquil November went by, December came in and I started to think about Christmas again. I spent the first fortnight of the month producing sets of pixie hoods and scarves for children. They were all made in red, white and green wool, patterned with Santas or fir trees or snowflakes. I was planning to sell them from a stall at the Christmas craft fair.

Then, one morning, I sat down to start on the last two and found that I had no green yarn. The tedious process of dyeing with indigo stock seemed too daunting that day, so I put my feet up by the fire instead, and listened to *Aida*.

It was when the tape finished and I went to the shelf for something more that I found my hand hovering over the one cassette box whose label was turned to the wall.

The Vaughan Williams tape – I hadn't dared play it for months. A longing for the music suddenly took hold of me, but . . .

Did I want to risk seeing Genevra again? Wasn't it asking for trouble? Now that this weird business seemed to have ended, wasn't it best to make one small sacrifice in the interests of continued peace?

Yet – I wanted so much to hear the tape again.

Chewing my bottom lip, I dithered – but then came a welcome thought. What if Mr Peplow's prayers had not been entirely in vain? It was perfectly possible, wasn't it, that Genevra might not appear any more?

Another lingering hesitation, then I laid a finger on the box, tipped it forward, pulled it from its place. Decided now, and moving swiftly before any cowardly change of mind could check me, I pushed the tape into the slot and jabbed at the button marked 'Play'.

Favourite pieces, sorely missed, filled the air as I sat by the fire again. Enjoying the music, but nervous too, I counted the tracks off, knowing their order.

Four more now, before the Tallis theme.

Three to go.

Now only two.

The one after this. Still time to switch off . . .

But I wasn't going to.

A final note, a breathless pause. The logs in the grate fell apart, collapsing into a heap of ashy-orange glowing cubes. I fixed my eyes on them and heard . . .

That single, drawn-out whisper of strings, so full of portent. Those deeper notes, like tentative footsteps, beginning to dance out a tune, growing more confident, stopping short, poised – and falling into that broad, slow melody.

I kept my eyes on the embers of wood, brooding on Genevra's story and half afraid to look around in case I saw her standing at the window once again. The music moved like an ocean swell, its tides and currents of emotion deep and strong. It might have been written for poor Genevra, for what her life became.

After it finished, I switched the tape off and stood for a moment, wondering what effect there would be. None, I hoped. Still, it was done now. Nothing for it but to wait and see.

For a while afterwards I pottered about, made myself a bite

248

of lunch and fetched some wood up from the cellar. Like anyone half-expecting a caller, I wasn't quite able to rest and settle to anything. At about two o'clock, I went out and sat on the terrace steps for a while like a one-woman reception, but no visitor deigned to appear.

Later, I wandered around to the back and up over the slope to the marble bench, where I stayed for nearly a quarter of an hour. The window of the bedroom where she died looked darkly out at me. I could almost imagine the face and form of a half-starved, aged woman there, but it was only light and shadow playing on the glass.

Finally, feeling the cold, I returned to the house and trotted upstairs to fetch a heavy cardigan. Coming out of my room, I was shrugging it on when something stopped me in my tracks and made me catch my breath.

At the opposite end of the landing was a tall, slim figure, slightly misty. Sure enough, in response to that music, Genevra was here again.

She was leaning over the banisters, looking down the stairwell, as if she had heard a call from below. A very young Genevra, probably about fifteen, and dressed in a skirt of pale blue, with a blouse made entirely of lace. The black hair was piled up in curls, and a cameo brooch was pinned in the frill at the base of her throat.

Briefly she bent her head, seeming to listen. And then all at once she was hurrying round the mahogany rail to the top of the stairs. Just for a moment, as she moved towards me, I saw an excited, smiling face, and then, in a flutter of swirling skirts, she swung around the newel and went running down the stairs.

It was all of two minutes before I moved, slowly went forward and peered down into the hall below. She had gone, of course, vanished completely, but the picture remained in my mind of that flushed and bright-eyed face. Imagination supplied voices too, echoing thinly out of the past.

Earnestina's, perhaps: '*Miss Genevra, Mr Lanyon's waiting in the sitting room.*'

Or possibly that of Mrs Penhale: '*Genevra, my dear, do hurry, David's here.*'

Well, I thought, dawdling downstairs, poor old Reverend Peplow might as well have stayed at home. The music was an invocation just too powerful.

Did I mind? Did I truly mind? Was I sorry for playing the tape?

Not really, I decided. Sooner or later, curiosity always had to be satisfied. And had it not been rather pleasing to see that eager, happy face? Some people said only sorrow left echoes, but it seemed that those good days before the Great War had left traces as well, and for that I was glad.

Later, I sat for a couple of hours in the basket chair, looking through the big bay window at the waning winter afternoon. A day of strange and subtle colours in the sky; clouds that were amber and grey and smoky mauve, bare trees black against them like heavy pencil strokes. Beach and sea, both pale and cold and lonely. I listened to Gregorian chant, thought about Genevra's life and mine.

That she was deluded I had little doubt. She never did have any phantom companion, except in her mind. Poor David had drowned and that was that. He had never returned from the sea, no corpse nor any shade of him. Perhaps he was the luckier one, better off than the grieving girl whose life became a pointless sacrifice.

And yet, I supposed, it had held for her a keen romance and dour drama unknown to normal people leading ordinary lives. Genevra's story was the stuff of poetry and folk-song, poignant and emotionally charged. Perhaps, without quite realising it, she had opted for that, chosen it in preference to mundane 'happiness'. Intensity of feeling was something she had never lacked, whatever else she had denied herself. The love affair had never palled, but lasted all her days, a passionate fantasy more stirring than anything real.

Twisted, pathetic? Yes, but so were many human situations if you looked at them closely enough. There were myriad ways to waste one's life – women stayed with violent or indifferent husbands, men spent forty years in jobs they loathed. By numerous everyday means, people destroyed themselves. Genevra, more extreme, more noticeably unbalanced, simply stood out from the rest by her eccentricity.

At least I had more sense. Self-sufficient, that was me, needing no one, suiting no one other than myself. When I grew old, I would not look back and say I simply tagged along in some man's wake, or followed paths which other people said were right for me.

When I grew old . . .

Something about the words suddenly chilled me. For hadn't I taken Genevra's place as the lone woman here? Might I not also grow strange in my solitude, ever more so with the passing of years? Would I, in my turn, one day become Trenarwyn's ghost?

Perhaps what I knew of Genevra Penhale should serve as a warning to me. What was it Jack had said not long ago on the quay?

'*One day you fall ill and no one's there. One day you hit fifty . . .*'

I shook myself. Weakness – this just wouldn't do. But his quiet voice persisted: '*You start to feel a sense of lack . . .*'

Lack of what? I thought crossly. It was all too easy to wreck a good situation by thinking something extra would improve it.

Yet . . . I pictured Jack, his smiling face. Hard to imagine him spoiling anything.

The music tape ended and switched itself off. Tiring of its melancholy, I changed it for *Scheherazade* and then sat down again.

A fortnight and it would be Christmas once more. Was I going to spend it alone? Well, I could. I'd enjoyed the last one by myself . . .

But what about next year and all the others to come after that? Would it always be quite such a pleasure?

Jack would be on his own as well, now that his grandad had gone. He would go down to the pub, I guessed, and probably have his lunch there. I was planning on having a piece of venison myself . . .

Did he like venison? I wondered, glancing towards the phone.

My Christmas pudding was already made. Too much, in

251

truth, for one. It would take me a fortnight to eat it all.

Unless I had some help.

I knew how delighted he would be if I made the invitation . . .

The telephone seemed to wait expectantly. If I picked it up, I'd be starting something. To encourage then drop him a second time would be unforgivable.

The sun began sinking as I debated. Beyond the window and the garden, the beach curved away and became indistinct in the distance. Like a road stretching out in front of me, a road with no one on it.

An empty road, a lonely life? Too much like hers?

I reached out, my hand poised above the receiver, and asked myself: What shall I do?

Then I lifted it, started to dial.